What the critics are saying...

"...Samantha Winston has created the perfect erotic novel with her romantic notions, hot sex scenes and her knowledge of polo. Although Rennie and Juan are made for each other, the problems they face come to life in a wonderful plot. Ms. Winston has a cast of secondary characters that rival any novel, putting this erotic romance in a category of its own. While many erotic novels seem to lack plot, *The Argentine Lover* sustains the reader with more than just sensual drama." ~ *Angie for Love Romances*

"...The Argentine Lover is a very sensual story. It flowed very well. The love scenes were well written and very intense -- just the way I like them. As one not understanding the rules of the game of Polo I found that it is a very interesting game as well as dangerous. I would recommend this story to all who want to experience a first. I would gladly share this story with all my family and friends." ~*Darlene Howard for Escape to Romance*

"...woman that at first I didn't think was a good match for Juan, but with grit and determination, her strength shone through and she proved me wrong...*Ms. Winston* delights readers with a fast-paced and romantic adventure with two very passionate and fantastic characters who learn how to love and to fight for what their hearts desire most...each other." ~*The Road to Romance*

Samantha Winston

THE Argentine LOVER

ELLORA'S CAVE
ROMANTICA PUBLISHING

An Ellora's Cave Romantica Publication

www.ellorascave.com

The Argentine Lover

ISBN # 1419952579
ALL RIGHTS RESERVED.
The Argentine Lover Copyright© 2003 Samantha Winston
Edited by: Allie McKnight
Cover art by:

Electronic book Publication: January, 2003
Trade paperback Publication: November, 2005

Excerpt from *My Fair Pixie* Copyright © Samantha Winston, 2005

Warning:

The following material contains graphic sexual content meant for mature readers. *The Argentine Lover* has been rated *E-rotic* by a minimum of three independent reviewers.

Ellora's Cave Publishing offers three levels of Romantica™ reading entertainment: S (S-ensuous), E (E-rotic), and X (X-treme).

S-ensuous love scenes are explicit and leave nothing to the imagination.

E-rotic love scenes are explicit, leave nothing to the imagination, and are high in volume per the overall word count. In addition, some E-rated titles might contain fantasy material that some readers find objectionable, such as bondage, submission, same sex encounters, forced seductions, etc. E-rated titles are the most graphic titles we carry; it is common, for instance, for an author to use words such as "fucking", "cock", "pussy", etc., within their work of literature.

X-treme titles differ from E-rated titles only in plot premise and storyline execution. Unlike E-rated titles, stories designated with the letter X tend to contain controversial subject matter not for the faint of heart.

Also by Samantha Winston:

The Argentine Lover

Polo Rules and Lexis

This book contains polo terms and foreign phrases that may be unfamiliar. For your convenience, a brief summary of polo rules and language has been provided.

A polo team has four players.

There are also two mounted referees on the field, and a third umpire in the stands.

A game is divided into 4, 6, or 8 periods called *chuckers* (or chukkas).

Each *chucker* lasts seven minutes. Players change horses after each chucker.

Players hit the ball with *polo mallets*. These are made of bamboo with hardwood heads. The ball is hit with the broad side of the mallet (not the points). The ball is slightly larger than a tennis ball and made of hard plastic.

Players can hook each other's sticks to spoil a hit. A *foul hook* is when a player hooks a stick in a dangerous fashion.

A *ride-off* is when one player pushes another player away from the ball. A ride-off must be shoulder to shoulder.

A polo field is 300 yards long and 175 yard wide. There are two goal posts 8 yards apart on each end. A *goal* is scored when the ball passes through the posts, (no matter the height).

Each player has a *handicap rating,* from –2 to 10 goals. *Ten goal players* are the best, and there are only about eight in the world. Most players are rated between –2 and 1.

Horses are traditionally called *polo ponies*.

At halftime, the spectators go onto the field and stomp divots to smooth the pitch for the second half.

The team scoring the most goals wins.

The most prestigious tournament is played in *Palermo*, a field right in the middle of Buenos Aires. Other big tournaments take place in Florida, California, England and France.

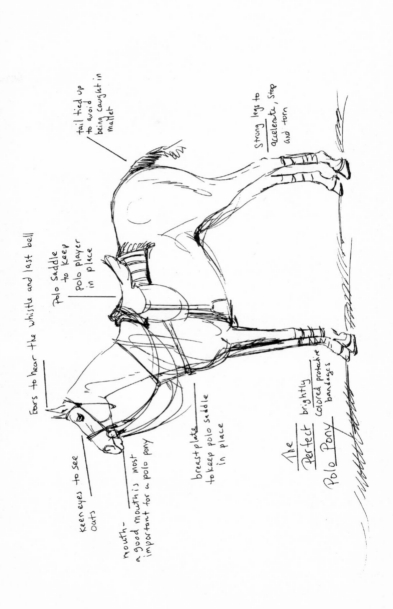

Ears to hear the whistle and last bell

tail tied up to avoid being caught in mallet

Polo Saddle to keep polo player in place

Strong legs to accelerate, stop and turn

Keen eyes to see oats

mouth -
a good mouth is most important for a polo pony

breast plate to keep polo saddle in place

The
Perfect
Polo Pony

brightly colored protective bandages

Prologue

Polo spectators huddled in their raincoats. It had rained earlier and the ground was soaked and getting cut up by the hooves of the eight horses galloping across it. Hitting the ball became more difficult as it lodged in hoof prints and bounced at crazy angles.

Juan Allistair missed the ball. He swore and pulled on his slippery reins, leaning heavily to the right to turn and try to get back to the play. His pony scrabbled for footing and bravely set off at a gallop again, chasing the opposing player who'd taken the ball and was now whacking it down the field. Juan's pony was just not fast enough, and although Juan leaned forward as far as he dared, stretching his arm out to try to hook his opponent's mallet, he couldn't reach.

Then the final bell rang.

"Thank God for that," sighed Juan, patting his winded pony.

At the pony line, his groom, Felipe, took his horse. Juan sat on the open trunk of his car, took off his spurs and put them in his polo bag. Larry, their number four player, was peering into the cooler, looking for a can of beer. "Jeez there's no more beer." He glared at his three teammates. "Can't you guys drink the cokes? I buy the beers for myself!"

Juan shrugged. "I don't drink beer," he said.

Andre Cruz, the number two player, echoed Juan. "Me neither."

Tom Wimsys, their captain and patron, rode up on his steaming pony and slid to the ground. Without a word to his players, he got into his yellow Porsche and drove off. Sally, his redheaded groom, took Tom's horse and led him away to be rubbed down and blanketed.

Juan watched his boss drive away, a bitter taste in his mouth. Being a polo pro, he thought glumly, was not what he'd imagined. He'd dreamed of fame, recognition, and fortune, of course. The reality was quite different. No one had told him his boss would only speak to him if he won, or that he'd be treated like the hired help.

Tom Wimsys had brought Juan on two weeks ago. And when he'd arrived at his new boss's house for the first meeting, Juan had been shocked at his directness and terseness.

Tom had told him, "I've been playing polo for four years. I want to play high goal now. I play number one. I pay the bills. Larry Ritter plays back. He's our token club player. At least one club member besides the patron has to be on each team here. You take care of your horses and mine, and get me another pro. Here are the keys to the west barn; there are two apartments there, one for you, and one for the other pro. There are also bedrooms and showers for the grooms. I'll be down at the stables tomorrow at ten to check out your horses. See you then."

Juan had found another pro to play with them, Andre, a Chilean. They'd started the season with three losses. Two had been close games, but today's game had been a fiasco.

Juan got in his car and watched Felipe as he left to collect his six ponies. Felipe mounted one pony and, holding their leads, juggled the ponies into position, two on one side, and three on the other. As he set off at a brisk walk, Juan could see that two of them were lame. He swore and leaned back on his seat.

The game had tired him out. A mallet had hit him when his opponent hooked his stick too high and his arm still felt numb. He winced as he flexed his hand. With another deep sigh he started the car. A drink would be welcome.

At the clubhouse, there was a large zinc cooler designed to look like a horse trough. It was filled with ice and soft drinks.

Waitresses wore white skirts like cheerleaders and yellow polo jerseys with a black number one on the front and the word "drinks" on the back. This group must have been working at the polo club for a few years, because they completely ignored the handsome, high-goal polo players — eternally broke — and concentrated on the patrons, whatever they looked like.

Juan grabbed himself a diet soda from the trough and looked around for a place to sit. Far off in another corner were the only two French polo players. They were drinking Perrier and having more success with the waitresses than the other pros.

These French players had the reputation for being crazy but excellent players. They came from a good family, and though they played on separate teams, they stuck together. Juan felt more secure with them than with the cutthroats from his own country. He also liked to hear French spoken, it reminded him of his mother, who had been French.

"Salut Pierre, Arnaud. Mind if I sit down?"

"*Pas du tout,*" said Pierre. He was the eldest brother, and by all accounts the handsomest, with dark chestnut hair and a pensive face.

"Not at all," echoed Arnaud. "We were just talking about the weather. If the rain keeps up they'll cancel the games, then what will we do?"

Juan grinned. "Rest my horses. It would be a good break for me if it did keep on raining. Half my string is lame."

"First year horses?" asked Pierre.

"Yes, they'll be good next year. This year we have to baby them. But my boss wants to win."

"Whose boss doesn't?" Arnaud laughed.

"What are you doing this summer?" asked Pierre. "After the season here in Florida, I mean."

Juan stared outside. It was still dreary, reminding him of his mood. "Going to England. My father lives there. He has a little farm in the north of Wales."

"Unusual, no? Aren't you Argentinean?" Pierre was curious.

"My father's English. He left Argentina when my mother died," Juan said.

The two brothers exchanged glances.

"Listen Juan…" Pierre began to say.

"We didn't mean to be so nosy," continued Arnaud.

Juan shrugged. "I don't mind."

"Do you live in Argentina?" "How long ago did your mother die?" The two questions came simultaneously from the incorrigible Frenchmen. They looked at each other and laughed.

"I still live on my family's farm in Argentina," said Juan. "My two older brothers are bloodstock agents for cattle. My mother died just after the Falkland war. My eldest brother was killed, and she died of sorrow. He was her favorite."

"Your brother fought in the war?" asked Arnaud, ignoring Pierre's elbow jabbing him in the arm. "Stop it Pierre, you're spilling my Perrier!"

"Yes, but he never actually got there. He was killed in a car accident on his way to the airport. A bus hit them." Juan winced at the memory.

"Mon Dieu, I'm sorry Juan," said Pierre.

"How sad," said Arnaud. "Our mother is dead also. I don't remember her at all. Pierre and I grew up in the stables where our father worked. He's an impoverished Baron. He sold all our land and the chateau after the war."

"How did you two start playing polo?" he asked the French brothers.

"Our chateau…" Arnaud said.

"Ex-chateau," corrected Pierre.

"Our ex-chateau," continued Arnaud smoothly, "was in the Normandy region of France, well known for its stud farms. The new owner raises racehorses, and like all the best snobs, joined the polo club."

"Where our father was already a member," put in Pierre.

"And our grandfather. Stop interrupting. Anyway, the new owner started to play polo. My father then said to this guy, give my sons your racing duds to train for you. So, we started playing polo with the chateau's polo team. We went to Paris every weekend. I trained horses all week long," said Arnaud.

"What about school?" asked Juan. His good humor was fully restored. The two Frenchmen's animated conversation was a welcome change from his captain's terse commands or his groom's mournful predictions about lame horses.

"School?" Arnaud laughed. "Pierre is very smart, he studied. He went to the university. I stayed on the farm and trained the horses. We mostly play polo in Europe. We've been to South America, to buy horses and to perfect our game, but it's a tricky business."

Juan nodded. "Very tricky, as you say." He flexed his hand over the table and winced. He hoped nothing was broken. He'd once played an entire tournament with a broken bone in his foot, and the memory still pained him.

A redheaded waitress came over to the table. "Want some more drinks?" She smiled at Arnaud, who was winking at her. She obviously thought his French good looks were worth a closer glance, because she dropped her pen on his lap and made a show of picking it up. Arnaud closed his eyes and feigned ecstasy.

Juan looked at his watch and said regretfully, "I have to get back to the stables."

He left, but not before Pierre and Arnaud invited him to their apartment for dinner that night.

"The best thing Pierre did this year was to seduce an Italian girl." Arnaud laughed. "Now she lives at our house and cooks for us."

* * * * *

Back at the stables, Juan saw Andre, the Chilean pro, cleaning his tack. "What happened?" he asked.

"My groom quit," he said grinning wryly. "She got pregnant and went back to England."

"You're kidding!"

"Nope. Not kidding." Andre shook his head. "Next time, I'm getting a male groom."

"I'll tell Felipe to help you out until you find someone else," Juan said.

"Thanks." Andre put a final brush to the saddle and put it back on the rack.

"You off?" Andre asked.

"Yes, I'm eating at the de Lancourts."

"The mad frogs?"

"You know them?"

Andre shrugged. "I saw them in Chile last year. They were more interested in the vineyards than in the polo fields. They bought cases of wine. Imagine! Frenchmen buying wine from Chile! They are loco, I tell you."

Loco or not, Juan was looking forward to seeing the Frenchmen again. They had managed to cheer him up, and right now he figured he could use some good spirits. After his loneliness at the stables, the Frenchmen's light chatter was a welcome relief.

He showered, checking for sore muscles and bruises. In the back of his mind, there was a nagging feeling that his life wasn't going as planned. He had thought he'd be missing Argentina, but he didn't. He missed his brothers, and his estancia, but that was it. He wondered if he missed Rosa, his fiancée. Then the hot water sputtered and died; a spray of icy water brought him back to the present. Juan rinsed off, shivering and cursing the ridiculously small amount of hot water at the stables.

That was another thing. He hadn't thought a polo pro would be lodged in the stables with the horses and grooms. Call it a form of snobbism—most of the pros he knew had luxury apartments, at least for the season. He was in a small room with no bathroom of its own. He shared a bathroom with Felipe and Andre, and if he was honest with himself, cleaning was not a priority. The place was beginning to smell. His room was full of dirty laundry, and as for food, well, he had a box of cookies under the bed, but otherwise his meals were taken at fast-food restaurants or microwaved in his little oven. He glared at his kitchen. That was another thing he hated, doing dishes. His sink was overflowing and he had forgotten to buy dishwashing liquid again.

* * * * *

Dinner was, as Arnaud had promised, wonderful. Juan had been eating frozen dinners for so long he'd forgotten how good home-cooked food could be. Afterwards, Juan realized how tired he was and begged off going out with the de Lancourts to the local nightclub.

When he pulled into the stables and got out of the car he gazed for a moment at the sky. He realized suddenly, with a shock, how clear the night was. For the first time in weeks the stars shone, twinkled and sparkled in the velvet sky. Juan rubbed his forehead and swore. His horses were going to get no rest.

The next day dawned hot and clear. The sun had returned to Palm Beach.

Chapter One

Rennie went into the church to get out of the sun. It was hot and her face was burning. She'd gone to the supermarket to buy the weekly groceries for her mother and herself.

The church was blessedly cool. The darkness made it hard to see at first; her eyes were a few seconds adjusting. Then she slid into a seat near the statue of the Virgin Mary and put her groceries at her feet. She rested her hot forehead on her arms.

After a while Rennie felt better so she raised her head to look around. The church was old by Florida standards; it was made of wood and had wooden benches instead of the orange plastic chairs Rennie had seen in other places. The floor was wooden too, and the church had escaped the worst of modern decoration. The statues were garishly painted though. The Virgin Mary looked like she had on a bit too much make-up, and the baby Jesus, suspended dramatically above the nave, was bright pink from head to toe.

Rennie liked the statue of Saint Francis the best. At least she thought it was him. Her religious instruction, like the rest of her education, was sketchy. The statue showed a man holding an eagle, and Rennie vaguely remembered Saint Francis protecting the animals. The statue's face reminded her of her father's. He'd had a reddish beard and piercing green eyes too. She noticed candles burning at the feet of all the statues and she went to have a look.

A card pinned to the wall read, *Big Candles 50 cents. Little candles 25 cents. Bless You and Have a Good Day*. It was a plain, white card. Nothing like her mother's new business cards. Her mother worked in a beauty salon in Palm Beach. Her business card, printed on shiny, pink cardboard, said: *Marilyn's Marvelous Manicures.*

"Rennie, I think you should enroll in beauty school," her mother had told her last week. "You're not doing anything interesting with your life, and we could set up a business together. We could call it 'Marilyn and Renée's Beauty Shoppe'."

Rennie's real name was Renée, but no one called her that.

As she thought about the future, tears welled up in her eyes. She blinked once and they rolled down her cheeks. The bright Florida sun would bleach all her dreams right out of her. Her dreams of fame and fortune. Her dream of having a house with a real garden. And even the simplest dream of finding a job she'd like, not doing manicures with her mother, or sticking curlers in some lady's blue hair. If only she had an idea of what to do with her life.

She looked up at the brightly painted statue and found her lips moving. "Help me, Saint Francis. Please. Help me get out of here. I don't want to be a beautician." The tears ran down her face faster and faster. "I don't want to be part of my mother's life forever." At these words she felt cruel. How could she? After all her mother had done for her… That made her cry even harder.

Rennie stood up stiffly, resolved to try to become a better person. She sniffed one last time and turned to the door. Her eyes were so blurred with tears she nearly bumped into someone on the way out. Slowly she started walking homeward.

"I will not daydream anymore," she told herself firmly. "I will work hard in college. I will help my mother. I will think about beauty school."

She wiped her face. The heat of the sun dried her tears in seconds, leaving silvery, salty traces on her cheeks. She sighed deeply and straightened her shoulders. "Only ten more blocks, just ten more blocks," she said.

* * * * *

On his way to the tack shop, Juan saw a little wooden church standing by itself under two fig trees. His mother had been devout, he'd gone to Catholic school, and his family went to church regularly. Although he hadn't gone to mass once since coming to Florida, he swerved his car into the parking lot and went into the church on a whim. After last night with the French brothers, Juan had realized how much he missed his mother and brother—he would light candles for them.

The darkness blinded him for a moment. Then he saw the girl. She was kneeling in front of a statue he recognized as Saint John from the eagle, and she was crying.

Her hair was the first thing he noticed about her. It was the color of sun-kissed apricots. It hung in a neat braid halfway down her slim back. She was dressed in cut-off denim shorts and a pale orange t-shirt that looked as if it had started out another color before being in a disastrous wash. Her feet were shod in plastic flip-flops, also orange, also faded.

When she turned around his breath caught in his throat. She looked like the Madonna his mother had hanging over her bed. The painting was old, Flemish, and the girl, by modern standards, was not beautiful. Her face was too round on the top, and her chin too pointed. Her brow was high and pale. Her eyebrows were pale too, like her hair, and her mouth was not the large, full mouth that was in fashion. It was small and folded like a flower. Like the Madonna in the painting, she had immense gray eyes as clear as rainwater. They were full of tears now, and red-rimmed, but her lashes were thick and dark. Probably mascara, he decided. When she stood up, he noticed she was tall and thin. Her arms were tan, and pale freckles dotted her nose.

As if in a daze, she walked out of the church right past him, and into the blinding sun. She smelled like fresh cut grass and her hair caught the light when she walked outside and flashed red-gold. Then she was gone.

Juan sighed and walked to the statue of the Virgin. He lit two candles and said a prayer for his mother and brother. He tried to think of Rosa too, but his thoughts kept straying to the slender redhead who'd been kneeling in the church. Why had she been kneeling in front of the statue of Saint John? He loved Saint John's the best of all the Gospels, but it was the most complex. He wondered at the significance the girl accorded to him.

Then his eyes were drawn to three large bags of groceries sitting under the bench. They were rather squashed as if they'd been shoved hurriedly there out of the way. He thought they must be the girl's so he picked them up and went to his car. He would try to find her.

* * * * *

In the end, she was easy to find. Her hair shone like a beacon from way down the dusty road. She'd taken the second left-hand turn and was walking slowly along the broken sidewalk with her shoes going clip-clap against her feet. She didn't walk so much as she floated. She stood straight, her thin shoulders pulled back by invisible wires, her head held high. She had long legs, tanned and smooth.

He slowed his car down to match her pace and leaned out the window to call to her. "Miss! Miss!"

She glanced over to him but kept walking. He noticed she looked nervous.

"Did you leave your shopping in the church?" he called.

At that she stopped, a horrified expression on her face. She clapped a hand to her mouth. "Oh no!" she wailed.

"Don't worry. I have them right here in the car."

She glanced quickly to the left for traffic then dashed across the road. "Thank you so much!" she said warmly. "I really appreciate you coming after me. That's so nice."

She smiled and he saw her teeth were white and even. Even her voice was delightful. Her hands were long and thin, like the rest of her. However, when she leaned up to the car window, he saw that her breasts were beautifully rounded, full and strained against the flimsy t-shirt. He felt a wave of heat rush through him. It was a strange feeling that encompassed her breasts, her scent, and the color of her eyes. Her lashes were *naturally* black and thick he saw.

"Do you live far? I'll give you a lift if you wish."

"Well…" She hesitated for a minute then smiled, getting into the car. "All right, it's not too far. Take the next road to your right, at the light. I live next to a chicken restaurant, you can't miss it." She giggled and the warm sound tickled his ears.

"My name's Juan," he said. "What's yours?"

"Renée."

"It's French," he said.

She looked surprised. "Yes, but everyone calls me Rennie. Actually, if you called me Renée I wouldn't realize you were talking to me. Only my father called me that."

Juan caught a trace of sadness in her voice as she said that, but didn't comment. Last night's conversation with the French players had reminded him just how painful the past could be even brought up with the friendliest intentions. "Is that the turn?" he asked, seeing a large sign with a red hen on it. The hen was dressed like a farmer holding a basket of eggs under her wing. The sign said "Den's Fryers", and something about going Cuckoo. Juan thought he'd probably go loco if he had to look at that sign all day. He'd been brought up in a household where good taste was considered very important.

"Yes, thanks. Why don't you come in and have something cold to drink? It's awfully hot out," Rennie said, as she gathered up her groceries. "I have iced tea in the fridge."

"Here let me get those," said Juan, taking the bags from her.

Rennie looked surprised. "Thanks."

Juan followed Rennie up the steps on the outside of an old wooden house. It was built colonial style and had once been a large, single family home. Time had divided the house into flats, and faded the paint and woodwork so that hardly a trace of the old mansion could be seen. All the doors were painted different colors now. Rennie's door was pink, he noticed. There was a pot of white geraniums near the door, with a bowl of cat-food shoved behind it.

The apartment was cool—closed shutters kept the sun out. Potted plants abounded, some on the floor, some on tables, and the furniture was mostly wicker, with cushions in a light, floral pattern. No paintings or posters hung on the walls, but there was a huge bookcase stuffed with books. Books overflowed onto the floor and were stacked neatly according to size. In a round bowl placed on a table, a goldfish swam in lazy circles.

Rennie put the groceries on the counter that separated the tiny kitchen from the living room and motioned Juan towards a chair.

"Have a seat," she said. "I'll just be a minute putting these away. What would you prefer, a soda or iced tea?"

"I'll have the tea," he answered. He sat in the chair next to the goldfish. The floor was bare, pine boards in the living room, linoleum in the kitchen. Everything was spotless. The apartment smelled nice, like flowers. There wasn't the smell of old tobacco. No smokers here, he decided.

He watched Rennie. Her movements were quick and decisive. Her hair was coming loose and tendrils hung around her face. Botticelli's Venus came to his mind; Rennie had the same grave look. She caught him staring at her and blushed.

"I look awful," she apologized. "It's this t-shirt, it's so old. I was just going shopping, and well…didn't think I'd be meeting anyone." She shrugged. "Here's your drink. Are you Cuban? I noticed your accent." She'd also noticed his good looks and his lithe, athletic body.

"No, I'm from Argentina."

Now he'd really caught her interest. She'd always thought Argentina sounded like an exotic and wonderful country. "Wow! That's far away. Is it nice there?" she switched to Spanish and spoke with hardly an accent. She was proud of her Spanish, and hoped the sexy Argentine would notice.

He grinned. "Where did you learn to speak Spanish?"

Score one for me, she thought. Aloud she replied, "In school, where else? Here in Florida we're mostly hearing two languages now. It's all over the radio and TV. I think it's great. I wish I could learn more languages. I'm taking French classes in college, but I'm not getting very far. Is Argentina nice?" she continued, suddenly conscious she'd been babbling about herself, something she knew was impolite. Besides, she wanted to learn more about him. "Are you here on vacation?" She settled on the sofa facing him.

"Argentina is wonderful."

Juan found himself telling her all about his life on the farm, and about his family. He spoke about his mother, and his brother, about his father moving to England and leaving him and his two older brothers in Argentina. He talked about polo, and the problems he was having with his boss.

Through it all Rennie listened with wide eyes. Clearly she was fascinated.

Juan couldn't remember feeling so much at ease with a person, or being able to talk so freely about his family. Even with his fiancée, Rosa, there was that frown of censorship that marred her face when he mentioned his father. She thought he was a criminal to run away to England after his wife's death. Rosa only wanted to talk about marriage and children and how Juan would run the farm when they were married.

Rennie was especially interested in polo, and laughed delightedly when he came to the part about Andre's groom running away.

"He found someone right away, didn't he?" she asked.

"Nope, I saw him this morning riding his horses out on exercise and mucking out the stalls."

Rennie looked thoughtful. "I wish I could be a groom," she said. "I can ride, and take care of a horse. Is the pay any good?"

When he told her she gave a shriek. "Oh please, please let me try! Introduce me to Andre, I'll work for half that, I'll learn quickly, you'll see, and work hard. Please, please? I promise I won't get pregnant and run away!"

"Are you serious?" he asked. His heart gave a strange flutter as he watched her face light up. Suddenly, the most important thing in the world seemed to be to make this serious, gray-eyed girl smile.

"Yes, a thousand times yes!" Rennie cried. "Just give me a chance, I know I can do it."

Juan nodded. "Okay, I'll let you try. You'll be on a trial basis for one week, and if all goes well we'll hire you for the rest of the season until mid-April. But I don't decide. It's Andre's decision. All right?"

"Okay," she frowned, "What do I have to wear? Hardhat and breeches?"

"No, hard-hats are only mandatory in England, although I think they're a good idea. Just any working clothes. You're going to get dirty. Can you come to the stables now?" he asked, checking his watch. "It's three-thirty, Andre should be there."

"Hold on a sec, I'll change."

She ran out of the room and he could hear her through the paper-thin walls digging around her closet for clothes. Soon she came back in, with jeans and a new t-shirt. Her hair was brushed and braided tightly and on her feet were low riding boots that looked old, in spite of the polish that made them shine.

She caught the direction of his glance and laughed self-consciously. "Aren't they sweet? They were my mother's when she was younger. Would you believe she used to be a terrific rider? You'd never guess now, seeing her, that she won a whole load of trophies. She had her own horse. Then she got married and had me. She gave me riding lessons for as long as she could afford it. I bet she's still better on a horse than me, even now. Here, look." She opened a drawer in the table underneath the goldfish and took out a photo album. She opened it and put it in Juan's lap.

In it, were snapshots of a woman dressed in impeccable riding togs on a large gray hunter. They were jumping over a huge fence in one photo, and a couple of newspaper clippings, faded and well worn were taped to the opposite page. He turned the page and saw the same woman receiving prizes, or jumping fences, always with the same horse. He tried to see the resemblance to Rennie, but couldn't. The woman was a pale blond with an austere expression on her angular face. She had wonderful style though, Juan could see that. She also looked familiar. He felt he should know her.

"Does she ride anymore?" he asked.

"No, not since I was born." Rennie sounded forlorn. "She had a problem when I was born, something to do with her back. She could never ride again." She stopped talking and looked away. Juan saw she was fighting tears, so he quickly changed the subject.

"Shall we go?" He wondered what Andre was going to say. He hoped he hadn't found anyone else. Suddenly it seemed important to keep Rennie close to him. He wondered if he was developing a crush on her.

* * * * *

Rennie was silent during the drive. Actually, she was petrified. She wondered what had prompted her to ask for the job. She'd never groomed before. She could ride, but she'd never taken care of more than one horse at a time. Juan said she'd have six to care for.

Furthermore, how was she going to tell her mother, or on a more practical note, get to work? She'd have to take the bus, and then walk through the club.

She was staggered by the size of it. They went through the front gate, and Rennie goggled at all the mansions lined up along the drive. There were tennis courts and swimming pools everywhere. There were real gardens here, with rose bushes, hibiscus and tons of other flowering plants that Rennie couldn't put a name to. She'd seen mansions before, of course. Palm

Beach had its Worth Avenue and the coast was one of the wealthiest in the world, but the polo club impressed Rennie. Everything impressed her. Arched bridges crossed the dark water of the canal. The landscaped gardens were beautifully groomed, as were the polo fields. There were huge expanses of perfectly mowed lawn with gleaming red sideboards running down their entire lengths. Rennie couldn't believe it.

Tucked in an endless orange grove, the barn was beautiful but unassuming. It was set amid four square paddocks and a tree-lined drive led to the parking lot in the back. Two other cars were parked there, a pickup truck, and a converted cattle trailer built to carry twelve horses to and from games.

Two apartments tagged on either end of the stables, and the stables themselves consisted of a double line of stalls built along a corridor in the middle of the barn. Each side of the barn housed twelve ponies. Twelve ponies faced out towards the orange groves, and twelve faced the parking lot and driveway. Each stall had a fan in it, and automatic watering troughs.

Rennie found her throat was so dry she couldn't speak. She trailed after Juan as he went towards the east side of the barn and hollered for Andre.

A curly head of black hair appeared. Was this Andre? He had a friendly face under all those black curls, decided Rennie. His nose had obviously been broken before and had been set crookedly. He also had a wicked-looking scar that cut his bottom lip into two pieces.

"Andre, here's your new groom," announced Juan in Spanish as soon as he'd opened the door.

Andre looked surprised. "But I wanted a man this time, not a woman. Where did you find her?"

"On the side of the road," joked Juan. "Why don't you give her a try, and if she doesn't work out we'll look for someone else. The advantage is that she's American. No problems with green cards or work permits."

Andre shrugged. "Okay by me. What's your name?" he asked her.

"Rennie. Rennie Piccabéa. "

"Piccabéa, Piccabéa. The name sounds familiar," said Andre, wrinkling his forehead.

Juan thought so too, and it suddenly dawned on him. "Your mother is Marilyn Piccabéa?" he asked, incredulous.

Rennie said, "Yes, she was. She is I mean." She was surprised they'd recognized her mother's name. Nobody ever had before.

Juan nodded his head. "Of course. I didn't recognize her from those old photos. She was on the Olympic team. Those little trophies, they were silver medals. Her horse was the Sergeant, wasn't he?"

"Yes, that's right."

"You could've told me," he said crossly.

Rennie flushed. "Sorry, I'm not used to talking about it. We never do. Anyway, it was a long time ago."

"How old are you?" Juan asked.

"Nineteen."

Juan tapped his chin pensively. "I don't remember her, but my father was on the English jumping team, and he used to talk about your mother when he spoke about the Olympics. He never knew why she stopped…"

Rennie tightened her lips. "It was because of me," she reminded him. "I was a breech birth and it hurt my mother's back."

Juan must have noticed the set of her mouth, because he looked abashed and said, "Sorry."

Rennie sighed. "It's okay. She married her trainer right after the Olympics. Then she had me."

"Your father was her trainer?" asked Andre. He sounded amused.

"For a while. Then he had an accident and died. My mother says we're cursed," she added, feeling suddenly worried.

"Poor kid!" said Andre. "Well, I don't believe in curses. You can start tomorrow at five a.m. I'll show you around now, and tell you what's to be done. The horses are all pretty good, except Pinto, the paint pony. He's a bit young." He turned and pointed to a truck. "That's the grooms' pickup, you can use that. You have a driver's license don't you?"

"Yes, I do." Rennie felt a huge weight lift off her chest. She had job and a car. *Oh!* she thought, *It must be Saint Francis. He's looking out for me.* Her skin prickled.

Her six horses were in the east half of the stables facing the parking lot. She would clean their stalls then see that their tack was clean and ready for use. She would feed and ride them twice a day, except on polo days, which were busier, but Felipe and Sally would be there to show her the ropes. She met Felipe and got along fine with him; he was glad she spoke Spanish. She would have to be at the barn every day at five a.m.—that was the part she liked the least. The best part was having most of the afternoon free. She hoped her mother wouldn't have a fit.

Actually, the best part wasn't the afternoon free. The best part was Juan. Rennie looked at him from the corner of her eye. He was, she thought, the most gorgeous man she'd ever seen. Maybe her life wouldn't be such a failure after all. Maybe, just maybe, she and Juan would get to know each other and fall in love. She took a shaky breath and shook her head. She'd have to stop daydreaming. Things like that only happened in fairy tales.

Chapter Two

Rennie drove the pickup truck home in a state of euphoria that lasted until her mother heard what had happened and just about exploded. However, underneath Rennie's seemingly fragile appearance was a steely determination. Once her mind was made up about something, it was impossible to move her. She simply narrowed her lips and waited until her mother's storm blew over.

Her mother knew this. She couldn't help trying though. When at last she sank, exhausted into the wicker armchair, she knew her daughter would go ahead and do whatever it was she wanted.

Marilyn knew she was doing the best she could for her daughter. She also knew she hadn't the slightest idea of how to raise a child in the kind of world she was now living in. She had grown up in Virginia, in a well-to-do family, surrounded by adoring parents, nannies and three sisters. Marilyn had been the tomboy of the family.

Her father was a horseman and had hunted every weekend. Marilyn had been the son he hadn't had. When she was five he'd seen her fearlessly leaping her pony over the stone wall enclosing the estate, and he'd taken her hunting ever after. The Sergeant was his gift to her when she was sixteen. She'd trained the horse herself, and she and the horse had gone all the way to a silver medal in the Olympics.

But her mother had died in a car accident while Marilyn was competing in the Olympics, and her father never forgave her for not flying back the second he'd called her. He could never understand how she could have stayed that one extra day to ride in the finals and win her silver medal. That she had cried the whole round, tears blinding her as she jumped, he never wanted to hear. She'd passed up the individual finals to fly home, but she couldn't let the team down. She'd tried to explain, but the damage had been done.

Then her father's re-marriage a year later and the birth of a long-wanted son had further strained their relationship. Marilyn had hated her stepmother from day one, when the woman she always referred to as "Father's Fling" came to the house and took over. Marilyn's older sister was married by then, and Marilyn had been running the household. But her father's "Fling" had fired the cook, the housekeeper was let go, and Jesse, Marilyn's beloved nurse, was told she was no longer needed.

Marilyn had thought that her two younger sisters, Rosemary and Frances would object. However they were only children, ten and twelve years old, and were completely bewildered about everything happening to them since their mother's death.

Then, just when she was feeling vulnerable and fragile, Marilyn had changed trainers, and she had met Ricky. Oh God, Ricky. She looked at her daughter's head bent over her beloved cat and felt tears well up. Why had she fallen in love with Ricky? He was all wrong for her. Everyone knew it, everyone told her. Her father had been livid, and had fired Ricky on the spot, but he'd just gotten another job. He'd been a good, no, he'd been a great horseman.

She'd fallen for him the second she'd seen him. He had dark russet hair that was cut short over his well-shaped head. His face was narrow and expressive, with bright green eyes that seemed to look right through her. He was not tall, but extremely well-made. And he could ride anything. He'd smiled his slow, mocking smile at her and said, "So, you're the famous Marilyn that Sergeant's been telling me about."

She was pregnant with Rennie three months later.

Oh, God, why torture herself? Why think of the past?

Wasn't it bad enough that her father hadn't accepted Ricky? That he'd cut her off without a penny? Then, before she could think of some way to make up to him, he'd died, thrown from his horse during a hunt. Her stepmother had refused all contact with her. A lawyer's call had informed her of her father's death. A letter had informed her that her inheritance was the Sergeant, and that was all. Another letter, from her sisters, told her not to bother coming to the funeral with her husband, so she'd gone alone, wrapped in a black veil to hide her growing belly.

Ever since that day, she'd regretted her actions. Regretted not flying home from Rome, regretted not making an effort to win over her stepmother, regretted falling in love with Ricky, and regretted not being able to be with her father when he'd gone hunting that day. She would have been able to save him, she was sure.

The one thing she'd never regretted was Rennie. From the moment she was born, a tiny girl with strange gray eyes and a thatch of fiery red hair, Marilyn had felt the strongest maternal instinct. She'd loved her with blinding devotion. Even though Rennie's birth had damaged her beyond repair so that she could never ride again, or even have any more children. Through Ricky's tragic death, and the loss of her beloved Sergeant, she'd hung onto sanity by loving and caring for Rennie.

Now Rennie was sitting calmly on the floor, waiting for her to sigh and give in. As she would. As she always did.

Marilyn rubbed her face tiredly and wished for the thousandth time she was still living in her mansion in Virginia, and that she could just call out to her nanny Jesse to come and help her. Jesse would come over, her face crinkled up with love and worry, and would take her in her arms and hug her, and say, "It's all right, honey child. Old Jesse is here. Lay your head on my shoulder now and tell me all about it."

Marilyn closed her eyes. She would say, "Jesse, I don't know what to do. My Rennie baby is growing up, and she wants to leave me. I can't hold her anymore. Lord knows I've tried. Nevertheless, blood will tell. Horses, horses are calling her, and she's going to leave. Those damn horses. Daddy was right though; they're the only honest things on earth. And the Sergeant was the best of them. He was the best." She opened her eyes, saw Rennie looking at her, her face pale and set, her bright hair a forever reminder of Ricky.

She looks like my mother, Marilyn suddenly thought. *But my mother was blonde, and pale as the moon. The only thing Rennie has of you is your coloring, Ricky, though not as vibrant. She's stronger than you are Ricky, though. She's stronger than I am. She's got something hidden way down deep inside of her that won't bend, and it's too strong to break. At least I hope to God it doesn't break. If it ever does, she'll be lost.*

* * * * *

"The whole thing never would have happened, if my mother hadn't won the silver medal in the Olympics. She made sure I learned how to ride." Rennie grinned crookedly at her best friend, Freya.

"Yeah, and now you got a job at the polo club! You lucky bitch, you'll probably catch the eye of some rich polo player and end up happy ever after."

"God, don't I wish!" Rennie sipped her cold beer and grinned.

The two girls sat at a table at the nightclub called 'The Last Chucker.' Located in town near the polo club, it was a popular hangout for grooms, players and the young people in the village. On the dance floor in the back a few couples were swaying to a slow country ballad, while at the bar, some men in jeans and wearing cowboy boots argued over a baseball game being shown on the television up on the top shelf.

Rennie was watching the game too—she loved the sport. Freya, her best friend since first grade, finished her rum and coke and worried about her upcoming real estate exam.

The girls had started coming regularly to the 'The Last Chucker' after Rennie got her job. Rennie now knew most of the crowd by sight, and some of the grooms greeted her. But most of the players just nodded coolly. There seemed to be an invisible line dividing grooms from players, and the line got wider when it applied to grooms and patrons. Most patrons were very wealthy and had time-consuming, high-stress jobs. Polo was their pass-time and a way of letting off steam. They lived in an exclusive world of their own, and Rennie rarely saw one of them outside of a polo game.

"Hey, isn't that your boss?" Freya asked.

Rennie turned, and saw Andre, his black hair tousled like he'd just crawled out of bed, walk into the club. He saw Rennie and gave her a friendly wave, then went to where a group of players and their wives were sitting. Rennie waved back, and was just about to turn away, when she spotted Juan. He was hesitating in the doorway, scanning the crowd.

"Holy Bat Britches," whispered Freya. "Who is that?"

"That's Juan. He's the one I told you about who got me my job," said Rennie.

"Wow! What a babe! Why haven't I seen him before?"

"I don't know." Rennie shrugged. "He doesn't come here very often. He must have come with Andre."

"Quick girl, wave at him," hissed Freya. She reached over, and to Rennie's dismay, yanked her shirt down, nearly popping her tits out of it.

"Stop it!" Rennie went to pull her shirt up again, and to her embarrassment, saw that Juan was looking straight at her. She gave him a little wave, trying not to notice her now low, low décolleté.

"Oh...My...God," said Freya. "He's heading this way."

"Jesus," said Rennie. "What am I going to say?"

"How about, 'Can I have your baby?'"

Rennie glared at her. "Very funny."

"What? Don't tell me you still haven't—you know what."

"You know damn well I haven't," snapped Rennie.

The Argentine Lover

"Shhh. Here he comes." Freya suddenly stood up and in a loud voice said, "Well, Rennie, I have to go back and study for my exam. Sorry to leave you all ALONE, you SEX VIXEN. Try not to get into trouble. See you!"

"What?" Rennie glared at her friend, who winked at her once, and slipped out through the crowd just as Juan arrived.

Rennie's mouth was dry, and she completely forgot about her shirt or the baseball game. She gazed up at Juan, incapable of uttering a single sound. For some reason, when he was near, her whole body seemed to go into overdrive. There were goosebumps all along her arms, and her nipples, to her embarrassment, suddenly started to tingle and stood up at attention.

* * * * *

Juan regretted coming to the nightclub as soon as he arrived, but Andre had talked him into tagging along. Once inside, Andre waved at someone and then spotted a group of polo players. Juan started towards them, but his eye caught a flash of red-gold, and he stopped. Sitting in the back, in a corner, was Rennie and someone with…green hair?

He narrowed his eyes and peered. Yes, the girl with Rennie had bright, blue-green hair, but that wasn't what captured his attention. Rennie was wearing a low-cut blouse that showed most of her creamy shoulders and a good deal of cleavage. He swallowed hard. He'd noticed her lovely breasts before, and now here they were, peeking at him from Rennie's neckline. What neckline? It was practically a waistline!

She noticed him, and waved. He swallowed, not surprised to feel his penis stir in interest. "Down boy," he said to himself. It didn't help. As soon as he thought about Rennie he wondered what it would be like to touch her soft skin. His cock seemed to like this train of thought and there was a definite stiffening in his nether regions. He took a deep breath, and to be polite, he went to say hello to her.

35

As he drew near, he heard the other girl say something, and then he heard the word 'alone', and then something about a sex vixen. Then she stood up and left. Maybe he'd misheard—after all, there was a lot of noise. Well, he'd say a quick hello and then go sit down with Andre and that crowd. He smiled at Rennie, who was staring up at him with wide eyes.

"Hi," he said.

"Hi." She blushed.

He wasn't sure why her cheeks were suddenly so pink, but he was entranced by the wash of color on her pale skin. And now he was stuck. He couldn't just leave her all alone here. He frowned. "Is anyone sitting here?"

"No. Freya just left."

"The girl with the green hair?"

"Isn't she something?" Rennie laughed, and Juan noticed her breasts moving as her laughter tickled his ears. His hand clutched at the back of a chair.

"Mind if I sit down?" His voice was a little hoarse, but it was a strain keeping control of his penis, which had suddenly decided to betray him by becoming as hard as a rock. He didn't wait for her reply, but sat down, leaning over the table; there— yes, that was better.

"What's up?" he asked, when he'd gotten hold of himself.

"Nothing." Rennie toyed with her beer.

"How is work?"

She looked up at him, her eyes dancing. "Wonderful. I can't thank you enough for telling Andre to hire me. His horses are fun to ride, and I never knew polo was such an exciting sport."

"Do you like it?"

"I love it. I wish I knew more about the rules, it looks complicated."

"It's not really," said Juan. "It's just a matter of getting more goals than the other team."

"I never saw a polo game before I met you," she said.

"Why not? The games are played all over Florida!"

"Yeah, in exclusive polo clubs." She grinned. "I was more into the beach volleyball crowd before."

Juan imagined her in a bikini, and then was glad of the table over his lap. "Um, so, what do you do when you're not working?"

She shrugged. "I'm taking classes at the Junior college, but I don't really know what to do."

"What classes?"

"I'm taking different language classes. I was going to major in Spanish and maybe become a Spanish teacher."

"Your Spanish is perfect," he said.

"Thanks." She tipped her glass up and finished her beer. Her pearly skin seemed to glow in the dim light. Juan saw a drop of beer on her upper lip, and wanted to lick it off. She caught his look, and for a minute she hesitated, as if she were going to say something. Then she stood up and said, "The team is playing tomorrow and I have to get up at four-thirty. I'd better go."

Juan nodded, a strange pang of longing striking him as she walked towards the door. He took a breath and let it out slowly. What spell had she cast on him? He tried to think of his fiancée, Rosa, but all he could see was bright apricot hair framing a pale face with immense gray eyes. He looked at the doorway. She was gone.

Chapter Three

Tom Wimsys swung and missed again. He swore audibly, and his wife, Carol, winced. The crowd loved it though.

The team was doing well today. Carol glanced at the scoreboard and smiled. five to two, they were ahead. The Argentine pro was outdoing himself, making goal after goal.

Juan *was* outdoing himself. He pulled his horse's reins and eased back a bit. No use tiring him out. His opponent missed the ball and now Juan swooped in and picked it up. He snapped a backhand shot to Andre who passed it along to Tom. Tom missed it, but Juan had anticipated and was there on the ball. He hit a cracking shot through the air and had the satisfaction of seeing it sail through the goal posts. The flagman waved the white flag. Goal! Six to two, then the bell rang marking the halftime.

Juan cantered over to the pony lines. Felipe ran up and took his pony. Juan slid to the ground and went to the cooler, taking advantage of the five-minute break to grab a soda. Out on the field the spectators started stomping divots, talking and laughing as they smoothed the pitch.

He stole a glance at Rennie, busy taking care of Andre's ponies. She scraped the lather off a tired horse then sluiced him off with water from a bucket. She tied him to the side of the trailer and went to get the pony for the fourth chucker ready. Juan loved the way her hair kept slipping out of her braid and falling around her face.

He took another sip of soda and tried to get a hold of himself. Here he was staring at Rennie when he should be concentrating on the game. But he knew that all his efforts on the field were for one thing only; to impress the pretty girl who was now swinging herself up onto the paint pony's back and checking that his girth was tight enough.

Satisfied, she cantered him around in a circle, warming him up. The pony was young, and bucked a bit, but Rennie had a marvellous seat and simply lifted his head up, kicking him on. She had enough training to get him onto the right lead and keep him there, and she knew just how to calm him and settle him down.

Juan admired her fluid style. Some people are natural horsemen and Rennie was one of them. Her body and the horse's were in perfect accord. With a subtle shift of her weight she swung the horse around and started him in the other direction. When she felt the horse relax and start to stretch out she slowed him down and walked him over to the side of the field. There she checked his girth again and put the stirrups down to Andre's length.

She turned and looked at Juan then, and he felt her gaze on him as if it had been a light touch. The bell rang and Juan turned his thoughts back to polo.

* * * * *

They won eight to four, and when the bell rang, signalling the end of the sixth chucker, the crowd roared its approval. Tom rode over and patted Juan on the back.

"That was some game, eh? I like our new groom. She's working out just fine. Finding her was excellent initiative. I can tell you're a serious guy. Good doing business with you." He nodded once more then rode off to the pony lines in a good mood.

Juan grinned. He was feeling more confident about himself. A compliment from the boss was a rare thing; Rennie was proving to be a good investment. There she was, taking Andre's pony and leading him away. Her hair had fallen out of its braid and hung in an apricot shine down her back.

Andre thanked her and sank tiredly into a folding chair.

"Whew, I'm beat. Hey Larry, throw me a beer, will you?" He laughed at Larry's sour expression and said, "Just kidding. Keep your beers. Toss me a soda. Hey Juan. Good game, man! You showed those guys."

Juan nodded and sat down in another chair. "It's nice when Tom's family shows up. He brings out the folding chairs and invites us to lunch afterwards."

Andre grinned at Juan. "Lunch by the pool. Sounds good to me."

"Maybe I'll go. I better go take a shower anyhow if I'm going to have lunch at the pool."

"Leave me some hot water," said Andre. "Last time I took my shower cold. "

Juan drove back to the barn. He took a long shower in his room and then rummaged around in his clothes to find a clean shirt for lunch. The apartment was a mess. Juan was not used to housework and couldn't keep up with the laundry.

A pile of dirty clothes was stuffed into an overflowing hamper, waiting for him to put them into the washing machine that was in the groom's shower room. With a sigh, he added his polo breeches to the already full hamper. He really was going to have to do something about the wash. Those were his last pair of white breeches. He couldn't find a thing to wear. Frowning, he picked out some clothes from the hamper. If he washed them and stuck them in the dryer, he'd have clean clothes. Why hadn't he thought of that before?

He heard the horses' hooves clattering on the cement walkway as the grooms finished hosing them down and put them back to their stalls. Then he heard Sally and Rennie laughing about something, and Felipe yelling at one of his horses to get off his foot. There was more laughter and swearing, and suddenly Juan felt the full weight of his loneliness as he stood in the tiny, Spartan apartment staring at the empty, white walls and hearing the sound of Rennie's laughter outside.

* * * * *

Rennie stood under the hot water and let her tired muscles relax. Grooming was much harder than she'd imagined. Taking care of six polo ponies was like taking care of six athletes. She was lucky to be working here though; she could take a shower right after the game and not have to drive back home all sweaty.

* * * * *

Juan was going to shove as many clothes as he could in the washing machine and then ask Felipe to start the damn thing. The last time he'd done it, he'd ended up with everything pink and he thought he must have pushed the wrong button. But which one was the right button? There were so many of them! There should be a law against making simple washing machines look like the control panel of a Boeing 747.

He glanced over to the shower and his breath caught in his throat. The shower stall had a frosted glass door, and Rennie — Rennie? he'd assumed it was Felipe! — was clearly visible, her back to him as she lathered her hair. He let his eyes feast on her long legs, her high buttocks and trim waist. The clothes he was carrying fell without a sound on the damp floor. His knees suddenly felt weak, and he was amazed to find his hands shaking. He backed up, intending to leave, but then Rennie turned around and he got his feet tangled up in his laundry and tripped, landing in a heap.

Rennie was standing with her head tipped up, face to the shower, rinsing the lather out of her hair. Her breasts were fuller than he'd thought, and tipped with shell-pink nipples. Her pubic hair was auburn, and Juan's penis was stiff with excitement.

With an effort he got up and staggered out the door, only realizing when he was outside he'd forgotten his clothes. He was naked. He didn't dare go back in though; he thought he'd probably go crazy if he saw her body again. He wiped his forehead with the back of his hand and went back to his apartment to get something cold to drink.

* * * * *

Rennie stepped out of the shower directly onto Juan's pile of clothes. With a frown, she recognized his polo shirt. She dried off and dressed, then stormed over to his apartment. She intended to give him a piece of her mind, but as soon as he opened the door the words died on her lips.

He was standing there, with just a towel wrapped around his waist. His shoulders were wide, and each muscle was clearly defined beneath his deep tan. A line of dark hair snaked from his belly button down, disappearing beneath the towel. As her eyes followed it, she blinked. The towel was pointing at her. She looked up at him, her whole body tingling.

He was staring at her with eyes that burned with a strange fever. Suddenly Rennie was conscious again of how attracted they were to each other. A sort of chemistry seemed to link them together, and instead of speaking, she swayed towards him and he caught her in his arms and kissed her.

* * * * *

He swung her around, closing the door with his heel. With his mouth fastened to hers, Juan let his tongue plunge in between her sweet lips. She parted them, and as he invaded her mouth, he felt his body starting to shake. He couldn't even think. All he could do was feel. Her lips were sweet and salty at the same time, and her teeth were sharp, with a little uneven edge in the front. Her tongue met his, timidly, then harder. She pressed against him, and his towel dropped to the floor.

Juan didn't know how they got into his bedroom, but he knew his hands were shaking so much he could barely undo the buttons of her shirt, so he ended up just pulling it off, popping buttons all over the bed. Rennie lay back on the covers without moving, her gray eyes immense in her white face.

Juan pulled off her shirt and her pants, and stared at her body. He'd never seen anything so lovely. It was as pale and delicately colored as a Venetian painting. Blue veins traced her throat and breasts; her hips were smooth curves leading from a narrow waist to her long legs. Her skin was like satin, like white coral, like seashells, and her hands were touching him, running down the length of his body, touching his sides, his chest and his belly. When she reached his penis and stroked it, it set him on fire, clouding his mind with the heat of passion. With a groan, he pushed her hands away. If she touched him again, he would come. Already his groin was tight with the effort of controlling himself. Taking a deep breath, he sat back and stared at Rennie's body.

When he parted her legs, he saw her labia, shiny and pink. Slowly, he drew his hand down her chest and over her breasts. He leaned over and drew a nipple into his mouth. Against his cheek, he could feel her heart beating wildly. It echoed his own. In his mouth, her nipple hardened, and he cupped her other breast in his hand. It fit perfectly. He massaged it, still pulling on her nipple with his mouth. Beneath him, she writhed, little mewing sounds coming from her throat.

Then he dipped his other hand between her legs. She opened them wider, and he touched her soft, curly pubic hair with his fingers, and found her slick and wet with desire. He touched her, finding the hard nub that was her clit, and gently circling it with his forefinger. Then, he lowered his head and kissed her there, letting his tongue stroke her. She grew even wetter, and her juice and scent almost made him lose his head. His body thrust by itself, seeking to penetrate. His cock was so hard and heavy; it was as if he'd never had a hard-on before. He couldn't even speak. He buried his face between her legs, licked her and stroked her, and felt her open and swell.

Finally, when he knew he couldn't hold off another second, he raised himself on his arms, and then slid into her body. She was so tight; it was like pushing into a closed fist. He was panting with the effort of not coming, but he could feel little spurts shaking him. Why was she so tight? He pushed harder, and then felt his penis slide into her, sheathing to the hilt. Within her, he felt hard contractions stroking his member, and that was it—he was lost.

"Rennie!" he shouted, as he drove into her body, his stomach contracting, ejaculating over and over, until he thought he was drained of every ounce of moisture in his body.

* * * * *

Rennie was breathing in quick gasps. She'd never seen a naked man, and she was unprepared for the intensity of her desire. When he touched her, her head literally spun. Her breasts ached for his touch, and when he sucked on her nipple, a deep tingling started and her belly began to throb.

He reached between her legs, and for the first time, she felt a man's touch on her most intimate parts. He seemed to know what he was doing though, and she gasped as he brought her to a fever pitch by stroking her clit.

And then he took her with his mouth. If his hand had felt good, his tongue was out of this world. It was so warm and wet. He tickled her clit and she arched her back, desperate for release. There was a pressure building inside of her cunt. It felt swollen and hot. She felt as if her body was melting, and at the same time she was as tense as a violin string.

When Juan lowered himself onto her she opened her legs instinctively. Everything she did was out of instinct. Arching her back, curling her legs around his, and drawing him into her, despite the sharp pain she felt. The pain was unimportant; all that mattered was getting him into her. She felt fullness between her legs that was different from anything she could have imagined. It was something between and ache and fierce heat— something so compelling she could not ignore it. The weight moved inside of her and became almost a part of her own body. She closed her eyes and let herself be swept away into the thrusts of Juan's hips.

When it was over, she felt as if a storm had passed overhead. The air was still. Juan was lying on top of her, his body trembling slightly. She felt an answering vibration deep inside her, and knew she wanted him to do it again.

She moved her hips, asking him with her body to satisfy her, and his body replied. They made love once more and this time Rennie concentrated fully on all the new sensations she felt. Her body knew what to do, she realized. It was a dance as old as time, what was more natural than sex? All her genes were pre-set for the act of love. It was the pleasure that surprised her the most. It left her panting, throbbing, and completely drained.

* * * * *

Juan was nervously and physically exhausted. He hadn't made love in so long. Rosa had never even let him touch her, aside from chaste kisses. She told him she would come to his marriage bed a virgin—what greater proof of her love for him?

He'd made love in England for the first time with a girl from the village who came to do housework for his father. Then there had been a few other times with different girls, in the stables or in the back of a car. But nothing had been like this. Nothing had felt so intense.

He rolled off Rennie and buried his head in his pillow, and despite himself, fell deeply asleep.

* * * * *

Rennie lay in the bed, her hands roaming over her body, quieting it. Her breasts and belly were sore, and when she moved her legs, a dull pain reminded her that this had been her first time. The pain was more an ache than anything else. Rennie savored it. It was a sort of proof.

She heard Juan's breathing deepen and even out. He was asleep. She didn't know whether to laugh or to cry. She would have liked to talk, to share her feelings and impressions but she was shy.

She slid out of bed without waking Juan and dressed, buttoning her shirt the best she could. She thought about leaving him a note, but had no idea what to say. Finally, she went to the showers. She separated whites and darks, put his clothes in the wash and turned on the machine. Then she went back home. She felt tired and depressed, and all of a sudden, she wanted to be back in familiar surroundings. She wanted the shelter of her own room.

* * * * *

When Juan woke up, several hours later, it was late. He didn't think of that though. Instead, he stared with growing comprehension and dismay at the small spots of blood on his sheets.

He realized that he knew absolutely nothing about Rennie. He'd assumed that she was like the other girls he'd slept with, because he himself was so inexperienced. His first reaction was to get dressed and go out to find her. As he slowly pulled on his pants the consequences of his act began to sink in. When he left the apartment, he didn't acknowledge Felipe's greeting. Actually, he didn't even notice him. His mind in turmoil he got behind the wheel of the car and drove off, unsure exactly where he was going.

Chapter Four

Juan arrived outside Rennie's apartment and turned off the ignition. He saw the pickup truck, so he knew Rennie was there, but he didn't go to her apartment right away. He tried to think of something to say, but he couldn't. His mind was a blank.

After a while he sighed and got out of the car. Perhaps when he saw her it would be easier. He had to explain, to tell her that there could be nothing serious between them. His path in life was already traced and she had no part in it.

Rennie opened the door. She was wearing a clingy dress that emphasized her slenderness. It was a pale yellow flower print, and Juan found it easier to look at than her face. Rennie smiled, but the smile died as he stood in the doorway.

"Why didn't you tell me you were a virgin?" He regretted the words as soon as he said them, but he couldn't call them back. He saw her flinch as if she'd been struck.

It wasn't how he'd imagined the conversation would go. But her presence was disturbing him. For some reason when he saw her, he wanted to gather her in his arms and bury his face in her neck. Her scent, light and fresh as it was, overpowered him. He felt his resolve weaken as his penis, remembering the good time he'd had with Rennie, grew uncomfortably stiff. He strode into the room and sat down on a chair quickly, to hide his treacherous member.

Rennie stood, a red flush creeping into her cheeks until Juan motioned her to a chair.

"We have to talk," he said firmly. "I have to tell you something right now, before we..." He was going to say, make another mistake, but Rennie was looking at him so hopefully, he said, "Before we do something we'll both regret."

She looked away quickly, but still didn't speak. He was beginning to find her silence unnerving.

"I think you ought to know that I'm engaged to be married," he said stiffly.

At that her cheeks flamed, but she still said nothing.

Juan was getting flustered. He was used to Rosa's incessant chatter and endless arguments to any of his statements. He didn't know what to do in the face of Rennie's silence. He remembered his mother saying, *It's easy to say silly things. It takes character to be silent.* The memory jabbed him as sharply as a spur.

"So say something!" he finally cried, out of patience.

"What do you want me to say?" Rennie's voice was steady. "What exactly do you want me to say? That I was a virgin. Yes. But I wasn't thinking of that when we made love." Her voice grew wistful. "I didn't think about anything, to tell you the truth. You surprised me, that's all. I didn't know you were engaged. You might have thought of that before." She sounded sorrowful at that.

Juan kicked himself mentally. She was right, he should never have made love to her. He felt confused. His mind was saying "leave, leave", but his body was saying, "kiss her, kiss her".

"You don't have to worry. I'm old enough to know better. I shouldn't have done it. You'll always have a special place in my life, though, as my first lover." She smiled at him sadly. "I thought I was in love with you. But we should have gotten to know each other better, I suppose."

"I'm sorry." Juan was sincere.

"Me too." Rennie blinked, sending two tears trickling down her alabaster cheeks. She looked so much like the picture of the Madonna over his mother's bed that Juan caught his breath.

"Don't cry, please."

"I can't help it. Please leave. I really want to be alone."

"I'm sorry," Juan muttered again, getting up and going towards the door.

He left without looking at her — he felt about two feet tall. Once in his car he didn't return to the stables. He went to the polo club to have a stiff drink. He *really* needed one.

* * * * *

Rennie sat for a long time without moving. She felt tears running down her cheeks but made no move to wipe them away. She'd had boyfriends before, and she'd even fancied herself in love, but no one had attracted her as Juan had. Nobody had given her the same sort of spark when he touched her, as if electricity had leapt from his fingers. She'd never once been tempted to give up her virginity to anyone until she'd met Juan.

And now he was gone.

He'd made it perfectly clear to her. She was nothing to him. She found herself wondering about his fiancée in Argentina and she thought that she was the luckiest girl on earth.

She sat until night fell, and her mother came home. Then she cried on her mother's shoulder, great, tearing sobs that wouldn't be comforted.

Marilyn took Rennie in her arms and hugged her tightly. "There, there. It's all right. You'll be okay, you poor baby. You poor, poor baby."

"I'm sorry." Rennie's voice was muffled against her mother's shoulder. "I feel like such an idiot. How can I ever face him again?"

"With your head held high." Marilyn was firm. "You're going to act like a lady."

"I'll try." Rennie sniffed. "Mom?"

"Yes angel?"

"Did it hurt so much when Dad died?"

Marilyn looked at her sadly. "Much, much more. I was crazy about your father. I couldn't believe it when he died." Her voice was bleak.

"Well, I can't believe Juan just left me," whispered Rennie.

* * * * *

The next day, at the club bar, Juan sat as far as he could away from everyone and ordered a double whiskey. He hadn't slept at all that night. Whenever he'd closed his eyes, he'd seen Rennie's stricken face. He'd left before Rennie came to the barn. He drove around aimlessly for a while, and then came to the polo club. He drank one double, then another. He was starting to feel good on his own there in the corner. Unfortunately he hadn't counted on Pierre and Arnaud.

The Frenchmen were on their way to a polo game in Boca Raton and had stopped in the club to grab some sandwiches.

"Hey Juan, guess what?" Pierre raised his eyebrow at Juan's whiskey then continued, "Miguel Andellero broke his wrist, and I'm supposed to take his place this afternoon. I wanted to find out about his horses, you know, before I played them. Well, he told me his best horse is one of yours. I'm glad I found you before I left, what can you tell me about Noche?"

Juan looked at Pierre and sighed. "Damn good horse. I had to sell her because I was flat broke and that bastard Miguel knew it. He wanted her for his boss, but wouldn't let me sell her to him directly. He bought her from me for five thousand dollars, and then sold her to his boss for twenty thousand. The bastard. Wouldn't even give me a commission." He stared despondently at his empty whiskey glass and wondered vaguely if it were his second or his third.

"Well, he's broken his wrist anyway," said Pierre with a shrug.

"Screw his wrist. Should've been his neck. The bastard. He plays dirty. I never would've sold her to him, but I was flat broke. Shit. There's no more whiskey in this glass." Juan tipped it to his lips and licked a drop off the rim. "I better order another."

"You better come with us. Whiskey is definitely not on the nutritionists' good breakfast list," Arnaud said.

Pierre nodded to Arnaud and they each grabbed an arm and hauled him to his feet. They walked him out of the bar, into the blinding sunlight, and tipped him into the back of their car. Juan tried to protest, but the Frenchmen didn't give him time to speak. Before he could gather his wits he was thrown back in his seat by Arnaud's quick acceleration. They roared out of the clubhouse parking lot, taking one of the narrow roads that wound through the club's manicured grounds.

They swerved past a trio of golfers who immediately dropped their clubs and plunged into a large hibiscus bush to avoid being run over. Arnaud leaned out his open window. "Get off the road you idiots!" he shouted.

"Um, actually, the golfers were on the sidewalk," Pierre remarked dryly.

Arnaud cursed, laughed, and bumped the car over a grassy strip back onto the road. "The sidewalks here are bigger than the roads back home in France," he explained to a gaping Juan. "Hell, we don't even have sidewalks," he continued blithely.

Juan rubbed a hand over his face and squinted at the sun. "What time is it?" he asked.

"About eleven. The game is at twelve-thirty, so we better hurry. I don't know why Miguel's boss called so late, he should have called earlier so Pierre could get ready. As it is we rushed out of the apartment as soon as we'd called Miguel to ask about his horses. Pierre, you left before you had breakfast, you better eat."

Pierre took a bite of the ham and tomato sandwich and gave the rest to Juan. "Here, you take it. I can't eat right before a game."

Juan looked at the sandwich and suddenly felt his stomach lurch. He barely had time to lean out the window before he vomited, sending a sour stream of liquid all over the side of the car.

"Merde!" Arnaud yelled. He slammed on the brakes, then, looking in the rear-view mirror and seeing the five-ton semi bearing down on them, accelerated, which didn't help Juan' stomach any. He vomited out the window again, and then weakly sank back into the seat.

"Merde," Arnaud repeated, while Pierre laughed helplessly in the front seat. "Why didn't you tell me you felt ill? I would have stopped."

"That's okay, I'll live. I think." Juan's head felt like it was caught in a vise and he slowly rubbed his temples. "Do you have a coke?" he asked, eyeing the cooler on the back seat beside him.

"Yes," Pierre answered

Juan took one and popped open the top. He sipped it slowly, it was icy cold and made his eyes water. "Thanks," he gasped weakly.

"De nada." Arnaud grinned at him through the rear-view mirror. "So, what were you celebrating all alone there in the bar?"

Juan sighed. "I think I just fucked up my whole life. That's all."

"That bad huh?" Pierre was sympathetic. "Girl trouble? Boss trouble? Or horse trouble?"

"Girl trouble, I guess." Juan took another sip of soda. "I made a mistake, tried to fix it, and made things worse."

"Sounds like a normal chain of events," said Arnaud, nodding sagely.

Juan thought of Rennie's face, so still, so white, and shuddered. "I don't think so," he said. "I screwed up big time."

The men were silent a while, and then Arnaud gave a shrug. "Life is too short to dwell on things you can't change," he said. "As a French philosopher so wisely put it, 'C'est la vie'."

"That's a bit simplistic," said Pierre reproachfully, but by then they were pulling into the Boca Raton Polo Club, and the talk turned to Pierre's upcoming game as a substitute player.

* * * * *

Juan and Arnaud left Pierre at the pony lines and walked back towards the stands. Miguel was sitting there despondently with his arm in a heavy cast. A polo ball had shattered his wrist and he'd spent five hours on the operating table while the surgeons fished for all the bits of splintered bone and tried to save his joint.

"Hello," said Juan cooly.

Arnaud, being more diplomatic, looked sympathetic and said, "How's your arm? I hope it gets better soon."

Miguel just shrugged and looked glum, so Arnaud took Juan's arm and led him to a seat near the middle of the field.

Pierre saw them and cantered over on a lovely blue-black mare to give them three polo mallets to hold for him in case he broke one.

"That's my Noche," said Juan, patting the mare's velvety nose.

"She's beautiful," said Pierre, shifting his leg forward and reaching down to check the girth.

Juan thought Pierre looked like an engraving sitting on the midnight-black horse, with his helmet in one hand, and the reins and his polo mallet held lightly in the other. His wavy, chestnut hair had copper highlights in it that contrasted with Noche's sleek black coat. Several pretty girls drifted over to admire the horse and rider.

Pierre grinned down at the girls and his dark brown eyes flashed.

One of the girls, bolder than the others, sidled up to him. Patting Noche, she looked up at Pierre and said, "What are you doing after the game?"

Pierre grinned. "Taking you for a drink, if you'd like."

The girl blushed and nodded, then went to join her giggling group of friends.

"Just put him on a horse and he gets all the women," griped Arnaud as Pierre tipped his helmet and cantered away. But there was no envy in his eyes as he watched his brother adjust his helmet's chinstrap and line up with the team for the throw-in. Instead he frowned.

"Worried?" Juan said teasingly.

Arnaud laughed and said, "I always worry when he plays and he worries when I play."

Juan bit back a teasing reply. The sport was dangerous and all the pros knew it. Instead, he said, "I hope he gets along with the horses."

* * * * *

The referee blew his whistle and tossed the ball in between the two teams lined up in the middle of the field, and the match was on.

Pierre and Noche got on well together. Juan grew more depressed as he thought of his own horses and compared them to Noche. She had been his best mare in Argentina, and now she belonged to someone else.

He decided to go get another coke—his stomach still felt queasy. So he left Arnaud and waded through the crowd to the bar. The girl behind the bar tried to flirt, but he didn't even have the heart to smile back at her. He thought that the day was pretty well ruined and figured things couldn't get much worse. Especially after Sally, Tom Wimsys's redheaded groom, saw him.

She waved, and with her mouth full of pretzel, called out, "Have you seen Rennie around?"

He shrugged and said, "I don't know." Conscious of being rude but unable to help himself, he turned his back to her and went back to the stands. The chucker was almost finished.

When the bell rang Pierre pulled the mare to a halt and walked her off the field. He waved gaily to Arnaud and Juan, and shouted, "Hey Juan, this horse is really great!" That cheered Juan up a bit.

The next two chuckers were closely fought, with neither team scoring a single goal. Then it was halftime and everyone went out on the pitch to stomp divots. Juan and Arnaud walked over to the pony lines to talk to Pierre, and found him chatting up the girl who'd talked to him earlier.

"That's keeping your mind on the game," joked Arnaud as the girl blew Pierre a kiss and went back to stomp divots. "Ever since Tina went back to Italy Pierre has been looking for a new cook."

"I have not," Pierre said reproachfully. "Tina wasn't just the cook. Anyhow, you're just jealous. Whenever I get on a horse girls fall madly in love with me. When you get on a horse they feel sorry for the horse."

"Nice. I'll remember that one." Arnaud laughed without rancor. "Do you think you'll win?"

"Who knows? It's pretty even. I'm going to play Noche again in the last chucker if it's close. She's really good! I can see why you didn't want to sell her, Juan."

Juan looked bleakly at the black mare standing in the pony lines. "She's good, that's for sure. And she's got heart. She'll try her best for you. Good luck."

Arnaud patted Pierre on the shoulder and they went back to their seats; the second half of the game was starting.

Pierre's team didn't do as well and they were losing by two goals as the last chucker started. The sun was beating down on

Juan's head; it was aching abominably, but he stayed in his seat to watch Noche.

The horses were shiny with sweat and the men were nervous. The referee blew the whistle to start the last chucker, and Pierre came out of the line-up with the ball. He took it all the way up the field and scored a goal before anyone could catch him. Noche was so fast that she looked like she was flying.

After that the other team was careful to mark him, and it wasn't until two minutes before the end of the game that Pierre got the ball back and scored another goal. The two teams were tied now, and the crowd screamed its enthusiasm.

The referee tossed the ball in, and there was a brief melee before Pierre tapped the ball out and then hit a long shot towards his goal. He set off at a fast gallop, and then Juan noticed that the other team had already sent a man up field to intercept Pierre.

The two players converged at a sharp angle. Pierre was caught unawares, not having seen the opposing player leave the throw-in. But the opposing player had misjudged Noche's speed and instead of riding Pierre off shoulder to shoulder, he crashed into Noche's hind-legs. There was a sickening crack and Noche was literally hurled to the ground.

In an instant there was a mad tangle of flailing legs and a confusion of color as both horses and both riders tumbled over and over. Arnaud gave a shout and vaulted onto the field before anyone realized what had happened. Juan, comprehending the seriousness of the fall, felt his head suddenly clear as if he'd plunged it into ice water.

On the field all was pandemonium as one horse staggered to its feet and trotted away, empty stirrups dangling against its sides. The other horse, the black mare, was still on her side. She didn't move. The two polo players were lying still on the field. Juan saw the ambulance start up and drive across the grass. Arnaud was kneeling at Pierre's side now, bent over him, talking urgently. Juan could see his lips moving, but he couldn't hear what he was saying. As if in a dream he stepped over the red boards lining the field and walked over to Noche. He couldn't feel his legs at all. He could have been floating.

The mare was breathing in great gasps, and Juan bent down and unbuckled her girth. She still made no effort to get up, and then Juan saw her front legs. Both of them were broken. The mare's eyes were rolling and she was grunting in pain, Juan stood up and started yelling for a vet, then he caught sight of Pierre and his voice died in his throat.

Arnaud had taken off Pierre's helmet and was sitting on the ground, Pierre's head cradled in his arms. He was rocking back and forth, and now Juan could hear him and chills went up his spine. Arnaud was singing a French lullaby. So softly he could hardly hear. He was singing tunelessly, in a harsh whisper, and between words he drew ragged breaths. Pierre was staring up at him with sightless eyes, his head thrown back at a weird angle, a bright wash of blood covering the side of his face and Arnaud's shirtfront.

The ambulance arrived and the rescue team leapt out and ran to Pierre, but Juan could tell there was nothing they could do. Pierre's head hung at an impossible angle in Arnaud's arms. His hair, with its copper highlights, blew softly in the breeze, but that was all that moved.

Juan stood next to Arnaud as the medical team tried their best to revive Pierre. There was a strange silence hanging over the field, broken only by Noche's harsh breathing. A vet drove his van out onto the field and erected a screen around the horse. Juan stayed next to Arnaud and didn't even flinch when the crack of the humane killer echoed across the field.

* * * * *

The next two hours were blurred for Juan. He took Arnaud's car keys and drove him to the hospital. There they waited until the doctors came out and told them there was nothing they could have done. Then they drove to Miami, to the French embassy, where Arnaud contacted his father and made arrangements to ship Pierre's body home to be buried. Then it was back to the hospital to give the authorities permission to release the body to the French consul, who sent messages by fax telling them what was going to happen, and where the body should go. All this was handled by Juan, who still felt like he was in some sort of nightmare, but would wake up eventually. He had trouble hearing things, words were wrapped in cotton wool, and he still had the impression that his legs and arms were numb.

Arnaud was even worse. The doctors kept asking him if he was okay, and he just kept saying he was fine, yes, thank you. Then he'd look around, see Juan, and frown, and ask him what day it was. He kept telling Juan that his father would take care of everything, that everything was fine. Just fine, and that Pierre was going to be all right.

Then Juan would have to say that Pierre was dead, and Arnaud would remain silent for half an hour, becoming nearly catatonic, then he would start all over again, asking what day it was.

Finally Juan asked the doctors give Arnaud some Valium, and he took him to his apartment at the stables and put him in his own bed. When the sun came up, Juan went outside and sat on the steps to wait for Rennie to come to work.

He lit a cigarette and watched the thin stream of white smoke spiral up into the dove gray sky. He had never felt so tired and so wide-awake. When Rennie came he would apologize again. Maybe something would fall into place. His life was as broken as a dropped jigsaw puzzle. He thought of Pierre and a tear found its way down his cheek.

As bad as he felt, it couldn't compare to how Pierre's family was feeling at this time. He looked at his watch. In two hours he had to be at the airport to pick up Arnaud's father. The old man had insisted on taking the first flight from Paris last night. He took another drag on his cigarette and felt the harsh bite of the smoke in his lungs. He hardly ever smoked, but now he needed something to calm his nerves.

He must have dozed off, because Rennie's car was there and horses' hooves made a crisp crunching sound as they trotted down the road. The white shells used for gravel made the roads ghostly in the moonlight, and at noon with the sun straight above they were blinding. But at dawn, with the sun rose pink on the purple horizon, the road was the palest, glowing, mother of pearl.

He watched as Rennie rode up, then, without speaking he went to help her. She said nothing either—she just handed him the lead ropes while she swung off her horse and took the saddle off.

He held each of the horses while she hosed off their legs, then he helped her put them in their respective stalls. The sun had cleared the horizon when they finished. They'd worked together in a silence that wasn't awkward, it was restful. Or maybe Juan was still feeling the edge of shock—he didn't know. He followed her into the tack room, intending to tell her what had happened, but when she looked at him, his throat closed up and all he could do was open his arms.

She came to him, her body fitting into his embrace, and when she tipped her head back, their lips touched. As before, Juan was lost. His mouth roamed over hers, then down her long neck, while his hands fumbled with the buttons on her shirt. He slid her shirt off, and then unhooked her bra, releasing her creamy breasts. They were heavy, warm, and he bent over to kiss them, pressing his lips against her soft skin, inhaling her scent. He took a nipple in his mouth and sucked hard, until it was stiff and long.

He could feel her hands sliding beneath his jeans, reaching for his penis, and then she touched him. He moaned, and then caught his breath as she unzipped his pants and released his cock. It strained towards her, touching her now bare belly. She pushed his pants down to his ankles and he stepped out of them. Their hands never left each other's body. Rennie held his cock lightly, as if she were afraid to hurt him. He moaned and thrust against her palms.

He took her beautiful breasts in his hands and cupped them, then rubbed them until her nipples were hard against his palms. Her hands explored his body, tracing the line of hair snaking from belly to groin. When she touched him, he could hear his heart pounding in his ears, and his penis seemed to jump in her hands.

And then she knelt down and slid her mouth over it. He staggered at the feel of her hot mouth enfolding his cock, and her tongue, swirling over his hardness. With her hand, she pumped him, while kissing and licking the tip of his penis. He couldn't stand upright. His knees gave out, and he collapsed and knelt in front of her.

She stared at him, her eyes feverish. His breath coming fast, he kissed her deeply, and then gently turned her around, facing away from him. He slid her pants off, and pulled her underwear down.

From behind, she was luscious. Her buttocks were perfectly shaped, and as he watched, she leaned down, propping her forearms on a pile of folded saddle blankets, offering herself to him. She spread her legs, and he could see her pink lips, swollen and slick with her desire. He touched her between her legs, slipping his finger a bit into her vagina, feeling the wetness gather. She moaned and suddenly rocked backwards, so that his finger penetrated her deeply.

A wave of desire nearly blinded him, and he grabbed her by her buttocks and put his penis right on the edge of her labial lips. They seemed to part, and he slid in. It was still a very tight fit, but she was so excited that her juices lubricated her and he had no trouble sheathing himself to the hilt. She came almost right away.

She uttered a cry and pressed her buttocks tightly to him, and he felt her contractions massaging his cock. She shuddered, as the throbbing grew and then he felt his control shatter.

He pumped in and out, and she cried out. "Juan! Harder, please, faster!"

Her words, the first she'd spoken, shattered the fog that had numbed him since Pierre and Noche had died. He blinked, suddenly as conscious and aware as he'd ever been. He felt everything as if it were magnified, including his fierce desire for Rennie. His body shivered, and he pounded into her, fucking her with all his strength, hanging onto her sweet buttocks, his fingers digging into her flesh as she twisted and writhed against him.

"More!" she cried, and suddenly he was coming—his back arched and he drove himself into her very core, emptying himself into her, panting as if he'd run a mile. When he was drained, he slumped against her back, trying to get his breath back.

Rennie slipped out from under him before he could say anything, and pulling her pants up, she grabbed her shirt and ran out the door.

"Wait!" he cried, but before he could untangle his clothes and dress, she was gone, gunning the pickup's motor as she drove off.

Chapter Five

Rennie drove home and showered. She couldn't believe what had happened at the stables.

He'd taken her by surprise, that was it. It was early, and she hadn't even expected to see him. His face had been strange too — his expression was like someone drowning, or someone about to cry. And they hadn't spoken, and she felt just awful.

No, that wasn't true. She felt incredible.

She hadn't known sex could be so wonderful. She turned off the shower and put on some underwear. Usually, she finished her morning chores at the stables, and then she napped for a while to catch up on sleep. Today though, she lay in her bed, but she couldn't sleep. Her mind was full of what she'd done with Juan. Just thinking about it made her ache with longing. She groaned, tossing and turning, feeling the sheets rubbing against her breasts and body.

Finally, she reached down, slipped her hand beneath her underwear, and fingered her clit. She was so hot it took one or two touches and she was coming, her hips rising as her whole body bloomed into a starburst of delight. Somehow it wasn't enough though. Now she needed something inside her, something to touch the deepest part of her — her own hands weren't enough anymore.

She rolled over, and with a strangled sob, managed to fall asleep. It was late when she woke up, and she felt groggy. But she had to exercise the polo ponies.

* * * * *

She trotted slowly back up the driveway with her string of ponies. They were shiny with sweat and tossing their heads, eager to eat. She slid to the ground and looked bleakly at where Juan's car was usually parked in the driveway of the stable, but it was gone. *He must be off somewhere having a good time*, she thought angrily to herself. Then she pulled the ponies through the gate and went into the barn.

Sally drove up just before Rennie finished cleaning the tack. She burst into the barn and grabbed Rennie by the arm. "Guess what! Oh my God, you'll never guess. Yesterday, at Boca Raton, Pierre de Lancourt was substituting for Miguel Andellaro. He was in a terrible accident, and he died on the field!"

Rennie went white and dropped the bridle she was trying to hang up. She didn't know Pierre personally, but she'd seen him playing, and she'd admired him. He'd been so tall and handsome and now he was dead. She'd known polo was a dangerous sport, but it had been an abstract thought, like thinking cars were dangerous and then being in an accident. She sat down abruptly on an upturned bucket and stared at Sally. She suddenly felt ill, and she thought she'd throw up. All at once she was worried about Juan.

Sally wasn't finished. "Juan was there at the game, he was with Arnaud when it happened." She pointed to the apartment at the end of the barn. "Pierre's father is there now. Juan went to the airport to get him early this morning. I saw him leave, and I asked him where he was going. He looked like a zombie."

Rennie pictured Juan and bit her lip. She wanted to cry when she thought about him. When she saw him this morning, he must have been hurting badly. "Where is Juan now? I don't see his car."

* * * * *

When Rennie finished her work, she went outside. Juan's car was still gone. Just then, a white-haired old man opened the door to Juan's apartment and stepped outside. He squinted his eyes in the harsh light and shaded his face with one hand, while leaning on a black cane with the other. He saw Rennie and nodded, but didn't smile. He looked so lost and mournful that Rennie found herself walking quickly over to him.

"Can I help you?" she asked.

The old man looked at her and shook his head. "Bonjour. Je suis désolé, mais je ne parle pas très bien votre langue, mademoiselle. "

Rennie bobbed her head shyly. "I know a little French. I'm learning it in school. *Bonjour Monsieur. Comment allez vous? Je m'appelle Renée.*" She smiled. "That's about all though."

"*Renée. Très jolie.* I am Julian de Lancourt." He nodded towards the stables. "*Très impressionnant.*"

Rennie blanched when he mentioned his name. She'd known who he was, of course, but hearing his name triggered a new rush of pain. How he must be feeling! "I'm so sorry about Pierre," she managed to say awkwardly.

The old man looked down at her. Despite his age he was very tall. His eyes were pale blue, and exceedingly sad. "*Merci,*" was all he said.

Then he offered Rennie his arm, and nodded his head in the direction of the stables. "*Montrez-moi un peu.*"

She led him around, showing him the horses and the tack room. They said a friendly hello to an open-mouthed Sally, nodded to Felipe who was busy rolling leg wrappings, and then walked into the coolness of the orange grove.

Julian de Lancourt examined an orange tree with interest, feeling its shiny green leaves and breathing in the delicate perfume of its white flowers. Rennie and the old man wandered through the dappled green shade of the orange grove in companionable silence, each nursing their private hurts. She wondered if it was instinct that linked them together. They walked slowly, for a long time, without smiling or talking, but the cool green shade was restful. Rennie hoped that Julian found it so as well.

* * * * *

As Rennie and Julian were emerging from the shady orange grove, Juan and Arnaud drove up the driveway. Juan was exhausted. He hadn't slept all night and his face was drawn. Arnaud was pale beneath his tan. Feeling like a sleepwalker, Juan transferred Pierre's things to Arnaud's car, and shook hands with the Baron. He noticed Rennie standing nearby, and his heart gave a lurch. He wanted to go to her, to say something, but he couldn't even bring himself to meet her eyes.

Rennie stood back diffidently as Julian bid farewell to Juan and thanked him for everything. Then the old man walked over to Rennie and gave her a tender hug. Juan heard him say, "*Merci ma petite Renée. Adieu. J'espère que ta vie sera heureuse.*"

Rennie hugged him back, holding him tightly for a long time. The old man's eyes misted and he stroked her bright hair. Then she stepped back. Juan shook the baron's hand, wondering what he and Rennie had talked about. Then he looked at Arnaud. "I'm so sorry," he said.

Arnuad nodded, shook his hand, and said, "*Merci*, Juan. You've been a tremendous help."

"If you need anything else, I'm here," Juan said.

Arnaud drove his father away. They were heading to the embassy in Miami before taking the plane back to France.

Juan stood by, watching Rennie, wishing he knew what to do. Life seemed full of pitfalls and illusions. He wanted to talk to her, explain how much he loved Rosa. Yet, perversely he wanted to hold her, as Arnaud's father had, and touch her apricot hair and breathe in her delicate scent. He wanted to lie down and sleep beside her for a hundred years. Instead he stood without speaking and watched her as she walked across the dusty driveway to the pickup truck and drove away.

Then finally he went into his apartment, collapsed on the bed, and fell into a deep and dreamless sleep that lasted until the next morning.

* * * * *

Rennie spent the following week trying to stay out of Juan's way. He played for Arnaud's team in another tournament in Gulf Stream so he wasn't around the stables as much as she had feared.

When Arnaud came back from France the polo players rallied around him, giving him their support and sympathy. Juan spent most of his time with Arnaud. They'd become good friends. Each had lost a brother, so there was a bond between them. Arnaud was busy though. He played on his team and on his brother's team as well. Being in two different leagues, he was able to do that.

Then the first tournaments ended and the polo season moved into high gear as the coveted Pasha Cup Tournament started.

There were three clubs in Palm Beach: the club in Boca Raton, the club in Gulf Stream and the club in Wellington. Each had its own leagues and trophies. However, the trophy everyone longed to win was the Pasha Cup. Offered by His Royal Highness, the Sultan of Brunei, the cup was fought for by all three clubs, between more than twenty teams. The finals were crowned by a huge costume ball given each year at the home club of the winning team. Invitations were extremely coveted. The Sultan himself attended the festivities, in disguise, so no one would know just which partygoer he was.

* * * * *

The tournament took place during the rainiest season Palm Beach had ever known. Countless matches were canceled, rescheduled, interrupted, and nerves were frayed. Tom Wimsys fired Andre, and hired a ten-goal player for his team. Andre's horses stayed. Tom Wimsys had bought them at the beginning of the season, and he told Juan to add them to his string. Juan rode them all one afternoon, and took two of the ponies. He kept Rennie on to help Felipe.

Juan was upset that Andre had been fired, but he was also secretly thrilled — he'd always wanted to play with Carlos Rubio, one of the best players in the world. It meant getting used to a new player in mid-season, though.

After the first week, unexpectedly enough, Juan's team was undefeated. The fact that Carlos Rubio had replaced Andre might have had something to do with it. Carlos was ten goals, and worth every one of them.

Carlos won the most valuable player award at the end of the Pasha cup when he led Tom's team to an astounding ten-to-two victory over the Shogun team from Boca Raton.

The ball would take place in Wellington, in a huge tent erected on the number one polo field. Invitations were sent off at once, in the colors of Tom Wimsys's team, blue and silver.

* * * * *

The Silver Birds
WINNERS of the PASHA CUP
and
HRH the Sultan of Brunei
Invite you to a COSTUME BALL
On the twenty fifth of March, at eight p.m. on field N° 1
RSVP imperative
Theme colors are Blue and Silver this year!

* * * * *

Juan looked at his reflection in the mirror and frowned. His hair was much too long for his liking, but he hadn't had time to go get it cut. He brushed it back and wondered idly how long it would be before he could put it in a ponytail. He imagined Rosa's face when she saw it. Her lips would pinch tightly and her whole face would seem to harden. He'd seen that look before on her face, when his father had moved to England, the week after his mother's death.

Juan turned away from his reflection, shrugged into his jacket, and fixed his tie. He smoothed a few wrinkles out of his pants with his hand then straightened his shoulders self-consciously. He was not looking forward to the party. He looked at the mask lying on his bed. Everyone on the team was wearing the same thing: silvery-gray blazers, white linen pants, and a blue mask with a silver beak and the great, staring eyes of an egret. All organized and procured by Tom's wife, Carol, for the team members.

The mask was beautiful, but it gave Juan a strange, claustrophobic feeling.

He got into his car and put the mask carefully in the back seat. The team was meeting at Tom Wimsys' house for cocktails before the party. Tom said he had an announcement to make. Juan wondered what it could be. He hated surprises and secrets.

* * * * *

Rennie finished cleaning the last bridle and stood up stiffly. She had been working double time lately. Felipe, Juan's groom had come down with the flu and Rennie was doing his horses as well as her own. She'd been feeling ill lately too; and yesterday she'd gone see her doctor. Luckily, there was a break in the tournaments, but the horses had to be exercised anyway, everyday. And fed, and cleaned.

She was tired and sore. The sun had set but the day's heat hadn't dissipated. Her hair stuck to her head and her face was shiny with sweat. It would be so nice to go for a swim. Maybe when she got home she'd go to the beach for a night swim. She didn't usually like to go at night, the sharks were voracious, but tonight she wouldn't even care if they ate her.

She was still depressed about Juan. Every time she saw him at the stables or at the polo games, her heart would tighten in her chest. She was in love. She saw him in her dreams—in her dreams he was holding her tightly, and they were making love again. She bit her lip and tried not to cry, but a tear escaped and wandered down her cheek. It slid down her smooth skin and trickled into the corner of her mouth. She tasted the sharp saltiness of it.

Sighing, she walked over to the barn door and peered out. Tonight the "crème de la crème" of Palm Beach would be at a sumptuous ball on the polo field. It wasn't fair; she had worked hard all month long for the team, and their victory had been as thrilling for her as for the players. The horses had been fit and ready to play because of her care. Yet, she hadn't been invited.

She watched from the shadows as Juan got in his car and drove away. As he did, something white fluttered to the ground. Rennie walked over and picked it up. It was the invitation to the ball. He must have put it on the roof of the car and forgotten it.

Rennie looked at the card, and then up at the stars. One in particular seemed to twinkle down at her. Suddenly she knew exactly what she was doing that night. She felt like Cinderella did when her Fairy Godmother showed up. The ball was in costume. Blue and silver. She knew just what to wear. Grinning broadly she ran to the pickup truck and roared down the driveway. At least tonight she'd have a good time.

* * * * *

In his spacious living room, Tom lifted his glass of champagne and toasted the team. Everyone was there. Even their ten year-old daughter Alice was going to the ball and she looked ridiculous in her long dress and feathered mask. Like a Spanish court midget, thought Juan with amusement.

Carlos was with his fiancée, Lucia. She was a very young girl from Argentina, and she looked like a princess. Her dress of gray watered silk flowed around her like molten silver and her mask was embedded with scintillating blue and white gems. She sat next to Carlos and sipped her champagne. On her left hand a diamond flashed. Carlos had given her a three-carat, blue diamond ring. It looked oversized on her fragile white hand and made her look vulnerable.

Juan surprised himself feeling sorry suddenly for the slender young woman. He dismissed his thoughts as fanciful and concentrated on Tom.

"I have decided to take the Silver Bird team to Europe this summer, "he announced with no preamble. "We will play in England in June and July, and in Deauville in August. The horses will leave in the end of April, and we'll join them in May. I've rented a chateau not far from Windsor with all the stable-room we need, plus accommodations for the grooms and players. There's even a practice field nearby, so we can practice all we want.

"So what do you say? Are you all ready to win the Queen's cup, the Cowdrey Gold Cup, and the French Open?"

The room erupted in cheers and incredulous voices. Carol gave a happy cry and hugged Tom, Lucia gasped and Carlos swept her up in his arms. Ten year old Alice whooped and spilled her champagne on the rug. The Wimsys's basset hound, Watson, lapped it up, ears dragging in the bubbles.

Juan didn't say anything. His mind was in turmoil. He'd been planning to go back to Argentina, marry Rosa and get his life into some semblance of order. Things were shifting like quicksand all at once, and he wasn't sure what he was going to do next.

Tom caught his expression and grinned. "Don't worry Juan, you're coming with us. I wouldn't let another patron snap up my secret weapon. You've been playing two goals more than your handicap since the start of the tournament. I'm counting on you, boy, to score the winning goals."

Juan smiled faintly and lifted his glass in a silent toast. Well, life was anything but boring, that was sure.

Chapter Six

The blue and white striped tent was enormous. A flickering path of candle-lit lanterns led from the parking lot to the party. A steady stream of costumed revellers flowed into the tent, pausing to admire the decorations as they wound their way down the flower-strewn walk.

Six arches twined with silver spray-painted ivy and blue and white flowers had been set up; one for each chucker. Pots of blue and white flowers were everywhere. Silver ribbons wound around the two goal posts on either side of the entrance to the tent. The tables were set with white lace and sparkling silverware. Silver candelabras on the buffet held long white tapers, and each table had a large birdcage hung over it, with little blue and white finches fluttering and cheeping inside them. Guests drifted around, chatting in an animated fashion, holding tall glasses of frothy champagne.

When the Silver Bird team walked in there was a spontaneous round of applause. Tom and Carol opened the ball with a waltz. Then the orchestra played a few bars of Beethoven's "Ode to Joy", and the party got under way.

Juan joined the line to the buffet and filled his plate. He was depressed for no reason at all. There were Argentine polo players at a table, but they made no effort to wave him over. Instead he drifted to an empty table in the corner and sat down. He didn't touch his food, but rather looked over the assembly and amused himself by trying to guess who was who.

It was easy to spot the Sultan. In his costume, he stuck out like an orchid among daisies. He was dressed as a toreador, all in blue satin, with a long, wicked-looking sword and a white silk cape lined with royal blue velvet. He wore a small white mask, and was surrounded by several woman dressed in blue velvet gowns. They wore Spanish combs in their hair and long, blue lace veils covered their faces.

Then there was a group of Renaissance musicians, all dressed in turquoise and carrying lutes and flutes. They wore enormous fraises around their throats. Juan wondered who they were, and how they would manage their dinner. He'd taken off his bird mask, and it was perched on the table facing him, its empty eyes staring up at the tent's gaudy ceiling.

A slender silhouette caught his eye, and he stared as a blue fairy drifted among the mortals. She wore a long dress made of filmy silk chiffon that floated like smoke around her legs. Her hair was a teal-blue cascade of ringlets hanging down her back to nearly behind her knees. She was wearing a white domino. Even her lips had been painted blue. She sported gauzy wings that shimmered as the light caught them, and she held a long silver wand in her hand.

Juan found himself staring at her as she moved across the room. She disappeared for a while in the crowd around the buffet, then re-emerged carrying a plate and holding a frothy glass of champagne. She hesitated a moment, then slowly walked towards him.

It wasn't until she sat down that Juan recognized Rennie.

"What are you doing here?" he asked stupidly, then flushed. "Sorry. You look wonderful. Where did you get the costume? "

"My neighbor. She played the part of the Blue Fairy in the Pinocchio play last year at the Children's Playhouse Theater. I remembered her costume and asked her to lend it to me. You dropped your invitation. I hope you don't mind." She smiled at him, and her eyes glowed. "I always wanted to crash a party like this. It's so beautiful. I never, ever thought I'd get to go to a ball."

She took off her domino and put it beside her on the table. "The rule is, when you're recognized you take off your mask."

Her face looked peaked beneath her make-up. Dark circles ringed her gray eyes, making them look bruised and incredibly sexy. She wiped her mouth and the blue lipstick came off. She smiled. "That's better, I bet I look more human. "

Juan didn't agree. With her mother-of-pearl complexion and her huge eyes framed by the waterfall of peacock-blue curls, Rennie looked like some dryad gone astray. She took a bite of crab quiche and had a sip of champagne. "Mmm, delicious. Don't you want your dinner?"

Juan nodded and started to eat. To his surprise, he found he was hungry. "It is good," he said, then laughed. "I wondered what happened to my invitation. Good thing I didn't need it."

Rennie nodded. "I didn't think you would." She pointed to the Sultan. "Isn't it exciting? A real live King. I'd love to meet him."

Juan smiled at her innocence. "He'd probably love to meet you. Go tell him you'll grant him a wish. "

Rennie said with a sort of sigh, "Everyone has asked me to grant them a wish tonight. Do you want one granted too?"

"Maybe." Juan thought a minute. "I wish that I could go back in time."

"How far back?" Rennie sounded wistful.

"Back two years. I'd save my brother, my mother wouldn't die, and my father would stay on the estancia."

"I wish I really *could* help you." Rennie waved her wand slowly in a circle in the air. "It would be so nice if this were a real magic wand."

Juan suddenly noticed tears running down her cheeks. "What's the matter?" he asked gently.

"I'm pregnant," she said, putting the wand down next to her plate.

He felt as if he'd just been punched in the stomach. His heart froze. "Say that again," he commanded when he could speak.

She just looked at him with her huge, gray eyes full of tears.

"When did you find out?" he asked. His voice cracked a bit.

"This evening. I went to the doctor's office yesterday. I wasn't feeling well, and as I'd had anemia very badly when I was little, my mother thought I might be getting sick again. She told me to visit Dr. Tobias. He's our family doctor." Rennie paused for a minute. Her face reddened.

Juan sat very still.

"And?" he said, his head feeling strangely light. Everything around him seemed terribly clear, as if a lens had shifted into focus something that had, for years, been blurred.

"He examined me, and then took a blood sample. He asked me if I could be pregnant, and I told him I hadn't thought about the possibility. He asked me if I'd had…had sex without protection." Her voice was so low he had to strain to catch the words.

"I said yes. He told me he'd call me and give me the results. He called me just before I left this evening. When he told me, I didn't know what to do. Will you help me?" She gazed at him imploringly.

"I'm sorry," she whispered. "I didn't know this would happen."

Juan sat and stared at her. They looked at each other without speaking. Suddenly Juan put his face in his hands. His shoulders started to shake, and Rennie leapt to her feet and ran over to him. "Oh Juan! "she cried, "I'm so sorry, I didn't know you were engaged! I won't cause any more trouble. I promise I won't bother you any more! Don't cry!"

Then he lifted his face, and showed her he was laughing. He laughed so hard he couldn't breathe, and she had to hit him on the back to make him cough.

"Oh Lord, my Lord. What a night. What a night." Juan was doubled over laughing and several people looked over at him curiously.

Just then, there was a drum roll from the orchestra and Tom Wimsys took a microphone. "Ladies and Gentlemen, thank you for all your support. The Silver Bird team has several announcements to make. I would like them all up here by my side, as well as my wife Carol."

Juan got up and caught Rennie by the waist. "Come on " he said. "You're part of the team. "

"I wasn't invited!" she said, panicking. "They'll kill me! "

"Stop being a goose. No one will kill you. Except maybe me." His voice was neutral, and Rennie shivered, but allowed herself to be led to the center of the room where the team was gathered.

"First of all," boomed Tom, "I'd like to thank His Majesty, the Sultan of Brunei, for this wonderful party." He waited for the applause to die down and went on, "Our team did itself proud this year, and I have decided to take them all to Europe for the summer season. You are all welcome to come cheer us on in Windsor and Deauville."

Rennie darted a wide-eyed glance at Juan. They were going to Europe? Oh no! He was going to leave her. She dug her fingernails into her palms. She would not cry. Not here. Not now. *Please*, she prayed to Saint Francis, her now patron saint, *give me strength*.

There was more cheering. "And I would like to formally announce the forthcoming wedding of Miss Lucia Garcida with my ten-goal pro, Carlos Rubio. They will be married here in Palm Beach as soon as we get back from Europe, in September. I hope you can all join us then." There were still more cheers, and some whistles and catcalls.

Tom grinned broadly and gave the microphone to Carlos, on his left.

"Thank you all for your support," said Carlos, "and for electing me best player. It is a great pleasure to play here in Palm Beach." He nodded to the crowd and with a wink, handed the microphone to Juan.

"I too have an announcement to make," said Juan, "Rennie Piccabéa and I are engaged to be married. We will marry before we go to Europe, where we will spend our honeymoon. *That* is called combining business with pleasure."

Rennie heard a roaring in her ears and thought she might faint. She stood, trembling, her eyes fixed on Juan. The crowd erupted in a roar of delighted applause, further adding to her incredulity.

Tom Wimsys stared open-mouthed at Juan, but his look was one of amusement, not anger. "When are you getting married?" Tom asked Juan.

Juan shook his head. "I don't know. As soon as we can. Come on Rennie, we've got to go tell your mother."

* * * * *

They departed, shaking hands left and right with well-wishers. Rennie couldn't feel the floor beneath her feet, and it seemed to her everyone was speaking in a foreign language. She tried to get her breath, but Juan pulled her out of the tent.

Rennie didn't speak until she got to Juan's car. "I have the pickup," she said.

"Sorry. You ride with me from now on." Juan pushed her into the car, none too gently, and they left the club in a squeal of tires.

"Okay, what's the joke?" Rennie was close to hysteria. "Are you serious about getting married?"

"Extremely. You asked me to get you out of trouble. I did."

"But…but I don't know if I want to marry you! I hardly know you!"

"We have all our lives to get to know each other. What does it matter?"

"What does it matter?" Rennie yelled. "Of course it matters!"

"Do you love me?" Juan asked.

"Excuse me?"

"I said, do you love me?"

Rennie looked out the window at the dark orange groves. She thought about the first time she'd seen Juan and about his hands on her skin. She thought about the way he smelled, and his voice, and the way the night air was blowing in through the open car window and making his dark hair an unruly tangle. "Stop the car," she said.

He did, and she leaned over and kissed him deeply. His lips were warm and he tasted faintly of champagne. She felt an electric shock run straight through her whole body at the touch of his skin. She sat up and looked at him, her eyes luminous in the dark. "Yes. I do love you."

He sighed deeply and then smiled at her. "Then I think we have a chance."

He reached over and took off her wig, tugging her hair out of its chignon and loosening it over her shoulders. "For now I will just tell you that I love your hair, Rennie Piccabéa. However, I think if you are patient I will learn to love you too. I have to tell you something very important about myself. I will never lie to you. I will never make empty promises. And I will never abandon you."

Rennie blinked back tears. "Thank you," she whispered. "I never thought I'd get even that. It's enough for me. I won't lie to you. Or at least I'll try not to." Her mouth trembled. "Sometimes lying is kinder than truth."

"I don't care. Let's just make a pact. No lies. No promises. We'll see how far we can go on that."

"Okay, it's a deal."

They kissed again, and the night air gently wafted the orange grove's sweet scent around them.

"Where are we going?" Rennie asked.

"Right here." Juan turned off the ignition. In the warm dark, the orange blossoms gave off a heady scent. Crickets chirped, and Juan slid his hand beneath Rennie's billowy gown. "Take it off," he whispered.

Rennie felt her heart start to pound. She complied though, after a hesitation, pulling it over her head. Juan took it and put it in the back seat.

"Now your bra," he said.

Her hands shaking, she unfastened her bra and took it off. Her breasts, once freed, felt heavy. Her nipples tingled. She wished he would touch her, and her nipples hardened just thinking about it. She felt herself get wet, and she shifted in her seat, arching her back.

"Now your underwear." His voice was less than a whisper.

Rennie swallowed, and then slid her underwear off. She was definitely wet. Her whole vulva felt swollen, and when she moved, she felt its slickness. She watched as Juan got out of the car, walked around it, and opened her door.

"Come for a walk with me," he said.

Rennie darted a glance around. Here in the depth of the orange groves, they were out of sight of the road and of any houses. The only sounds she heard were the crickets chirping, and her own breath, coming fast. She stepped out of the car. Her cunt was so swollen with desire that when she walked she could feel her thighs squeezing her labia together.

Juan led her into the orchard. He stopped in front of an old orange tree, and then, taking off his jacket, he laid it on a low branch. He took Rennie and swung her up, so she was sitting on that particularly low branch. Then her legs opened wide, her knees spread apart. She felt the night breeze cool against her hot cunt and she spread her legs wider, feeling suddenly terribly wanton and sexy.

In the dark, in the orange grove, the wind whispered in the branches and stirred shiny strands of her hair. The feel of the tree bark against her hands and the way the branch swayed as she moved, made her feel as if she were an elf, or a wood sprite; she didn't feel human.

Instead, desire for Juan made her blood pound in her ears and made her nipples stand up in aching, hard points. She wanted to feel his cock sliding into her body, until he filled her completely. Then she wanted him to pound into her, slam into her, until she screamed with her release. Just thinking about it made her stomach clench. She wanted him now.

Rennie leaned back and spread her legs further apart, showing Juan the auburn bush between her legs and the shiny pink lips wide open. Her round breasts with their dark nipples ached for his touch, but instead, his hand went to her wet cunt. He slid a finger into her and probed delicately.

"I think I have a ready, red-hot redhead here, what should I do?" He tried to keep his voice level, but there was a definite tremor in it.

Rennie arched her back and offered herself to him. "What ever you want," she gasped. The feel of his finger inside her made her desperate for more.

Juan undid his pants and pushed them down around his ankles. Standing, he thrust himself against her. He cupped his hands around her buttocks and guided her onto his stiff cock. "Now that's what I call hot," he said, his voice hoarse.

He stopped, withdrew ever so slowly, and stayed there. Rennie gasped and tried to pull him into her again, but Juan was teasing her now with his cock, pulling out then drawing it in circles around her labia.

"I love watching your face," he whispered. "In the dark, in the moonlight, your skin is like white satin. Your face is flushed with desire, your cheeks are like roses." He leaned over and kissed her.

His tongue probed and her mouth opened, her lips parted. Slowly, he drew his tongue across the inside of her lip, then entered her mouth, slowly, so slowly. At the same time, he teased her with his cock, rubbing it up and down her pussy. She writhed against him, begging for more. He thrust into her, until his cock was sheathed to the hilt. He kiss deepened at the same time.

Then, perversely, Juan pulled out, ignoring her efforts to pull him back into her hot pussy. Instead, he leaned over and took her breast in his mouth. Her nipple hardened on contact, and he sucked hard on it. His hand found her other breast, and he took her nipple between his thumb and forefinger and pinched it gently. Rennie moaned, rubbing her slit against his thigh, reaching for his cock. When her hands found him, he uttered a moan, and thrust back into her tight vagina.

He tried to hold back, she could feel his body stiffen with the effort. When she cried out with pleasure, his whole body responded. She sensed he was about to ejaculate, and she grasped him tightly around the waist, burying her head in the crook of his neck.

Rennie moaned and moved back and forth. She was so excited she knew she was going to come any second. She didn't try to hold back though, she could feel Juan starting to shiver and she bit her own arm to keep from crying out. Her body started to shake and she wrapped her legs around Juan's waist and held him tightly against her while he spurted into her. She felt his climax hitting her womb. It set her off completely. Her body convulsed madly—she lost track of where she was. With a cry she arched her back and shoved herself as close to Juan as she could. Shaking with the force of her orgasm, she would have fallen off the low branch if Juan hadn't grabbed her.

"Hey! Stay with me," he teased, his voice tender.

Sighing, she rested her forehead against his shoulder and let her tremors fade.

Afterwards, Juan helped her off the branch. She didn't feel odd, standing in an orange grove at midnight, naked. Juan was there, and for some reason, whenever he was with her, she felt at ease.

"Do you want a tissue?" he asked, reaching into his pocket, as they reached the car.

She nodded, and took it, wiping herself off before pulling on her lacy underwear. Juan helped her fasted her bra, his hands lingering on her full breasts. Then she put her dress on, they got back in the car, and went home.

* * * * *

Marilyn was sleeping when her daughter came in. She woke up immediately though, she slept as lightly as Mr. Marmalade did; the orange cat sat perched on the chair. It wasn't Rennie's quiet whisper that woke her; it was the deeper sound of a man's voice. She got up, wrapped herself in her bathrobe and went to the living room to investigate.

For a minute she was confused. A woman dressed in a long, filmy blue gown was sitting on the sofa. She was wearing wings too, she saw, and carried a silver wand. For a second she thought she was dreaming. Then she saw it was Rennie.

A man was sitting next to her. He was slim, and looked very young, with wavy, sable-brown hair, and dark, smouldering eyes. His pale face was narrow, and he had a wide, sensuous mouth. He looked up when she walked in, but didn't seem startled, rather he took a deep breath, as if he were preparing himself for a confrontation.

"Marilyn Piccabéa," he said, with a trace of an accent she couldn't place. "I am Juan Allistair. I have come to ask for the hand of your daughter in marriage."

Marilyn gaped at him. For a second all she could register was the name Allistair, which sounded familiar somehow. Then she remembered Rennie telling her about the Argentine boy. Rennie was staring at her toes, she was wearing silver pumps, and she held a blue wig in her hands. She was twisting the long locks in her hands and Marilyn took it out of her hands and smoothed it out. She did it mechanically, still staring at her daughter.

"Rennie?" Marilyn's voice wavered uncertainly.

She looked up at her mother and nodded. "It's true, we want to get married."

Marilyn sat down heavily on a wicker chair and asked Juan, "Why? I thought you were already engaged to another girl. That's what Rennie told me. She told me that..." Her voice died and realization hit her. "Oh no." She turned towards Rennie. "Oh no. You're not pregnant, are you?"

Rennie nodded.

"But, but that doesn't mean you have to get married! We're not in the dark ages for God's sake! You're too young to get married! Rennie!"

"I'm not." Her voice steadied and as she looked at her mother the light hit her eyes obliquely, making them look like pools of molten silver. "I love Juan. I don't think age has anything to do with it. Some people will always be too young to marry. Some people will do all right. I honestly think we'll sort it out. Babies are wonderful. You always told me how happy I made you, was it a lie?"

"No, of course not." Marilyn had a sudden recollection of Rennie as an infant and smiled softly. "Babies are special," she said. Her hands came up and covered her mouth.

Juan was sitting in the shadows, his face hidden. He watched the light play across Rennie's face and marveled at the pure lines. He felt as if he'd found something that he'd been searching for forever, and the impression he'd had, ever since the day of Pierre's death, of a fractured future, was somehow mended. Rennie turned to him and smiled, and he smiled back. Life was never boring, he thought, and was getting very sweet.

Chapter Seven

For the polo season in England, Tom Wimsys needed another Argentine player. Carlos called a cousin in Argentina, helped him arrange for his passport and had him get on the first flight available. When Juan picked him up at the airport, the eighteen year-old four-goal player looked like something the cat dragged in.

"Hi, I'm Sebastian Rubios," the boy said, staggering out of customs and limping over to where Juan stood, holding a sign with Sebastian's name on it.

"How was your flight?" Juan asked politely, though from his appearance it couldn't have been good.

Sebastian grimaced and replied in fairly good English, "Awful. The plane it was late. It stopped everywhere. At your customs, they make me empty my bags. They took my sticks. My helmet is stolen."

His jade green eyes were red-rimmed with exhaustion and sunken. His long black hair hung lankly around his angular face. He was a nervous wreck.

Juan had no idea what to say, so he resorted once more to pleasantries. "Have you ever been out of Argentine?"

"No. I never even took an airplane before. I barfed all the way to Rio, and then I didn't have anything left in my stomach. I tried to sleep, but there was a storm and I thought I was for sure going to die." He grinned and kissed the silver cross hanging on a string around his neck. "Gracias Jesus, I'm here at last."

"You're Carlos's cousin?" Juan was curious. He couldn't believe this long, awkward, beanpole of a boy was related to cool, self-possessed Carlos.

"Not really. My mother worked as a maid for his uncle's wife, Señora Rubio. The Señora's husband got the maid pregnant and the result was yours truly. I grew up on the estancia, as far away from the family as possible, of course. But I liked to ride, so they gave me a job breaking ponies when I was ten. I think the Señora probably wanted me to break my neck but I did so well I was hired to work in the stables. I break all the horses for the polo. Ever since I am ten. I also break most of the bones in my body," he held a crooked hand out for Juan to see, "but I heal quick." He kissed his cross again. "Gracias Jesus."

His shoes were new, which explained the limping gait. He kicked them off in the car and examined his blisters ruefully. "At the farm, I hardly ever wear shoes," he said. "My mother got these for me the day before I left. And this." He looked fondly at the cross around his neck. "Gracias Mama," he murmured. Then he closed his eyes and fell asleep.

Juan looked askance at the boy lying with his head thrown back. His hand had been badly broken and reset crooked, and his nose and jaw had probably shared a similar fate. His jacket was too tight, and his jeans worn nearly through the knees, but everything was as clean as possible and showed signs of careful mending. Sebastian looked both fragile and tough, and Juan found himself liking the kid.

* * * * *

Tom was less than thrilled when he saw the boy stagger out of the car and nearly fall in a heap, but Juan laughed and hauled him to his feet.

"He's just about done in from his trip," he explained, and took him to the bedroom allotted him next to the laundry room. Juan had been pissed when he saw that the boy was getting the tiny room, and had even dared ask why he couldn't have the second efficiency apartment. The one Andre had used. Carlos raised his eyebrows and said that the boy would be much more at home in the smaller room. Juan hadn't argued, but now he surveyed the room ruefully as the boy tossed his bags on the floor and ran a skinny hand through his hair.

"Well, it isn't the Ritz," said Juan, "but the showers are hot, and the neighbors are fairly quiet." A horse snorted in agreement and the boy laughed delightedly.

His name was Sebastian, but everyone called him Sebi. When he emerged the next day, rested and clean, Juan nearly didn't recognize him. He'd washed his hair and it hung in jet-black curls around his narrow face. His skin was dark from the sun, and his eyes were two blazing, emerald chips under fierce black brows. When he grinned Juan saw that some of his teeth had been broken and never capped.

He looked like a young pirate, Juan decided.

The team was busy getting ready for the last tournament of the year before flying to England. The Argentines sent their passports to the British embassy for their visas, and the Americans simply made sure their passports were up to date. Rennie had a brand-new passport with her married name on it.

Sebi fit right in. He took orders from everybody, and worked harder than anyone, even Felipe. He was diffident without being shy, outspoken without being insolent. He had an incredible way with horses. He could literally ride anything. After a week he'd sorted out the most difficult ponies and had even helped Tom's daughter Alice with her pony, Jingles.

Alice followed him everywhere. The seven-year difference in their ages didn't seem to matter, they got along well, and Sebi never seemed to mind her incessant chatter as she tagged around after him, poking her nose into everything he did.

Ten-year-old Alice was in heaven. Sebi was her hero, and she worshipped him from the moment she saw him riding Bruja, the unbroken mare Andre had managed to sell Tom as a polo pony.

* * * * *

85

The last tournament was over. Palm Beach shrugged off its polo boots and britches and hit the beach. The sun was burning the ground, scorching the once verdant polo fields and turning them into hard, dry, brown plains. When the horses galloped over them now it was like galloping on a snare drum.

Juan loved it. One day, when the sky was a big, brass bowl radiating nothing but heat onto the burnt ground and the air was shimmering with mirages Juan took his gray mare out and galloped her madly up and down the fields, just for the noise.

When she was white with foam and heaving for breath he took off her saddle and got on her bareback. Then he galloped her straight at the canal and jumped her in it. The mare disappeared for a minute under the dark green water, then came up and swam strongly to the opposite side. She heaved herself out of the water, Juan clutching her around her neck. Then she shook herself like a dog. Laughing, Juan slipped off her back, and when she was done, he patted her and jumped back on.

They trotted the long way back towards the stables, picking up the saddle on the way. Then they cut through the orange groves where Juan ate his lunch: ten ripe oranges.

He sat beneath an orange tree, the gray mare tethered nearby. Bees buzzed in the blossoms, and in the distance came the sound of tractors in the fields. He leaned against the tree trunk and closed his eyes. Since asking Rennie to marry him, he'd been having second, third and fourth thoughts. His first letters had been to his grandmother and to his father, announcing the news. He didn't think he'd get an answer from either of them.

He wrote to his brothers, and predictably, they wrote back angry notes telling him to forget about getting a bigger share of the estancia. His share was a small house on the north end of the farm—three hundred acres, and not an inch more. The house was pretty, but needed work. And for now, he had a herd of about thirty horses grazing on his land—his future polo string, he hoped.

The hardest letter had been to Rosa, and he was sure he'd made a mess of things. He'd tried to explain, but how could he? How could he tell Rosa — the girl he'd known all his life — that he was marrying someone else? He sighed and thought of Rosa. He pictured her, with her long, dark brown hair and serious eyes. Her face, a perfect oval with classic features was pretty. But she inspired no passion. When he tried to think of her nude, all he could imagine was her mouth drawn down in a disapproving frown. In his imagination, he tried to take off her shirt. Imaginary Rosa slapped his hand away and gave a haughty sniff.

He hadn't really been looking forward to their wedding night, despite her declaration that she was 'saving' herself for him. When he'd tried to touch her breasts, she'd always pulled away, and when they kissed, she'd kept her mouth tightly closed.

Rennie, on the other hand, was proving to be a sensual, uninhibited woman. Their mutual inexperience was a plus — they had no preconceptions about what was right and what wasn't. Just last night, when she'd slid into bed with him, she'd bent over, offering herself to him. He'd become terribly aroused by the sight of her smooth buttocks and labia, highly visible when she leaned forward. Her cunt was a mystery to him — he hadn't had the leisure to explore a woman's body, so he could spend hours stroking, touching and looking at her.

Last night, Juan had stroked and licked her until she was sopping wet with desire. Then, after penetrating her vagina for one or two strokes, he thought he'd like to try her anus. She made him use a condom for that, but that was fine with Juan. Then they'd had fun experimenting with anal penetration all night. They found out it was best done very slowly — that when Rennie had an orgasm he felt it more when he was sheathed up her butt, and that he could penetrate her with his cock and his fingers at the same time. He recalled the violent contractions he'd felt as she'd come, and his cock hardened again.

Rennie's body was long, lean and flexible. She could lift her legs up and drape them over his shoulders while he penetrated her, driving right to the very heart of her. She was just as curious about this body as he was about hers, and he looked forward to the night time, when she joined him in his bed, and they found out what made each other tick. Juan felt his cock twitch. Her touch was magic—just her hand brushing accidentally against his pants set him on fire. Just thinking about her made him horny.

Uncomfortable, he shifted his hips, but then unzipped his pants and took his cock out. He pumped it hard, imagining Rennie's smooth, white buttocks in front of him. His hand tightened and he thought of her hands reaching back and parting them, showing him right inside her cunt. Her moist, pink flesh contracted around his fingers, and he loved to slide them in and out while he watched.

His penis, remembering the good time it had gliding in and out, throbbed almost painfully. Juan closed his eyes and imagined himself with Rennie, gently pushing his cock into her ass, while his fingers were buried in her sweet cunt. He gave a shivering cry, and then he came, spurting all over his hand. His head fell back against the tree trunk. "Oh Rennie, what you do to me, woman," he groaned.

Juan dressed, and then got back on the mare. It was late afternoon, and he still had some things to do before joining Rennie in his bedroom.

The mare trotted contentedly along. The green shade was cool and dappled her pale coat. She was going to Miami later that evening; the horses and grooms were all flying to England late that night. The polo team would join them in one week. Juan's job today was to tire the gray mare sufficiently enough so that she didn't give anyone any trouble during the trip. She had so much nervous energy she could be impossible.

Juan kicked her in the flanks and she broke into a smooth canter. He caught sight of a small white shadow flitting through the trees a little ways away, and he recognized Alice and Jingles.

She yelled to him, and they raced each other the last few hundred meters back to the stables. Juan pulled up a little to let Jingles swoop in through the gate inches in front of him.

"I won!" screamed Alice, throwing her crop into the air. "I won!"

She flung herself out of the saddle and hugged Jingles around the neck. Jingles was huffing and puffing like a little steam engine. His eyes were bright, his nostrils flaring. He too was going to England; Alice wouldn't leave with out him.

The only sad face was Watson's. He couldn't go to England because of the six-month quarantine for dogs. He was going to stay at the house with the maid. He trailed mournfully about, getting in everyone's way and making a nuisance of himself.

Juan and Alice hosed their mounts off and made sure they were safe in their stalls before they went to the back yard and jumped in the pool. Juan swam a few laps, and then went back to the stables to rest. He didn't want to admit it, but he was nervous. He and Rennie were getting married the day before the team flew to England together, and it was all he could think about.

Chapter Eight

The wedding day dawned hot and clear. After waking up early and trying to get over her nerves by walking to the beach for a swim, Rennie took a cool shower.

Her mother, Marilyn, wandered around the house with a tragic face, and occasionally went into Rennie's room to stare at the ugly brown suitcase on the bed filled with Rennie's meager wardrobe. Rennie saw her mother sit on the bed, pick up Mr. Marmalade, and hug the old tom so tight he meowed. He, too, knew something was amiss. He wouldn't leave Rennie's room where he sat on the top of the suitcase all day long.

In the afternoon, the heat was nearly unbearable. Huge, dark storm clouds moved sluggishly along the coast and the few, fat raindrops that fell sizzling onto the pavement didn't cool the air down a bit.

* * * * *

Juan also woke up early that day. He'd packed his clothes and cleaned the little studio the best he could. He and Rennie were spending their wedding night there. Neither of them wanted to go to a hotel.

After he'd finished cleaning, he went outside and wandered around the empty stables. From across the paddocks and through the orange grove came the sounds of laughter and splashing in a pool. It was Sebi and Alice; he recognized Alice's shrill voice. He thought about walking over and taking a swim, but he lacked the energy.

He went back into the apartment and lay down on the narrow bed. The ceiling seemed too close and the walls were leaning in. He suddenly felt as if his marriage was a trap he couldn't escape.

He'd never really thought about marrying anyone except Rosa, and even that had been pushed to the back of his mind. It was something he was going to do after he became a famous polo player and made a fortune. Then he would think about marriage. Now, before he'd even had time to complete one polo season and his bank account was still in the red from buying horses, he was getting married.

He shuddered. Where would they live? The little house on the estancia was nice, although it didn't have electricity yet. That could be fixed. His horses were doing well, and back home at the ranch, he had thirty more in training. But he had to pay the bills. The domadors cost money, and the horses had to eat. Just thinking about it made him dizzy.

Then there was the baby to think about. Or rather, not to think about. Not quite yet. He'd start thinking about a baby when he could accept being married. Another shiver ran through him. Sleep, that's what he needed. He would think about everything later, when he'd rested a bit.

He closed his eyes and slept until the sun falling on his face through the window was suddenly blotted out by a shadow of a black cloud. He woke up and glanced at his watch. He swore and got stiffly to his feet. He had less than half an hour to get ready.

He jumped when Sebi pounded on the door. He wanted to borrow a tie. Juan took a deep breath and told himself to calm down. His nerves were getting the best of him.

* * * * *

Rennie put on her wedding dress. Her mother had made it. It was creamy white satin cut on the bias with short-sleeves and a scoop neck, and there was a simple, white, lace veil that Rennie draped over her head.

When she was done, she looked at herself in the mirror. The girl staring back at her had the same gray eyes as she, the same cinnamon-colored hair, the same slender silhouette, but it wasn't her. This girl was older, and more solemn. The sparkle in her eyes had changed to a soft glow. Marilyn had done her make-up for her, making her eyes immense in her pale face, and putting more definition on her mouth. She rarely wore lipstick, and it made the reflection in the mirror even more of a stranger. Her face was stronger though, with a new set to the chin. Even Marilyn noticed it.

"You look so grown up," she said, coming in the room and smoothing Rennie's veil down. "I feel like you're someone I've never met before. Who are you Rennie? What are you thinking about right now?"

Rennie looked at her mother soberly. "I'm someone who knows she has an uphill battle in front of her. I have to make Juan love me as much as I love him. I feel like I'm entering an arena, not a marriage. I am going to fight all the way though, Mom, I'm going to make this marriage work, you'll see."

"I bet you will sweetheart," said Marilyn, hugging her daughter tight. "But I want you to know that what ever happens, my door will always be open for you and your baby. You will always have a room in my house, forever and ever. I will never turn you away."

"I know," Rennie bit her lip to keep from crying. "And that's what makes it so easy for me to leave."

"I hope that's a good thing," said Marilyn. She hugged Rennie once more, and then heaved a great sigh. "Well, we better get going. The groom will be waiting for you."

"I certainly hope so," Rennie gave a little laugh. "God I'm nervous."

* * * * *

When Juan saw her coming down the aisle in the little church, he had a shock. He had been in sort of a fog since the morning, not really registering what was happening around him. When he saw Rennie, the significance of it all suddenly hit him. He was getting married. The girl next to him was carrying his child. He wouldn't be able to go back to Argentina to live on the farm. He would have to either stay in England or live in the United States until he made enough money to go home and buy an estancia.

And did he really want to do that? He'd never doubted that his future would consist of raising cattle and horses. His studies had all been agricultural. What did he know about anything else, including marriage and raising a child?

He felt, at that instant, as if his feet would lift off the floor. As if the hot breeze that was blowing in through the open window would pick him up and carry him away. He thought he would disintegrate. His life was shattered beyond repair, and it had all happened because the slender redhead standing next to him stirred something in his heart that hadn't been moved before. Something deep inside him, some sort of instinct that was imprinted somehow into his very genes had reached out to this girl and touched her, and bound her to him in a way that was irrevocable.

"I do," he heard himself saying, and the sun broke out from behind the clouds and slanted down from the sky to hit the statue of St. John, making its paint glow and the gold feathers on the eagle shine.

* * * * *

Rennie noticed that too, but for her it was still the statue of St. Francis. The one she'd prayed to, and a superstitious shiver went up her spine. *He's protecting us*, she thought fervently. The thought was like a lifeline in the turmoil of her mind. Rennie was terrified. She was frightened of being pregnant, frightened of getting married, frightened of flying to England the next day on a huge silver metal plane which had no business flying in the sky in the first place.

She was positive they would go plunging to their deaths, but at least that way all her worries would be over and she wouldn't have to go through the pain of childbirth, or the agonies of a divorce.

Suddenly she heard the priest repeating her name. He'd been saying the wedding vows while she'd been thinking about airplanes! With a start, she forced a wide smile, and said, "I do."

* * * * *

The reception, organized by Carol Wimsys, was a huge success. Rennie and Juan floated around the party, arm and arm. Rennie sipped her iced tea and tried to smile at everyone. Juan greeted most people by name.

Rennie squeezed his arm. "I feel like I'm dreaming," she whispered. "Did Carol really invite all the people in Palm Beach?"

Juan grimaced. "And all their friends. My God, I never thought the wedding reception would be so crowded. Look, there's the girl with the green hair."

"That's Freya."

"The one that gave us the blue sparkly vibrator as a wedding present?" He raised his eyebrows at Rennie and grinned. "What kind of thank you note will you write her? Will you tell her how much you love to use it?"

Rennie laughed at that and felt her nerves untangle a bit. "She's a sweetie, but I hope she doesn't drink any champagne."

"Why?"

"She's fond of skinny-dipping in pools."

Juan looked at Freya. She was tall and thin, but had big breasts straining against a tight halter-top. If she did go skinny dipping, Juan thought, she'd be a sensation. The green hair was a bit odd, though. It clashed with the polo set.

"I feel really strange," said Rennie. "I can't believe we're really married." She felt herself blush and gave a nervous laugh. "You don't regret it, do you?"

Juan looked at her gravely and she felt her heart skip a beat. "No." he said, and kissed the tip of her nose.

"I'm going to get another coke. Are you all right with your drink?" She nodded, and he left Rennie for a minute and went towards the bar.

Rennie sipped her iced tea and felt better. It was still sultry out. She saw Betty Ramirez dive into the pool and for a moment felt like doing the same. Burr Chester, one of the club's polo patrons, was awfully handsome, she reflected. And he was nice too, helping Betty out of the pool and fishing for her shoes with the pool skimmer.

Most of the polo people were nice. She still couldn't put names on half the faces, but everyone had been so sweet.

She smiled as Juan pulled up a chair at sat down beside her. She was so much in love with him. If only he loved her too.

He'd taken off his tie and stuffed it in his pocket. He glanced up at the sky. "I bet it rains tonight. I can't wait to get to England. We're going to have a good time. You'll love it there. And just think, no more grooming." He grinned.

She smiled back, but it was a strained smile. "I'm terrified about the plane," she confessed.

"Don't worry! Statistics prove it's a lot safer than driving." He kissed her gently on the lips. "You look tired. Do you want to leave now?"

"We have to cut the cake," she said. "It's a tradition here in America. Then I toss my bouquet to the ladies. After that they make you put on a blindfold, and you have to take off my garter and throw it to the men."

Juan looked interested. "You're wearing a garter? Can I see?"

She shook her head. "Not right now! Come on, let's go cut the cake, I feel like something sugary." She wondered what the custom was in Argentina, but she didn't want to ask, she was afraid it would make him think about his ex-fiancée.

She led Juan to the desert table and her mother came over. When they saw the bride and groom standing in front of the cake, the guests gathered around.

Rennie and Juan cut the cake and handed plates around. Rennie envied Juan's easy assurance with everyone. He joked as he handed the slices out, and he never seemed to forget a name. Rennie just smiled shyly and tried to look as if she belonged to this crowd. Only her mother and her friend Freya were familiar to her though.

Betty came to get some cake. She still wore her wet dress, but her dark hair was neatly brushed. She'd taken off her bra too, and Rennie's eyes widened at the sight of her huge breasts clearly outlined by the wet fabric.

Nearly everyone else's eyes widened too, and Diana nearly choked on her cake. "Well I'll be!" she exclaimed. "If it isn't Betty Big Boobs. Here darling, have some cake. So sorry you're all wet, but isn't it a perfect occasion for showing your new tits to one and all?"

Betty smiled graciously. "Sweet Di, always thinking of others. Your husband did tell me he wanted a closer look earlier."

Rennie gasped in shock, but everyone around her simply laughed. Rennie looked at Diana, but Diana was eating her cake and grinning along with everyone else. Would she ever be able to fit in here? Even Juan seemed amused.

Before Rennie could gather her thoughts, Carol clapped her hands.

"Girls!" Carol grabbed Diana by the arm and led her to one side of the pool. "Rennie, it's time to throw your bouquet. All you unmarried ladies go over there!" She pointed to a spot behind Rennie.

A group of giggling girls soon formed. Ten year-old Alice joined them. Lucia and Betty stood in the front; behind them was Freya. Rennie turned around and threw the bouquet of white roses over her shoulder. There was a scuffle, and both Lucia and Betty ended up holding the bouquet. They looked at each other for a split second, and then both let go as if the flowers burned their fingers. Alice Wimsys, leaning forward to see what was going on, caught the bouquet before it hit the ground.

"I got it!" she crowed, holding it aloft and prancing about. "I caught the bouquet!"

"Come here Juan!" boomed Burr Chester, standing by a chair. He grabbed Juan's arm and turned him around. "Rennie, you too!"

Rennie giggled and told Juan, "Don't look so scared, all you have to do is take off my garter and throw it to the guys."

"Yes, but first," Burr took a scarf from his wife and brandished it in the air, "I blindfold you!" He deftly tied the scarf over Juan's eyes and waved his hand to show that he couldn't see. "Now, you will kneel down and take off your wife's garter."

Rennie stifled her laughter behind her hand. She slipped off her lacy garter and handed it to Kurt, Burr's son, who was making motions with his hands telling her what to do. Then Kurt hastily pulled up the leg of his own pants and pushed his foot into the garter. He sat on the chair, and nodded to Rennie.

"Here I am, Juan," she said, trying not to giggle.

Burr spun Juan around a few times and faced him towards the chair where Kurt sat, waving his hairy leg in the air. Juan put out his hands and groped forwards, suddenly encountering Kurt's hairy leg.

"What the...!" Juan yelled and stood up. He tore off his scarf and grinned sheepishly at the laughing crowd. "I *knew* it wasn't Rennie," he said, "But I was hoping it wasn't Kurt!" He grabbed Kurt's leg and pulled off Rennie's garter. "Here, catch!" he cried, tossing the garter into the air.

There was a scuffle and Moshie Stern came out of the fray with the lacy garter clutched in his hand. There was a moment's silence, then shrieks of laughter. Moshie was ten years old. Everyone knew he was a child prodigy, who played the piano, the harp and the violin, and had skipped five grades. He was now in eleventh grade, and was at the head of his class. Even

Rennie, who didn't know half of the crowd at the wedding, knew about Moshie Stern. He'd been on television several times.

"I got it," said Moshie, in his strange, adult-sounding voice. "Does that mean I have to wear ladies underwear from now on?"

His older brother Isaac cuffed him on the head. "No dummy. It means you got the garter, that's all." Isaac could have been sore that his little brother was three grades ahead of him, but he clearly wasn't. Moshie might be able to explain quarks and trigonometry, but he was a complete failure socially. He had no common sense at all—he was once seen outside in a severe thunderstorm trying to catch a lightning bolt with one of his father's golf clubs. The fact that he was only three at the time didn't change anything. He was weird, and everyone knew it.

His father played polo; he was the patron of the Kosher Chicks, named after his first deli. Moshie's two brothers played polo, David was eighteen and rated two goals and Isaac was rated four goals. Isaac could ride just about anything with four legs, and some girls in the club claimed he could ride the two-legged variety just as well.

His parents would have liked Moshie to take up riding, but Moshie was allergic to horses. He was allergic to anything he disliked, actually. It was common knowledge that his subconscious produced the most amazing hives the doctors in Palm Beach had ever seen.

"It's mind over matter," he told his despairing mother, and continued to try to bend a metal bar with his thoughts.

Isaac tried to take the garter away from Moshie, there was a scuffle, and they fell into the pool. This caused some consternation because everyone knew Moshie was allergic to chlorine, but he was so engrossed in trying to get the garter back he forgot to sneeze.

Kurt pushed Sebi into the pool, but it was purely by accident. Kurt was trying to put his shoes back on and he tripped.

Sebi, however, possessed a keen sense of justice, and as soon as he had hauled himself out of the pool, he pushed Kurt in, shoes and all.

Juan pushed Sebi back in, "to keep Kurt company," he said laughing, though Sebi was spitting like a mad cat and furious about wrecking his new jacket.

Moshie was out of the pool now, but decided that his mother should take a swim, and shoved Magda Stern into the deep end where she sank like a stone, being weighted down with fifteen pounds of jewelry.

Her husband dove in after her, which prompted a general rush towards the pool. Moshie's father was also the president of the club, and what he did, everyone did. Soon there were twenty club members swimming around imitating their beloved president while the junior club-members dove to retrieve Magda's jewelry.

Betty Ramirez seemed peeved not to be the only contestant in the wet t-shirt contest, so she decided to out-do Wendy Strokeson and Sadie Dupree who were both flaunting impressive bosoms beneath wet, transparent garments. She peeled off her dress and went topless.

Diana Chester, standing near Rennie, said acidly, "If tits were brains Betty would be smarter than Moshie."

Freya took off her dress too, and she wasn't wearing anything underneath it. Moshie suddenly decided he wanted to learn to swim, and jumped back in the pool, next to her.

Rennie giggled when she overheard Moshie, in his ultra-precocious manner, say to Freya, "What's your name baby?" And when he puffed out his chest and blurted, "I caught the garter, my dad's the president, and if you let me touch your breasts I'll buy you a car when I'm sixteen," Rennie burst out laughing.

Freya, with her usual aplomb, replied, "My name's Freya, and come back when you're sixteen, okay?"

Rennie saw Moshie nod vigorously. "Fair enough, can I look all I want though?" he said.

Freya nodded, but Moshie's mother caught him by the hair and pulled him out of the pool. He yelled like a skinned cat. Isaac took his place and, obviously having overheard Moshie's conversation, said, "Hi, I'm Isaac, and I'm sixteen."

Rennie waved to Freya, and then went to find Juan. "How about we leave before everyone remembers whose wedding it is," she suggested.

Juan nodded. "Let's go."

They found Carol and Tom and thanked them, then Rennie went to see her mother. She realized with a pang of sadness that she wouldn't be seeing her mother for weeks. Rennie gave her mother a huge hug. "I love you," she said.

"I love you too, darling." Marilyn wiped away a tear. "Write every day, all right?"

Juan shook hands with Marilyn. "Don't worry," he said to her. "I'll look after Rennie." Then he led Rennie through the crowd and out the back gate. Once outside, he gave her a soft kiss. "You look so beautiful," he said. "I wish I'd told you before."

Rennie blinked, surprised. "Thank you," she whispered, strangely touched.

* * * * *

"It's your wedding night, what do you want to do?" Juan asked.

They were in his small apartment, and the noise from the party came in faintly through the window.

Rennie looked at him, and a faint blush stained her cheeks. "You're going to think I'm silly," she said.

"No, tell me."

"Well," she was really blushing now. "I've always wanted to make love in a horse's stall. The horses are all gone now, so they're all empty," she said. "We could take our pick."

"A stall?" Juan gaped. He hadn't expected that. A horse's stall wasn't exactly romantic to him.

"What do you think?"

Juan reconsidered. He pictured Rennie on her hands and knees, her incredible hair trailing in the fresh straw. He grinned. "All right, on one condition."

"Name it."

"I want to use Freya's wedding present," he said.

Her eyebrows rose and she turned pink. "Have you ever used one before?"

"No, I haven't really done very much, sexually speaking." He cleared his throat nervously, wondering if he should admit that he'd only made love a few times before he'd met her. Maybe she'd think he was not macho enough, or something.

"So we'll have fun learning together," said Rennie. Her expression turned mischievous and Juan's reservations dissolved instantly. "Let me get that sparkly blue sex toy." She rummaged through the gifts until she found it. "It says to wash before use. Hang on half a sec."

She vanished into the bathroom and there came the sound of running water. Juan waited impatiently, his penis stirring with interest. When she returned, he frowned. Had she changed her mind? There was no sex toy in her hands.

"Where is it?" asked Juan, frowning.

Rennie smiled. "You'll have to search for it. In the stables. Come on."

Juan closed his eyes, reached out and touched her arm. His hand slid over to her shoulder, followed the line of her collarbone, and dipped down to cup her breast. Beneath the satin, her nipple hardened at his touch. "Is it inside you?" he asked, his voice breaking a bit as his imagination suddenly ran wild. He reached between her legs.

"Not here," she said with a giggle, pushing him away.

He led her outside then into the stables. The boxes were empty, and one was full of fresh straw. "Perfect," said Rennie, and she pulled him inside. It was dark, but there was enough light for Juan to see Rennie's outline, and when she smiled, her teeth were a white flash.

Rennie made him undress first. When he was standing nude, she knelt in front of him and ran her hands up his legs, over his knees and thighs, between his thighs, to his groin.

In the dark, he couldn't see her, but he felt her hand even more keenly. At her touch, his penis suddenly grew hard. It reared up, touching her on the face. She opened her mouth and slid her lips over the tip of it. Juan reached out and grabbed at the wall to steady himself. The feeling of her lips, teeth and tongue on his sensitive penis was making his head spin.

Rennie purred deep in her throat, and the vibration tickled the tip of his cock. He trembled, and leaned harder on the wall. Rennie sucked and licked, her mouth opening and closing around him. She cupped his balls in her hand, her fingers dancing along the hypersensitive skin between his thighs and behind his testicles. As if she was starving and wanted to devour him, she sucked greedily on the tip, then ran her lips along the length of his cock. He felt little electric surges within him, and her tried to push her away.

"I'm coming," he said hoarsely, trying to stop.

Rennie pulled back long enough to say, "I want to taste you," and then she slid her mouth over his penis.

He wasn't sure he could come in her mouth. He'd never done it before, and he'd never had a real blowjob before. The feeling was incredible. He shuddered and gasped as suddenly his control left him and his cock spurted into her mouth. He thrust as gently as he could, holding tightly to her head.

When he was finished he sank down into the straw. "Sorry," he gasped. He wondered if she'd hated it, or if she was disgusted by it.

"Don't be sorry." Rennie licked her lips. "It was interesting."

"Just interesting?" He was worried.

She grinned, and the moon suddenly peeked from behind the clouds and shined into the stall. In its silvery light, he realized her eyes were very bright. "Why don't you reach down and see?"

He reached under her dress, and as his hand slid up her thigh, he expected to encounter silk underwear. Instead, he encountered her skin. Smooth skin.

Surprised, he lifted her dress above her waist.

"What did you do?" he asked.

"Shaved." There was definitely a teasing note in her voice now. "Freya told me to try it. She says it drives her boyfriends crazy. Do you like it?"

Juan wasn't sure. He moved her into a patch of bright moonlight and stared. Instead of her auburn bush, there was smooth skin. Her mound of Venus was satiny soft. Her outer lips were visible now, and within them, the coral-colored inner lips of her labia.

Smiling, she spread her legs. Inside her vagina was the blue vibrator. It was just like a penis, and even had some round balls at the end. Juan's cock suddenly decided he thought that shaving and vibrators were terrific. He was aching to penetrate into this newly shaved territory. But before that, Juan had to explore.

"Lie down," he said.

She did, and opened her legs wide with that mixture of artlessness and wantonness that drove him wild. The vibrator was halfway in, and he took it, sliding it all the way inside her. The sight of her pink flesh stretched around the base of the blue vibrator was straining his control. Slowly, he slid it in and out, one hand on his cock, pumping himself while he pushed and pulled on the vibrator.

"It vibrates," said Rennie, in a breathless voice. "There's a little button."

He took the vibrator and turned it on, pressing his hand to it to feel. It did vibrate—and it made a soft humming noise. Rennie uttered a surprised shriek and ground her cunt against his hand. "I'm coming already!" she cried, and arched her back.

Juan thrust the vibrator in and out of her taut pussy while she writhed and clutched at the straw. Her thighs tightened around his hands and he saw her stomach contract. "That was a surprise," said Rennie, between little gasps.

It was a surprise. Juan had never really watched a woman in the throes of an orgasm before. His cock was so hard he thought he'd probably explode.

He drew the vibrator out and kissed her deeply on the lips. The moonlight turned everything to silver. Her eyes, her skin, even her shiny cunt. Juan found himself wondering if she was even human. Maybe she was part fairy. At any rate, she was bewitching, and he slid his mouth over her lips, her chin and down her neck. When he reached the hollow at the base of her throat he paused, breathing in her light scent, his eyes closed. He tried to concentrate on what he was feeling. He felt the prickly yet soft straw beneath them, the cool night air on his naked back, and his calloused hands touching Rennie's soft skin. "Do you mind that my hands are so rough?" he asked her.

"No," she murmured. She moved her hips suggestively. "I like it. It feels, I don't know, masculine, somehow."

Relieved, Juan reached down and probed into her vagina with his finger, and found her slippery and still swollen with yearning. When he penetrated her, his finger slipping into her hot, tight flesh, she arched her back and uttered a plaintive cry. He loved to feel her muscles contract around his fingers. He pressed his mouth to her, to feel it with his tongue.

Her clitoris stood up—a hard nub, begging to be rubbed. He touched it with his tongue, flicking it until she writhed beneath him. His penis quivered and he realized he was about to lose his control. He gave one last, long kiss to his wife's clit, tonguing it until she writhed against his mouth. Then he reared up and plunged into her. She was so wet, he slid in smoothly. He felt his cock hit the end of her womb. "Did I hurt you?" he asked, trying to hold still.

"No! Juan! Go faster!" she begged, her voice ragged.

He thrust hard, urged on by her cries and her hands.

She grabbed his hips and pulled him in then pushed him back. He wanted to stop, he wanted to slow down, but he couldn't. The taste of her in his mouth, the memory of her sucking his cock, her small cries as she writhed beneath him, and her fingers digging into his back all pushed him over the edge. "I'm coming!" he cried, and he shuddered once very hard. His seed shot out of his penis and he gave another hoarse yell.

He felt her start to quiver and he leaned over and held her tightly. Then she burst into tears.

Fear stabbed him. Had he hurt her? What happened? What had he done? "What is it?" he cried.

"It's the last time we'll make love," she sobbed.

"What are you talking about?" He pulled back and stared at her. In the moonlight, tears glistened on her cheeks.

"Tomorrow we leave for England, and we're all going to die. But at least I'm going to die with you," she wailed.

Juan sagged in relief. "Yes, in my arms. You nut. I want you to repeat after me. Airplanes are fun, airplanes are safe, airplanes are the best way to get from one place to another."

Chapter Nine

Rennie threw up eight times on the flight to England. Juan slept. He was tired. Rennie and he had made love nearly all night long. His dreams were full of her creamy skin and coppery hair, her full breasts and her long legs. He slept with a smile on his face.

Rennie was glad he was sleeping and not witnessing her nervous sickness. Every time the plane's engines changed rhythm slightly, every time there was a tremor from turbulence she would turn green and race towards the bathroom. She was so uptight that her jaw ached from clenching her teeth, and her heart raced so much that she was exhausted. Finally, an hour out of Heathrow, she fell asleep.

She woke up when the plane touched the ground to see Juan leaning over her with a grin.

"We're here!" He sounded so happy she managed to smile back. Then she dug around in her bag for another mint—she'd eaten almost three whole rolls during the flight. Then she realized that they really had landed, and that she was still alive. The relief made her feel giddy.

The polo team disembarked, although not together. Tom, Carol and Alice were in first class. Juan, Rennie and Sebi were in coach, and Lucia and Carlos were in business class—there hadn't been any more room in first class.

* * * * *

When she got out of the plane, Rennie looked out the huge glass windows looking over the parking lots. She flipped a lock of apricot-colored hair out of her eyes and stared at the rain falling outside. "It looks dreary," she said. "And cold."

Juan laughed. "It's only May here, it'll be cold to you. The English call this spring, though I don't agree. It will get warmer by June, maybe. I remember one year we had our coats and scarves on right through August."

Rennie shook her head. "It's so different from Florida. It's so gray. Everything is gray — the sky, the buildings, the cars, and the rain. I feel like I've gone colorblind. It's so strange." The only splash of color came from the yellow slicker a policewoman wore as she directed traffic.

Rennie and Juan stood at the window a moment, looking out at the rain, then went to the baggage claim area to get their luggage.

Rennie only had one suitcase. She didn't have any clothes that were suitable for England. She'd grown up in a hot climate, and didn't even have a decent pair of jeans. She wore an old cashmere sweater that her mother had found at the bottom of her closet. Marilyn had managed to mend the hole in one elbow and make it look presentable. Rennie was glad of its soft warmth, though she was jealous of everyone else's warm coats.

Sebi and Juan had Barbours. Juan had an old one, and Carlos had taken Sebi shopping in Palm Beach for a new one. Alice had a wool duffel coat. It was bright red with a matching red scarf. Carol had a mink coat. It was reversible, and she put the fur side on the inside. It was three-quarters length, dark and supple. It looked wonderful to Rennie. Lucia had a white jacket. It came from the polo shop and was waterproof and windproof. Carlos had the same jacket in dark green. They looked very sharp.

Tom had a Blue jacket with his team logo in silver upon it. He pointed proudly to his jacket. "I have three others like this for you guys," he told Juan, Sebi and Carlo as they gathered around him with their baggage.

Rennie hid a grin. They would go to the polo games looking like quadruplets.

Tom rented four cars for his team. Carol, Carlos and Juan all followed him out of the parking lot. Rain made everything shiny-slick. Rennie stared out the window with wide-eyed wonder. *This is England*, she kept thinking. *I'm really in England!* She didn't talk to Juan. He was silent and seemed preoccupied. She was too tired and excited though, to fret.

Two hours later they drove into the courtyard of what Alice referred to as "Their Summer Castle". The rain slackened and stopped suddenly, and a shaft of pale sunlight lit the old manor.

Rennie was intimidated. There was a full staff waiting for them. Mrs. O'Brian, the cook, Daphne, the governess, and Sarah and Tolly, the maids, all dressed in identical short black skirts with starched white aprons. There was a gardener named Bill, who worked in an orchard around the back, between the manor and the stables. The apple and cherry trees were all in bloom. It was the first time Rennie had seen them and she thought that the trees looked like brides.

Juan and Rennie had a room in the west wing overlooking the orchard. It was called the Ruby room. Tolly, the maid, who was short and quite pretty with dark hair cut in a bob, showed them to it and lit the fire for them. There was a tiny fireplace, and the floor was covered with an Oriental rug. The walls were papered with a Victorian rose pattern, and the curtains were made of rose-colored poplin.

"I hope you like it here," said Tolly.

Rennie smiled. "It's wonderful."

"Are you the newlyweds?" she asked, tilting her head.

"Yes," said Rennie. The words still sounded strange to her and she wondered if she'd ever get used to being married.

"There is a complementary bottle of champagne in the fridge," she said, pointing to the little bar. She bent over to show them, and Rennie saw Juan's eyes widen. Tolly's skirt was so short it showed she didn't wear any underwear at all. She had on black lace garters though, holding up her sheer stockings.

Rennie hit Juan's arm and he rubbed it, grinning sheepishly at her.

"It's a demi bottle," said Tolly, looking back over her shoulder. She winked at Rennie. "That means it's half size, like me."

When Tolly left, Juan leered at Rennie and said, "I want you to run out and buy a garter. And next time you wear a dress, I hope you don't put any underwear on."

"You'll be sorry," said Rennie demurely, walking to the fridge and getting the bottle of champagne.

Juan took it from her and kissed her lips. "The man of the house usually opens the champagne." Then he stopped and put the bottle down, clapping his hand on his forehead. "Oh no!" he cried, "I forgot!"

"Forgot what?" Rennie wondered what he was so upset about. Nothing serious, she hoped.

"Come here," he said sternly, and he opened the door to their room. He pointed out into the hallway, his eyebrows drawn in a ferocious scowl. "I said, come here."

Rennie frowned. "Why?" Her nerves started to fray a bit. He looked so stern, suddenly. The thought that she hardly knew him crossed her mind. Had she done something wrong? What was it? Slowly, she walked to him, then past him into the hallway. "What is it?" The next moment she shrieked as Juan suddenly swept her up in his arms.

"I forgot to carry you over the threshold," he said, and he carried her into the room and dumped her on the bed. Laughing, he caught her by the waist and kissed her. "You have no idea how worried you looked," he said, grinning at her.

Rennie rolled her eyes. "If you think that is romantic, you have another thing coming."

"I do?" he looked pleased, not cross, and Rennie pushed him away playfully.

"I thought you were the man of the house."

"I am. Why?" Juan asked, standing up.

"Because I would like some champagne, please."

"You can' t have any, you're expecting a baby," he said sternly.

"The doctor said I could have half a glass to celebrate."

Rennie was glad to sit on the velvet-covered chair in front of the fireplace and warm up a bit, sipping her champagne. There was a wicker basket full of firewood, and Rennie felt as if she'd stepped into a fairy tale, complete with handsome prince. It was a magical place.

* * * * *

The team decided to meet every morning at eight to ride the horses and practice on the polo field next to the stables. Rennie soon got used to the cool weather and went for long walks every morning. She and Juan woke up at sunrise. They were both early risers, and while Juan went to the stables, Rennie put on her new boots and walked for miles through the countryside. She thought she'd never get used to seeing such a palette of greens, and she'd had to ask the gardener the names of all the different flowers she saw. Azaleas and rhododendrons were blooming in the woods, and their incredible fuchsia and hot pink hues set the forest ablaze. Parts of the wood were carpeted in bluebells, and it looked as if the ground was reflecting the sky.

There were public walking paths all over the countryside, and Rennie soon found her way to the village through the woods and made friends with the woman at the post office shop and the ladies at the teashop.

She was alone for her walks, but she liked the solitude. It gave her time to try and sort out her feelings about her marriage. She loved Juan, and she was determined to make everything work. But she was afraid Juan regretted marrying her, and she was terrified to ask him. She didn't want to hear him say he was unhappy. So she walked for hours, the forest calming her frazzled nerves, the English countryside never failing to enchant her.

* * * * *

After they had been in England three days, Juan's father called and asked Juan to come to visit. They decided to drive to Juan's father's farm, so they packed their bags for an overnight trip.

When Juan told Rennie about the trip, she unearthed a map of England. She had no idea where Wales was. She felt so uneducated compared to everyone, but at least she was trying to learn.

"Juan?" she asked timidly, the map spread on the table in front of her. "Can you show me where your dad's farm is?"

Juan came and leaned over her shoulder. He put his finger on the map. "This is where we are. The castle is here, in the Cotswolds, not too far away from the city of Bath." Rennie nodded. Bath was beautiful and she'd enjoyed seeing the ancient Roman ruins.

Juan drew a line with his finger. "London is there, to the south east, and the polo clubs are scattered around the English countryside." Juan pointed out Cowdray Club to her, and Cirencester, which was the closest club to their summer castle. Windsor palace and polo grounds were not too far either; the Berkshire Club was near Windsor.

Then he rested his finger on the place that jutted out in the southwest of England. "That's where my father lives. That's Wales. My father's farm is in north Wales in a region called Snowdonia." His voice held no trace of emotion, so Rennie couldn't tell if he was happy to go see his father. She glanced up at his face, but it was pensive.

He caught her looking at him and smiled crookedly. "You're going to love it," he said.

* * * * *

Rennie thought Wales was beautiful.

"Even in the pouring rain, the countryside is incredible," she said. "Oh, look at that place, it's gorgeous!"

"Do you like it?" Juan slowed the car and pulled into a cobblestone drive. "This is my father's farm."

"Oh Juan." Rennie was speechless with delight. She loved the stone cottage Juan's father lived in. It was a square, slate-roofed building set in the middle of a rainy garden. Large trees grew around it, and there was a hedge of rose-briar growing up over the gate and all along the fence.

Juan's father came out to the car to meet them. He wore a faded green overcoat and large rubber boots. He held an umbrella over his head, and the effect was very like a scarecrow striding suddenly out of the rain. He bent over the car and extracted their suitcase, then opened Rennie's door for her. She stared up at him. He had long, gray hair tied back in a ponytail. His eyes were bottle green.

"So, you're Marilyn's daughter," he said, and stared down at her for the longest time until Rennie felt very uncomfortable.

"I'd like something hot to drink. You know, the weather has taken a turn for the worse, and we're standing in the pouring rain," Juan remarked dryly.

"Come into the cottage," said Juan's father with a sigh, ducking through the gate where the rose-bramble caught at his shoulders, then leading the way down a flagstone path crowded by hedges of fragrant sage and lavender.

"What a lovely place, Mr. Allistair," Rennie said sincerely.

"Call me Rupert," said the green-eyed man, holding the front door open for her.

Rennie stepped through a narrow doorway directly into the kitchen. There was a huge stone fireplace on one wall with a fire crackling merrily in it. A wooden table was surrounded by an odd assortment of chairs—no two matched, but all were wood and painted white. A stone sink juxtaposed a more modern white enamel one. Piles of *Horse and Hound* magazines slithered over one counter. Rose-patterned dishes were stacked haphazardly in an old glass fronted buffet, along with a collection of glasses and teacups.

A large orange tabby got up from his seat near the window and yawned hugely, giving Rennie the sudden, creepy notion that Mr. Marmalade had somehow been magicked to this timeless place.

"That's Jude, the farm cat. He comes inside when it rains," said Rupert, seeing where Rennie was looking.

"He must be here every day then," said Juan ironically.

Rupert took a seat near the fireplace, motioning for Rennie and Juan to sit where they liked.

"*Como estás?*" asked Juan, and his father shot him an irritated look.

"I'm fine, thank you," he replied.

"*Y los...*"

"We're in Wales lad, speak English please." There was no malice behind his words, just a sort of fatigue that Rennie couldn't fathom.

"Sorry." Juan shook a cigarette out of his pack and lit it, tossing the match into the fireplace. "How's the sheep industry?" Rennie watched him smoke with a concerned frown. She'd noticed that Juan only smoked when he was stressed.

"Good." His father shrugged. "I can't complain."

"What do you have now?" Again, Juan's bland voice troubled Rennie. Why were the two men so formal with each other? They weren't acting like father and son at all.

"Well, I still have the Merinos for the wool in addition to the Welsh Mountain sheep, of course. White and black ones. I'm starting a small herd of Lleyn and Llanwenog. And then there are the rarer breeds." He seemed to relax talking about his sheep, and Rennie caught a glimpse of the young man he used to be when he smiled boyishly.

"Why so many sheep?" she asked.

"I'm not really breeding them for wool or meat," he explained. "Though I do use the Merino's wool for the money. I'm more of a bloodstock agent. I'm trying to keep the bloodlines pure, and I've started a safeguarding program for some of the older Welsh breeds, as well as for rare breeds from around the world. It's rather interesting, if you like that sort of thing.

"I do think it's a shame that farm animals have become so homogenized around the world. I'm hoping to convince farmers to start diversifying. The thing will be to find the best examples of the rare breeds so that they will be able to compete with the more familiar farm animals.

"However, the main source of income out here is the hunting. I rent out the land come autumn to a hunting club. I can fix the quotas myself. Last year, for example, there were ten red deer and fifteen roe-buck bagged, and of course the pheasants. More than four hundred of those, I suppose. I raise them here, it fixes them on the land, you see." He paused. "Sorry. Am I boring you?"

"Not at all!" Rennie said. She liked Rupert and wished Juan would be nicer. As if reading her thoughts, Juan leaned forward and smiled at his father.

"You always did like shooting," said Juan. "Is it good money?"

"It keeps the farm's head above water." Rupert grinned at Rennie. "Want to see the farm?"

Rennie nodded. "Sounds good to me," she said. "When do we go?"

"As soon as it stops raining," Rupert said.

Juan looked out at the drizzle and sighed. "I don't suppose you have anything to eat besides lamb chops? "

"I usually cook them on the fire," said Rupert blandly.

* * * * *

Rupert showed them to their room. Juan remarked on the changes he noticed. "I see you finally got an indoor toilet," he

114

said to his father. "And the bathroom has been redone. It looks nice."

"I thought you might like that," said Rupert. "What do you think, Rennie?"

"It's just perfect," she said. The room was large and Spartan, with unvarnished wooden floors and an old wardrobe standing against one wall. The stone walls were whitewashed, there were no curtains, and on the floor were two sheepskin rugs. A black sea chest was at the foot of the bed, and the patchwork quilt on the bed was the only colorful thing in the room.

Under the window was a marble-topped dresser. Juan walked over to it and ran his hands over the smooth white stone.

"So that's where it went," he said softly.

"I shipped it over." His father shrugged.

"Why?" Juan sounded curious.

"I don't know. There were so many things I could have taken to remind me of your mother I suppose. The painting. The needlepoint chairs. But every morning your mother would wake up and go to this dresser. She would open the top drawer and take out her brush and comb, then she would sit down and I would brush her hair. She had the most beautiful hair. She was French, you know. Her hair was the color of horse chestnuts. Deep brownish-red. I never got tired of seeing it. It had gold in it, and black. Deep red and dark brown. Every morning the first thing she touched was this dresser. That's why I took it."

Rupert went to the dresser and opened the drawer. He took out an ebony box and opened it. There was a silver brush and comb in it. Rennie could see they were in pristine condition. "I bought her a new set every year," he said sadly. "She hardly used this one."

"Papa..." Juan put his hand on his father's shoulder, but Rupert moved away. Rennie wished he'd let Juan comfort him; he seemed so sad.

"I never understood how she could love you boys more than she loved me," he said. "Especially Luke. When he died, so did she. She never saw how much I needed her too."

"Papa!" Juan's voice seemed strained.

"Sorry." He looked up and a wry smile twisted across his face. "I put the dresser in the guestroom so I wouldn't see it."

Rennie hesitated in the doorway, feeling out of place, as usual. This was between Juan and his father, but her heart ached for both of them.

"Okay, so let's go back to the kitchen," Juan said, sounding sad.

"The rain's stopped," said Rennie. "Shall we go see the farm?" She was desperate to get out of the house now; it was far too quiet when they all stopped talking. She didn't feel too uncomfortable, but she could tell they were each unhappy with each other. If only they would stop acting so formal and relax. She wondered if there was a radio or a television set she could turn on as a distraction.

They put on raincoats. Rupert had a wall with a line of coats hanging from it. Everyone chose the one that fitted them the best. Rennie hadn't bought a coat yet, but she found an old brown oilskin jacket that fit her fine though it was a bit short through the sleeves.

They saddled three ponies and rode around the farm. Part of it was in a steep valley, and Rennie was amazed at the hills — Florida was so flat! She loved getting a peek at the ocean from the very top of the tallest hill, but most of all she adored the sheep. They were in small pastures, separated by woodsy hedges and streams, and seemed to come in all sorts of sizes and colors. They looked absolutely miserable in the rain though. Their wool was soggy and muddy, and their long faces looked, well, Rennie searched for a better adjective, but could only come up with sheepish.

Three other men worked on the farm with Rupert Allistair. They each had two dogs with them, and Rennie was given a demonstration of sheep dog work.

Over another hill was a large forest and Rennie thought she caught a glimpse of a herd of deer running like red smoke through the trees. "Was that deer?" she asked, pointing.

"Yes. You've got keen eyesight. We're lucky to see them at all; usually they're well hidden this time of day," Rupert said.

The fields were planted in long, alternating strips of cabbage and grain. There were pheasant everywhere; they ran through the underbrush, and sometimes they would explode upwards with a loud, whirring noise that startled Rennie. When a cock pheasant launched himself in the air inches from her pony's nose, she gave a shrill cry and nearly tumbled off backwards. "Don't laugh!" she said to Juan.

"I wasn't laughing at you," he said, his voice teasing. "I was just comparing your expression to your pony's. He looked so calm, and you were so scared."

"He was scared too," she said, giving her pony a pat on the neck. "But he's a better actor than I am."

The horses they were riding were sturdy pony types with pretty heads. They were bigger than ponies though, and Rupert said they were Welsh cobs. Rennie thought they were lovely, and she especially liked their names: Llewelyn, Rugby and Leekie. She was riding Leekie, a gray gelding.

* * * * *

"She rides like her mother," said Rupert to Juan.

"I wouldn't know," Juan said.

"Why? Doesn't she ride anymore?"

Juan glanced at Rennie, riding a little ways ahead. "No, she hasn't ridden since Rennie was born."

"Oh. And her father? Does he still ride?"

"No. He died before Rennie was born. Did you know him?"

Rupert frowned. "Knew of him more like it. A good horseman. I didn't know he'd died though." He was silent for a minute, then said wistfully, "She was such an amazing rider."

"Rennie rides well too. I suppose I should let you know, she was my groom in Palm Beach. I thought I'd tell you before you heard from someone else."

"What's wrong with that?" Rupert looked amused. "Don't tell me you're getting as snobbish as the rest of them? I suppose you're going to inform me next that she's pregnant, and that's the only reason you married her. You don't have to explain anything you know. I don't care that she's not Argentinean, or English. Or French. I don't care if she was a dancer at a strip joint. If, you love her and she loves you, that's good enough for me. You forget boy, we're not in Argentina now—land of the virgin bride. Not that I'd wish that fate on anyone."

Juan was startled. "What are you talking about? You married mother in Argentina. You loved her."

"The first few months were hell. She cried whenever I touched her."

Juan flinched. "Things got better."

"I should bloody well hope so. We had you boys." He frowned and looked off towards the ocean, barely visible through the gray fog. "On a clear day the Irish Sea is so blue you'd think you were in the Caribbean." He paused, and then said, "She always loved you boys more than she loved me though."

"You already said that." Juan scowled. He was angry for some reason. He leaned back in his saddle while his horse slithered and scrabbled down a steep muddy bank. Suddenly his horse stumbled and he was pitched off into a deep puddle.

"Are you all right?" Rennie reined in her pony. Rupert was laughing too hard to talk though, and this made Juan even angrier.

"What a bloody awful country," he stormed. "Always raining and muddy and gray."

"I think it's beautiful," said Rennie. "Look at the mist on the hillside. It's so romantic." She looked at Juan and smothered a laugh. "You're all covered in mud," she said. "Let's go back and take a bath."

Rupert smiled faintly. "You haven't seen Argentina yet, have you?" he asked Rennie.

"No. I'm looking forward to seeing it though, Juan has told me so much about it."

"He has?" Rupert waited while Juan scraped most of the mud off himself and climbed back up on his horse. "I suppose he's told you there's no mud."

"Of course there's mud," Juan said tightly. "Sometimes it's so damn muddy we're stuck at the farm for weeks on end. No cars can get in or out, and we have to go shopping in the gig."

"It sounds wonderful," said Rennie. She looked at Juan and gave him a puzzled frown, but she didn't say anything about his obviously foul mood.They continued down the hill in silence. As soon as they arrived on level ground Rennie said mischievously, "Race you back to the farm!" and kicked her pony into a canter.

Leekie was not as fast as Llewellyn or Rugby, but she had a head start, so the fat, gray pony managed to clatter into the cobblestone courtyard ahead of the two bigger horses. Rennie threw her arms around her shaggy neck and hugged him. "What a sweet pony you are," she said.

"You shouldn't be racing in your condition," said Juan sternly. "You might have fallen."

"Like you, in the mud." Rennie was unfazed. "We didn't go very fast, just a little canter. Why are you being so stuffy? Come on, smile a bit. Don't you think it's lovely here? I really like it. I hope we'll be able to come back soon."

"Of course you will," said Rupert, who'd overheard the conversation. "I insist you come back whenever you want."

Juan didn't reply. Silently he unsaddled his horse and turned him out in the rain-drenched paddock.

* * * * *

While Juan soaked in the huge white-enamel tub, he tried to figure out his mood. Why was he so angry with his father? Why was he being so churlish?

Juan had adored his mother, and the fact that she had a marked preference for his older brother Luke never bothered him. Luke had been like a god to him while he was growing up. Everyone had spoiled Juan, being the youngest. He'd never lacked attention.

When his brother and mother died, he'd turned towards his father, but Rupert had left. *That must be it*, he thought sourly. *I'm pissed because he ran away. Just when we needed him the most, he ran away.*

Juan ducked his head underwater and washed his hair.

Coming up for air, he decided that he was being unreasonable. His father left, but he had been nearly twenty years old, and he'd had his own life. As far as his father had known, he was to have gotten married to Rosa and started his own life with Rosa's family on her farm. His two older brothers were married already and had their own lives. Why should Rupert have stayed on the farm? What would he have done? His sons had started their breeding program, and Rupert had liquefied all his assets to help get them started.

The more he thought about it the more he decided he would have probably done the same as his father. Rupert had grown up on this farm, and he'd come back to it, that was all.

He looked through the open door at Rennie, lying on her stomach on the bed reading an old *Country Life* magazine. She turned the pages slowly and every once in a while would fold the corner of a page down to mark a house she particularly liked, he supposed.

Whenever Juan saw her, he was filled with a sort of wonder. He tried to imagine the baby inside her but he couldn't. He floated in the warm water and tried to see into the future, to see Rennie pushing a little stroller, or holding a baby to her breasts. The image was so erotic that he got a hard-on and the top of his penis poked out of the water.

"Rennie?" he called.

"Yeah?"

"Could you come here a minute? Someone wants to see you."

She walked into the bathroom, her hair tangled and curling around her shoulders. Her shirt was partially unbuttoned and one of her lacy bra-straps was just visible.

"My master calls?" She smiled coyly at him, and then started slowly unzipping her jeans. She shrugged out of them, peeling them off and tossing them on the bed. Then, facing away from him, she bent over and pretended to fiddle with her toes. Exposed, her naked pussy looked fragile. It was still a shock seeing it like that. But Juan loved being able to see all of her, and especially, to be able to touch and taste all of her.

"Come here," he said, moving to the side of the tub. She did, stopping when he seized her hips. Then he pulled her so that his mouth was level with her pussy.

"Spread your legs," he ordered, and she did. With his tongue, he parted her labia and found her clit. It was already stiff, and he licked it greedily, until she was thrusting her hips against his face, begging him to take her. Then he fondled her, touching her all over, slipping his fingers into her swollen cunt until she was panting, hanging onto the side of the tub.

"Get in," he said, his voice thick with desire. He turned her around, facing away, and bent her over. Kneeling, he put some soap on his cock, to make it slippery, and then pushed it gently but firmly against her anus. She tightened up for a second, but he reached around in front of her and found her clit. He rubbed it, and she relaxed and let him push his cock into her beautiful round ass. The feeling was incredible. She was so tight he couldn't even move. He wished he could stay like this forever, with his cock buried in Rennie's body, his arms wrapped around her. He thrust, but only very gently.

She gave a little cry of delight. "That feels so good," she gasped. "A little harder, please!"

His hands slipped over her soapy body. He dipped his hands lower, parted her smooth labia, and touched her clit. He stroked her, keeping time to his thrusts. Her breathing grew more labored, and it turned him on. Feeling his cock start to quiver, he slipped a finger deep into her vagina.

"Do you like this?" he asked, unsure.

"Yes!" Rennie cried. "More, harder!" She opened her legs and pressed against him.

That nearly sent him over the edge, but he managed to hang on. Breathing hard, he put one finger in, then two, and thrust hard. He felt her coming, and as before, the muscles in her anus contracted so hard it was like a massage on his cock. With a groan, he exploded inside her, holding on to her body tightly while his body bucked against her back.

Later, when they'd gotten their breath back and could speak, Juan looked at Rennie gravely. "Do you think we'll be happy?" he asked. He didn't know why he brought that up. He wondered if it was because of what his father had said about his mother; and about him being jealous of his own sons. That had shocked him more than he cared to admit. He was starting to think love might be a hindrance to a happy marriage.

"You mean in the future?" Rennie put some soap on her hands and started to work it into a foamy lather. She spread her fingers in a large circle and then blew a soap bubble from them. It floated for a second in the still air before coming to land on Juan's knee. "I think so." She looked serious. "I'm happy now. And I intend to make this marriage work you know. I don't give up easily. I know we didn't have a great start, but I'm going to try my hardest to give it the best I can. Sounds corny doesn't it? But I mean it."

She leaned over and kissed him on the lips. "It helps to have such a sexy guy to work with."

Chapter Ten

"Do you think I'm sexy?" Rennie stood in front of the mirror and raised her arms. She turned around and inspected her back. "I think I'm too skinny, don't you? Tolly is curvier than me."

"Tolly?"

"Our maid." Rennie giggled. "It's funny to say, 'our maid'. I've never had a maid before. Tolly's more of a friend though. She stays and chats when she comes to clean. She's got the cutest little maid outfit."

"I wouldn't mind seeing you in one of those," Juan said. "Does she still not wear underwear?"

"She says she hates underwear," said Rennie. "Tolly has bigger breasts than I do. I'd love bigger breasts. What do you think?"

Juan glanced at her then back down at the schedule he was trying to work out. He wanted to see when the team was playing, against whom. "Mmm. You're fine," he said.

Rennie frowned. "You didn't even look at me!" she complained. She shrugged and then looked at herself again. She was naked and the greenish light filtering through the tree branches outside made her look like a mermaid, she thought. Her skin was pale and smooth, and her hair was loose, hanging down past her shoulders. She tipped her head and her hair slid down her back, tickling it. Then she spun in a circle and her hair floated around her like a red-gold cloud.

Facing the mirror once more, she cupped her breasts in her hands. They were large and full. Her thumbs drew circles around the nipples, making them stiffen. She glanced at Juan but he was engrossed in his papers.

She turned around again and jutted her hip out, striking a pose. Then she turned sideways and examined her tummy.

The telephone rang and Juan reached over to answer it, his eyes still fixed on the papers spread out in front of him. "Hola. Oh, hi Stan. Thanks for calling back. I'm looking at the match schedule for our team, and I wanted to know if you've got the umpire list."

Rennie sighed with boredom and stopped listening. Stan was one of the secretaries working at Windsor polo club. She admired herself in the mirror and struck some more poses, bending way over to catch a glimpse of her bare pussy.

* * * * *

Juan hung up and looked at her, surprised. "What are you doing? Posing for Playboy?"

"No. For your information, I'm just fooling around. I'm bored." Her eyelids were lavender with fatigue, and Juan thought she looked incredibly sexy.

"Oh yeah?" Juan sat and watched her for a minute. Her body was giving him an enormous erection. He grinned. There was one thing he'd been meaning to try. Why not now?

He got up from his chair and walked over to Rennie. On the way he grabbed a belt from the back of the chair. Before she could react, he grabbed her and threw her on the bed. She squealed and twisted, laughing when he tickled her under the arm. Then he slipped the belt around her wrist and attached it to the bed. He reached for a silk tie lying on the floor and deftly tied her other arm to the bedpost. Her legs were next, and before Rennie could wriggle out of his arms, she was tied to the bed, spread-eagled.

Juan could hardly get his pants off in time. Watching her twist about, trying to get loose, was the most exciting thing he'd ever seen. His cock was about to go off without him. He fumbled with his buttons, got his zipper caught in his shorts and tore them off. Leaving his shirt and socks on in his hurry, he bent over her pussy, panting. His hands shaking, he parted her labia and pressed his mouth to her cunt. She let out a surprised cry and raised her hips, opening her legs even wider. She cried out again as his tongue found her clit, and a rush of wetness filled his mouth.

"I can't wait," he moaned. He grabbed his twitching cock and pushed it against her cunt. He just had time to plunge into her before he came, groaning and thrusting against her.

Juan pulled out and looked down. Her cunt was spread wide open, and his sperm, like thick cream, dotted her wet flesh. Without thinking, he bent down and took her in his mouth, licking and sucking at her. The taste of his own cum was strange—not sweet, not sour, and with a slight tang. She'd said it was interesting, and it was.

His cock grew incredibly hard, so hard it hurt. He had to be inside her. Now! Before he knew it, he was plunging back into her, and he fastened his mouth on hers.

She drank his kisses, nibbling on his lower lip, her tongue probing deeply into his mouth. He shattered again, and with a whimper, he drove himself into her, harder and harder. Her legs and arms, held spread wide apart, excited him even more. His orgasm was never going to finish.

Blinking, he sat up. Rennie was staring at him, her face flushed.

"Did you come?" he asked. He was a bit embarrassed about getting so carried away. He'd never lost his head like that.

She shook her head. "A little, not much."

He bit his lip. "Sorry. I was too quick. Don't move."

"As if I was going anywhere." She blinked. "What are you going to do?"

"Do you remember Freya's wedding present?"

Now her cleeks flamed scarlet. "I left it in Florida," she said.

"No way I was going to let you do that. I brought it with me," Juan said with a sexy grin. He reached into his drawer and drew out the toy. He wiggled it. "Realistic, no?"

He was glad it was smaller than his own penis, though. He wondered if all men were like him, or if he was normal. Was it normal to want to watch something penetrate his wife's cunt? When he thought about that, he got horny again.

Rennie pulled at her ties. "For an alien, maybe." She batted her eyelashes. "Are you going to use that on me?"

"That's the idea." Juan sat next to her and stroked the inside of her thigh. He pushed a button, and the machine started to hum. "Whoa! Tickles!" Juan laughed and then looked at Rennie, a wicked light in his eyes. "Want it inside of you?"

Rennie writhed. "Please," she gasped. Her hips lifted towards him, begging.

Softly, he touched her labia, tracing circles with the tip of the vibrator. Then he held it gently to her clit.

"Oh! Too strong," she gasped, panting.

"Sorry."

"Put it inside me," she begged. "Please, oh hurry, please."

Her face was very flushed. Juan slid the vibrator into her pussy, watching as it entered her, then pulling it out and teasing her again with it. He held it just to her lips, then, when she shrieked in frustration, he plunged it into her. He kept it there, while she bucked and thrashed against him, her eyes screwed shut, the muscles in her stomach contracting.

Juan watched avidly, his curiosity about Rennie's body growing. He wanted to ask her what she was feeling and exactly how she liked it, but right now her eyes were shut and all she seemed capable of saying was "faster, harder, yes! Oh yes!"

Finally, her body relaxed and she opened her eyes. He shut off the vibrator. "Was that better?" he asked.

"Hmmm. Yes," she purred.

"I'm going to take a shower," he said to her. He couldn't suppress a wicked grin. He loved seeing her tied up. She was his prisoner. He decided he was going to fulfill this macho fantasy. He kissed her breast. "Are you comfortable?"

"Yes," she said.

"The ties don't hurt?"

"No."

"Good." He kissed her other breast and then got off the bed.

"Hey!" Rennie raised her head. "Aren't you going to take it out of me?"

"No, I'm leaving it in." Juan looked at her cunt, and the vibrator still inside of her, just the blue end sticking out. It moved up and down a bit as she contracted her muscles around it.

"It has sparkles in it," he said, not bothering to hide his teasing grin.

"Juan!" she shrieked. "Hey! Come back and untie me!"

"No, I like seeing you like that. You'll just have to wait until I'm through with my shower. Don't yell, or one of the maids will come to see what's going on."

"Beast!" she cried, but he just waved and went into the bathroom, shutting the door behind him.

* * * * *

After Juan left, Rennie tried at first to escape, but couldn't. The feeling of being helpless and tied up was incredible. She realized she could never have done this with anyone else but Juan. She trusted him.

She couldn't help being aware of the vibrator inside her. It was heavy, and very smooth. It had warmed up quickly, gotten hot even, and now it was still inside her. She moved her hips, tightening her muscles around it. When she rocked back and forth, it massaged her insides. The feeling was agreeable, no, it was more than agreeable. Little tremors ran through her, and soon she became fully aroused again. Her nipples stood straight up, and her heart was pounding. She rocked faster, tilting her pelvis so that the vibrator moved a bit. She wished she could push the button again. She felt her vulva contracting, she wanted to come.

Just as she thought she couldn't stand it anymore she heard the key in the lock. In her state of heightened arousal, she could only stare as Tolly entered without looking, a stack of towels in her arms, as she did very evening. Tolly turned, saw Rennie, and froze. Then she gave a huge grin.

"My, aren't we in a fix?" she said archly.

"Can you help me?" gasped Rennie, sure her face was scarlet with embarrassment.

"Oh no!" Tolly said. "That torture is soooo good. Maybe some other time, my dear." She paused, and her tongue darted to her lips. "I'd love to see your handsome husband come in and finish what he started. Tell him I said so, all right?" Then, with a wink, she left, closing the door behind her.

For a minute Rennie lay there trying to imagine what Tolly must be thinking. Then she decided she didn't care. If someone didn't push the button on the vibrator, she was going to go crazy. She listened to the sound of running water, and when the shower stopped, she nearly sobbed in relief.

Juan strolled casually out of the bathroom, a towel wrapped around his waist. He stopped when he saw her and pretended to be surprised.

"What? You're still lying there? Why, what a lazy girl!"

"Turn it on," begged Rennie.

"Your wish is my command," said Juan in a deep, sexy voice. He reached between Rennie's legs and touched the button. Instantly, a low hum came from inside her, and Rennie arched her back, welcoming her orgasm.

Juan watched as she came. His face was getting red and he was breathing hard. Before Rennie had stopped convulsing, he leaned over and took Rennie's breast in his mouth. He sucked on it, hard, and lifted his towel up. Rennie saw Juan's hand grip his cock and he started to stroke himself.

"Let me go," said Rennie.

Juan untied her, and Rennie reached over pushed Juan's hand away. Juan sighed and stood still, shivering a little. Rennie took his penis into her mouth. It was smooth and tasted faintly of soap. She licked her tongue around his head, finding the little opening and darting the tip of her tongue into it. Juan gave a low growl. Then he leaned closer to Rennie, massaging her breasts with both hands.

Rennie loved when Juan did that. It was so erotic she felt herself creaming again. The vibrator was still humming between her legs, and Rennie reached down and started pushing it in and out. At the same time, she sucked hard on Juan's cock.

Juan gave a cry. As the vibrator sank into her, Rennie pushed hard with her hand, holding it all the way in, while Juan moaned and bucked against her, his cock sliding in and out of her mouth.

Juan's towel fell to the ground. He arched his back and uttered a hoarse cry. Rennie could feel when Juan was about to come. Tiny tremors shook his cock. Then there was a rush of liquid filling her mouth. That made Rennie come again, and her orgasm was violent, her pussy and buttocks contracting like mad. Afterwards, Rennie stroked Juan's cock, marveling at the satiny feeling. He lay down beside her. Cupping her breast with one hand, he fell asleep, a sated smile on his face.

Rennie watched him fondly. He might not love her, she thought, but he certainly loved her body. And that would have to be enough for the time being.

Chapter Eleven

The next day was the first game of the season for the Silver Bird team. At the field, Juan bought Rennie 'The Little Polo Handbook', a comic pamphlet telling a little about the rules of polo. "All the spectators have one," he said.

"It's so cute!" Rennie flipped the pocket-sized, spiral-bound pamphlet open. "The drawings are precious Oh, I love this one. It's called, 'The Perfect Polo Pony'."

"And there is a page on the end for autographs," said Juan, pointing.

"I won't forget to ask my favorite player to sign mine," said Rennie.

"How about a kiss for luck?" he asked.

"Is that in the book?" Rennie grinned.

The game was a close one. Rennie was watching her husband play, sitting in the stands for the first time. She was nervous, but not so nervous that she didn't notice the looks the Argentineans were giving her.

Juan had broken off an engagement to a girl back home to marry his groom, a girl he'd only known for three months whereas he'd been engaged to Rosa for nearly five years. Supposedly the ex-fiancée was heartbroken and had refused to see anyone. The Argentineans whispered together and Rennie overheard them, getting more uncomfortable by the minute.

The last chucker started with both teams tied. Sebi had been terribly nervous during the whole game, and had missed several easy shots. Now, in the last minutes of the game he suddenly found his swing and hit two fabulous goals through the posts. Then Juan intercepted a ball and dribbled it all the way to the goals, flicking it through the posts with practiced ease. Rennie stood up, applauding madly. She was proud of Juan, and thrilled that he'd played so well.

The crowd screamed its encouragement to the opposing team, which had Gonzalo Tomalli playing with three Englishmen, but the Silver Birds finished three goals ahead, winning their first game of the season. There was a flutter of polite applause, and Alice standing by the pony lines, screamed "Way to go Silver Birds, we won! " Her voice sounded as shrill as a gull's to Rennie.

Juan could see Rennie up in the stands, she was standing up and cheering. She loved watching polo, unlike some polo wives who couldn't be bothered. After the game, she'd massage his neck and back, and that usually led to some more intimate massage games. Rennie knew just where to rub, too. And when he won his games there was an added excitement, the kind that a herd stallion must feel when he's beaten his rival off, thought Juan with satisfaction. The mares sensed it too. Rennie was much more receptive on winning days.

His thoughts were interrupted when his boss came up to him and said, "Good game tiger, way to go!"

Juan grinned back, but it was a strained grin. On the field, he'd come face to face with one of Rosa's cousin's. Well, Gonzalo was a cousin once or twice removed, but he was related somehow. He'd been like ice. He hadn't said a word to Juan. He'd even refused to shake his hand after the game. Juan had a sinking feeling that all his other fellow countrymen would treat him the same way. He was not looking forward to the rest of the season.

* * * * *

Rennie was slower to feel the heat, but she spoke perfect Spanish, and it wasn't long before she understood what was being said about her and Juan.

Rupert had warned her that it would be difficult to become accepted. Rennie had just stared at him and said, "Why should I worry? I'm not looking for friends. You never find them when you're looking. I'll just wait until someone comes along who wants to be friendly, and I'll be glad to get to know them."

"It matters a great deal for Juan's polo," said Rupert gently. "I know it sounds ridiculous, but polo is a matter of relations. There are hundreds of talented polo players out there who never get jobs because it's all word of mouth. Patrons don't hire the pros, other pros do. And their wives whisper in their ears. It's as simple as that."

Rennie had blushed then, embarrassed. "Well, I won't be much of a help, will I then?"

He shrugged. "I don't know. Maybe if you can't charm the other polo players or their wives you can work on the patrons or their wives. Not that the wives are easy to find, most of them are at the hairdressers or in their lover's beds when the game starts."

Rennie remembered Rupert's warning as she stared bleakly at the backs of six women after their third game. The women were all wives or girlfriends of players. Rennie had run into them when she walked into the clubhouse to get some hot tea. Juan was refereeing the next game, and she was alone.

"Hello," she said shyly.

"Hola," said one girl, about her age, with long black hair and flashing dark eyes. Rennie thought she was just lovely.

However, the other women had simply stared at Rennie as she ordered her tea. Then the oldest woman, who was very thin with straight, brown hair and freckles, came over to her. Rennie thought she looked nice. She had twinkling green eyes, and she was small-boned and pretty in a wholesome way.

"Hola," she'd said. "So, you are the girl Juan Allistair married in Palm Beach."

"Rennie. My name's Rennie. Yes, we got married just before we came here. What's your name?"

"I'm Clara Dimenti. My husband is playing today against yours. So, when is the baby due?"

Rennie was not used to such bluntness, but she decided it was just simple curiosity. "In December."

"So, you're what, three months pregnant? You're awfully skinny."

Rennie smiled, but she was starting to feel uneasy. "Well, I'm sure that will change soon. Do you have any children?"

Clara nodded proudly. "I have five children."

"How amazing!" Rennie exclaimed. "You don't look like the mother of five, congratulations." She thought she was being perfectly friendly, but Clara had yet to smile once.

"So, you and Juan got married when you were already two months pregnant."

Rennie found her cheeks getting hot. "That's right." She tried to smile. "That happens sometimes."

"Well, that might be a tiny bit of comfort to poor Rosa."

"Who?" Rennie glanced at the other women standing behind Clara and wondered what they were smiling about. Rosa? The name wasn't familiar.

"Rosa who? You mean you never heard about Rosa? The girl who was engaged to Juan? He never told you?" Clara was clearly disbelieving.

"That really is none of your business," said Rennie stiffly, wondering how she could change the subject. Juan had never mentioned his ex-finacée's name, and she had not wanted to pry.

"She is my first cousin," said Clara. "So it is my business what happens to her. Especially when a *puta Americana* screws her fiancée and gets knocked up and has to get married."

The other women gasped at that, obviously they thought Clara had gone too far. So did Rennie.

"That's enough," she snapped. "I really don't think I need to discuss my private life with you."

"Even if Rosa commits suicide?" Clara hissed.

"If she does that's her own choice," Rennie was surprised to hear herself sound so cold. Actually, she was horrified, but she'd be damned if she showed it. "I certainly won't feel responsible."

"You wouldn't, you don't even know her. But I do. I grew up with her. And I tell you, if anything happens to her, I will personally hold you responsible."

"Me?" cried Rennie. She glanced at the other women who were nodding in agreement.

Rennie might have looked a bit like Botticelli's Venus, with her downcast eyes, strawberry blonde hair and her pale mouth. But her temper was her mother's. The Piccabeas were Basque, well known for their terrible tempers and irascibility. Pure, icy rage took hold of her. "I don't know who you think you are lady, but let's get one thing perfectly straight. Juan did not *have* to marry me. I didn't ask him, he asked me. So if he didn't marry your precious cousin Rosa I guess it's because he didn't want to. Is that clear?" She was trembling with fury.

"Just stay away from us, you hear?" sputtered Clara, her green eyes narrowed.

"Why?" asked Rennie sweetly, going straight for the jugular. "Are you afraid your husband will think I'm more beautiful than you? Afraid he'll want to have sex with me and not you anymore?" She bit each word off at the end. "I don't want to come near you anyway. You're meaner than a rattlesnake."

Clara gaped, at loss for words, and then marched over to her friends. She turned her back to Rennie, and the other ladies did the same.

Rennie stared at their backs and muttered bleakly, "Way to go Rennie, so much for making friends with the Argentines."

She couldn't even take comfort in her surroundings. When she'd arrived at the club, she'd imagined something a bit cosier, but the Windsor tearoom was nothing more than a large cafeteria with long, brown, Formica tables and plastic chairs lined up like soldiers. Behind a counter three, large-boned women stood selling plastic-wrapped sandwiches and slabs of homemade cakes. The women could have been triplets. They had round, shiny faces with pink cheeks and red noses, and their hair was pinned in tight gray buns on their heads.

Rennie took her Darjeeling tea and wandered towards the back of the room. Huddled in her jacket, she watched the drizzle streak the glass. From where she sat, she could see a quarter of the polo field where the Highlander polo team was thrashing the Pouey Bears. Juan was refereeing that game, and from time to time she caught a glimpse of him. He sat on his horse with ease—his long legs encased in high leather boots, his white breeches gleaming in the dim light. He raised his whistle to his mouth and blew a foul. Hand pointing to the sixty-yard line, he cantered out of Rennie's sight.

* * * * *

The polo season left very little time free for the pros; when they weren't exercising their horses, they had to play or referee other games. Juan woke up at six a.m. to go to the stables every morning. Sometimes Rennie went with him. She still loved to ride, and thought if she were careful she'd be able to ride until she started to show. Juan didn't like to see her on horseback though, knowing she was pregnant, so out of respect for his wishes she soon stopped riding in the morning. She missed it though.

Her walks through the woods grew longer, and she stopped nearly every morning at Miss Rose's Tea Shoppe on High Street. Rennie loved Miss Rose's fresh scones, and she took some back to Juan every morning. He ate them when he finished at the stables.

* * * * *

Juan thought about Rennie as he cantered his horse around the exercise track. She was often on his mind. He also thought about Rosa, but the guilt was starting to fade—he'd never really been in love with her. He'd gone along with her plans all along, but they'd never been his plans at all. He was finally taking control of his life and the feeling was like hesitating at the top of a very high cliff. He wanted to jump, but wasn't quite sure his parachute was going to work.

Felipe took Barco, and Juan thanked him. He patted the sweating horse absently on the neck and started back to the manor house for breakfast. Rennie had been trying to get him to walk with her to the village to meet someone named Miss Rose at the bakery, but Juan hated walks. So far, he'd managed to put her off. However, he thought he might as well accompany her one morning. The scones were delicious, and a walk with Rennie through the forest might be nice.

Out of the corner of his eye, he caught a movement in the orchard. Standing on tiptoes, he could just peer over the top of the stone wall. He wondered if it was Alice, climbing the trees again. She'd been asked to stop by the gardener, and that had provoked a war between them. Now, Alice was always trying to sneak into the orchard, and the gardener was always trying to catch her.

But it wasn't Alice. It was Carlos.

He was with Sally, Tom's groom. She was sitting on the stone wall, her legs opened wide. Carlos, standing up, thrust himself against her. His pants were down around his ankles. He stopped and Sally tried to pull him to her again, but Juan could see that Carlos was teasing her now with his cock, pulling out then pushing partway in before pulling out again.

Sally was leaning back and Juan felt a pang of lust as he saw the dark, curly bush between her legs and the shiny pink labia wide open. Sally's shirt was open too, and two round tits, like little birds, peeped out.

Juan decided to stay and watch. Sometimes it was good to have a couple cards up your sleeve, especially when dealing with someone as slippery as Carlos. He'd never tell anyone, but Carlos had disappointed him, and he wouldn't put it above him to try to do something sneaky behind Juan's back. He wouldn't mind having something to use as a bargaining chip, Juan thought wryly. Juan had no illusions now. He knew how ruthless Carlos really was and he was pretty sure he'd been the one to get Andre fired.

He'd seen Carlos punching a horse in the eye during a game when a rival player was getting the better of a ride-off. He'd seen him reach over and yank on the reins of another horse to slow him down, or even catch someone's leg with his own to unbalance them. Nothing the referees ever saw though, and usually on the far side of the field, far away from the shrieking fans. Who'd really shriek if they knew what a dirty player their polo god was.

This wasn't to say Carlos was the worst one out there. No. The player who'd sabotaged his own teammates' horses was perhaps the biggest snake. Of course there were some pros who'd actually try and hurt someone, as if polo wasn't dangerous enough. Juan thought of Pierre de Lancourt and his mouth tightened. He couldn't think of Pierre's death without wrenching grief.

To get his mind off it, he turned back to the scene in the orchard.

* * * * *

Sally grabbed Carlos by his shirttails and pulled him into her.

"Whoa!" Carlos chuckled. "I wasn't going to go anywhere, not with that waiting for me." He cupped his hands around her buttocks and guided her onto his stiff cock. "How's that?"

Sally moaned, moving back and forth.

Carlos came a second later, first jerking himself out of her then spraying the ground with his milky semen.

Sally stared at him with wide eyes. "Why'd you do that?" she gasped.

"In case you're not on the Pill," said Carlos, stuffing himself back in his pants and zipping up. "I don't want any trouble.

Look what happened to Juan. I'm engaged to be married, in case you forgot."

Sally gaped at him, tears suddenly appearing in her eyes. "I wouldn't cause trouble," she sniffed. "I love you."

Carlos looked at her warily. "That's what I mean," he said. "Let's get this straight from the beginning, shall we? I like you. You're a very pretty girl, and I'm attracted to you. Physically. Got that? I like to screw but with no strings attached. If you can deal with that fine, if not, well, let's just say it was fun, but never again."

Sally swallowed her pride. "I'll do anything to keep you with your cock buried in me up to its hilt. I only have to think about you to become sopping wet." She wiped the tears out of her eyes and managed a shaky smile. "Come on," she said. "I know that you're already engaged, and I don't mind. Please, you have to believe me. I'm on the Pill. I'll even show them to you."

She slid off the wall and lay down on the ground. "Come here," she pleaded, "Feel how much I want you."

Carlos grinned. "All right." His hands roamed from her throat down to her breasts, still pointing cheerfully out of her shirt. He rubbed them hard, making the nipples even longer and stiffer. He caressed her triangle of crinkly auburn hair and her long white legs. Her underwear was still caught on one ankle, her jeans were on the ground underneath her, and her knees were apart, showing him her moist pinkness. She looked like the goddess of spring, with the white apple blossoms falling around her and the long spring-green grass framing her body. He licked his lips and undid his pants again.

"You're really on the Pill?" he asked, his voice getting deeper. "Well, might as well take advantage of the situation. Mmmm." He slid a finger into her and probed delicately. "Are you sure you want me?"

Sally arched her back and offered herself to him. "Yes, I want you," she gasped, "whenever, and however."

* * * * *

Juan thought Carlos was a shit screwing around in the apple orchard. Not only was it heartless, but he could get caught, which would cause a row and piss Tom off. Juan glanced at his watch. Only seven a.m. and Lucia slept until at least ten every morning. Alice, the pest, was a late sleeper as well. She didn't get to the stables until nine—everyone could hear Jingles as he whinnied and kicked the door to his stall, which was his good morning greeting to Alice. Tom was in the States so Carol would stay in bed late too.

The house seemed empty as Juan crossed the hallway and mounted the stairs. The sound of a Hoover came from the back of the house, and he guessed the maids were busy getting the breakfast room ready. He thought of Tolly, and grinned when he remembered the first time Sebi had seen her. Sebi's mouth had dropped open, and his eyes had widened until Juan thought they'd fall out of their sockets. Now Sebi followed her around like a puppy, desperate for another glimpse of her treasures. Tolly knew it, and teased him unmercifully, letting Sebi see beneath her skirt, even artfully spreading her legs on occasion so he could get a good hard look. Afterwards, Sebi usually bolted for his bedroom.

Juan walked soundlessly down the thick carpet in the hallway, and as he opened the door to his room the smell of fresh biscuits greeted him. They were on a plate on the little table in front of the window. Rennie was sitting there, waiting for him. She had a white men's shirt on and was wearing jeans. She had put her hair up in a loose chignon, which Juan adored. He loved seeing her hair slip down, tendril by tendril. It's bright apricot blondness seemed too light to remain restrained. Rennie was always exasperated by her hair, she complained that it was too straight, too fine, too red, but Juan couldn't take his eyes off it, and half-jokingly threatened to divorce her if she ever cut it.

"How were the horses?" she asked.

"Good." He hesitated. He thought about mentioning Carlos and Sally, but he knew he'd better keep it a secret unless he needed to use the information. He picked up a light, flaky biscuit and bit into it. "Delicious as usual," he said. My compliments to Miss Rose."

Rennie smiled. "She would love to meet you. Why don't we go to the village at teatime? We'll take Alice, she'll like that, and I'll try and persuade Lucia to come with us."

"No, just you and me." Juan leaned over the table and kissed Rennie on the mouth. Seeing Carlos and Sally had given him ideas. He reached over and unbuttoned her shirt, then slipped his hand under her bra. "Nice," he said, giving a little squeeze.

Rennie yelped and said, "They're awfully tender. I think they're growing."

Juan leered at her. "Good! Can I see?"

Rennie shrugged out of her bra and Juan narrowed his eyes, looking closely. "I believe you're right," he said after a minute. "And the left one is growing faster than the right one. I'd better help it along," and he took it in his mouth and pretended to blow it up like a balloon.

Rennie shrieked with laughter and pushed him away. "Grow up!" she said teasingly. "You're about to be a father, try and set a good example." As she said this, she grew serious. "And I wanted to talk to you. Your dad called this morning while you were riding. He wants us to come and visit him between tournaments. I said we would. I really like him. I wish you'd make more of an effort to get along."

Juan scowled. "I do make an effort."

"You don't. Every time he starts to talk you close your ears. I think he wants to tell you something, but you won't listen."

"All he talks about is my mother and how sad he is that she's gone," said Juan. "Didn't you notice? He's never once said the same thing about Luke. My brother died too, and it's like he never existed. My father was always jealous of him."

"And you loved your brother," said Rennie gently. "I can tell, but I think that the reason your father never mentions Luke is that he loved him too. He loved him so much that to talk about him would be too painful, so he doesn't. It's a protective reaction, don't misread it. When he's ready to, he'll mention Luke. But for now it would be too hard."

Juan cocked his head, considering. "I never thought of it that way," he conceded. "Maybe you're right."

Rennie smiled. "I think so. I wish Freya were here. I miss her."

"I miss her present. Where did you hide it?"

Rennie blushed. "Oh, somewhere."

"Did you ever, you know, sleep with your friend?"

Rennie raised her eyebrows. "Where did this come from?"

"Just wondering. It's sort of one of my fantasies—seeing two women together."

"Oh?" Rennie's face broke into a grin. "Well, that's one dream we might be able to have come true."

"How?" He was getting hard just thinking about it.

"You'll see." She kissed his chin, then his throat, unbuttoning his shirt to run her hands over his chest.

"When?" Juan closed his eyes and let her unzip his pants and take them off. His penis was stiff and very heavy. He thought about Carlos and Sally in the orchard and a little moan escaped his lips.

"My sexy baby," said Rennie, taking his cock in her hand and guiding it to her cleft.

She was standing, her back to him, bent over slightly so that he could penetrate her. He put his hands on her back and thrust forward, sliding slowly into her tight, wet passageway. It took a few thrusts before she could take him completely. She was narrow, but the feeling of her vaginal muscles clenching around the tip of his penis when he withdrew it, drove him wild. He thrust harder and harder, and holding Rennie tightly so she couldn't pull away. His cock slammed into her, and he felt her womb hitting his tip—he hit harder, twisting and thrusting upwards, his hands grabbing Rennie's buttocks, while he drove into her again and again. The friction was making his cock hot, or maybe it was just Rennie's hot cunt. Oh God it was good.

She was braced against the bed, meeting his thrusts with sharp cries, her own body writhing, offering herself to him, legs wide open. Getting a hold of himself, he thrust once again, hard, then drew out. He wanted to calm down a bit, make it last longer. His arms trembling, he held himself away from her although his cock was stiff, and pointing straight up. Rennie gave a little cry and, reaching between her legs, grabbed his penis.

"Come back!" she said, pulling him towards her. Her hand clenched him tightly. It was too much. Before he could enter, he was coming, spurting all over her hand. Before he had time to go soft, she gave a cry and rammed backwards, forcing his penis into her vagina. Now he felt her contractions as she came. He tried to still himself and concentrate on the sensation, while his cock plunged deeper and deeper within her. Breath coming hard, they stood like that for a moment, joined together, then his penis slid out of her, and she collapsed on her bed, her whole body glowing.

"Lets take a shower, then go for a walk," said Juan, on a whim.

Chapter Twelve

Rennie and Juan walked down the drive, arm in arm. Her hair was bright red-gold in the spring sunlight. People's heads turned when they saw Rennie. Yet she never noticed. She walked on a cloud of her own, her eyes dreamy, and her feet light.

Juan saw the church first. He tugged her arm. "Let's go in there, I haven't been to church in a long time," he said.

They walked into the darkness of the old stone church. At first, all they could see were the flickers of candle light from the votive candles placed near the altar. Then the beautiful colors of the stained glass windows glowed as the sun moved from behind a cloud.

"Look!" Rennie breathed. "Isn't that pretty! All those colors. And the pictures! My, I've never seen such a lovely window."

Juan walked down the aisle, his practiced eye taking in the stories of the scriptures as he went along. Each window represented a stage in the story of Christ. There was Jesus in the desert, and there he was with St. John the Baptist standing in the Jordan River. The dove was just above his head.

"Oh look!" said Rennie. "A pigeon!"

"It's not a pigeon." Juan frowned. "It's a dove. Actually, it's just a symbol. You know that."

"I do?" Rennie looked confused. "Symbols aren't things I'm familiar with. In fact, I get symbols hopelessly mixed up with signs." She added with a light laugh.

"You do know who this is, don't you?" Juan insisted. "The first time I saw you was in church. You were praying beneath the statue of St. John."

Rennie shook her head. "It must have been someone else."

"No, I got your groceries for you, remember?"

"Oh. That's true. Were you in the church? I didn't see you. I saw a lady lighting a candle. I was praying in front of St. Francis..." She hesitated. "I thought it was St. Francis. He had a bird."

"It was St. John, and the eagle."

Rennie smiled. "Well, that's nice to know. St. John and the eagle." She looked around the church for a familiar sight. "Well, there's the Virgin Mary," she said triumphantly, pointing to a stained glass window showing a woman kneeling at Jesus' feet.

"It isn't," said Juan. He was horrified. Rennie didn't know the first thing about religion. He'd thought he'd found a good Catholic girl, after all, he'd first seen her in a church.

"Don't you go to church?" he asked. "Do you...do you believe in God?" He was almost afraid to know the answer.

"Of course!" Rennie raised her eyebrows. "I went to church once or twice."

She looked up at the ceiling and at the nave. "It sure is pretty here," she said. "It would make a nice place to have a wedding. The church we got married in wasn't half as nice. This one is so old. Do you think they built this church when Jesus was alive? Is that why it's so beautiful?"

Juan sat down on a bench and stared at Rennie. He couldn't believe that she was so ignorant. Not only of the church, but also of time.

"Jesus was born nearly two-thousand years ago," he said.

"Well, how old is this church? In America, everything is so new. It's much older here in Europe." Rennie sounded hopeful. "Why are you so upset? It's an easy enough mistake to make. Are we going to the cocktail party tonight at the Pouey's? I saw that the team was invited. Carol put the invitation on the table in the hallway. What should I wear?"

Juan didn't answer. He was trying to put Rennie back into perspective. The girl he thought he knew; shy, pious, a bit gauche, was in fact completely pagan, uneducated, and ungodly. He shook his head again and sighed. He was deeply bothered. He looked over at Rennie again, seeing her from a different angle. He wasn't sure if he liked this new perspective.

* * * * *

Rennie glanced back at Juan and she felt her nerves starting to frazzle. He was making a lot out of her mistakes. She knew she wasn't particularly well-educated, but she hadn't thought that it was that important. He was staring at her now with something like resentment in his eyes.

Rennie blinked back tears. Being pregnant had the added inconvenience of making her particularly emotional. Almost anything could bring on tears. She'd managed to keep herself from getting homesick by writing long letters home to her mother and Freya nearly every day. She'd even managed to stop thinking about having a baby, or that she was married to someone she didn't know very well.

She was crazy about Juan. She loved his hazel eyes, green one moment, brown the next. She adored running her hands through his silky hair, and feeling the hardness of his muscles when they embraced. But all of that was just physical. Juan was more than just a handsome man. He took his responsibilities seriously. Family was important to him. He was honest and hard-working. She also loved his kindness, the way he insisted she call her mother every two or three days so she wouldn't get homesick, and the way he complimented her on her looks. Her loved her looks, but that was a problem. She could never hope to hold him by her body alone. Especially now, when it was about to change so radically.

"I'm sorry," she said. "I don't know anything about religion. You never mentioned the fact that it was important to you. It's also true that I know nothing about Jesus, or his place in time. I never studied about him at all."

"BC," said Juan. "AD. Do they mean anything to you?"

"Before Christ," Rennie whispered miserably. "And something else. I don't know. After Death?"

"Anno domini," Juan nearly hissed. "It's Latin."

Rennie relaxed somewhat. "Oh!" she laughed weakly. "I never took Latin in school. They didn't even offer it. I took Spanish." She flinched at Juan's scornful "phhfft!"

"I'm sorry," she repeated. Her face twisted a bit and she managed to smile again. "Why don't you teach me? I'd love to learn about it all."

Juan sat in silence, looking at his young bride. He had no idea what he was really feeling. Deception, perhaps yes. Disappointment, surely. Pity? Sorrow? Where could he go from here? Could he teach her? No doubt he could, but the relationship he was looking for with a wife was not that of a student to a teacher. He was well-educated and cultured enough to want to be able to converse. He loved to argue. With Rosa he'd debated for hours about such things as Divine Right, the Pope, and any number of things. Rennie probably didn't even know the Pope's name.

"Speak to me." Rennie slid into the pew beside him and took his hand. She pressed it to her lips and caressed it.

"Not here!" He snatched his hand away, shocked. What would she do next? Toss him on the floor and ravish him? The idea fluttered through his head and he was horrified to find himself getting a hard-on in front of the statue of the Virgin Mary.

Rennie seemed torn between the urge to laugh and cry. "Let's go please," she said. "I want to go to town."

Juan waited until his unruly erection subsided a bit before standing up. It was amazing how intense his physical reaction was to Rennie. Somehow, that confused him more than anything. He resolved to speak to a priest about it as soon as he went to confession.

He glanced at Rennie and sighed. Her Madonna-like face was smooth as alabaster, her copper hair ringing her head in a fiery nimbus. She stood tall and poised in front of him, her clear gray eyes guileless and faintly hurt. Her mouth was trembling slightly and he longed to kiss it, to press her to himself and to…he sat down rather suddenly. "You go ahead. I'll meet you back at the manor for lunch. I think I want to…to pray a bit."

Rennie didn't bother to hide her hurt. Tears filled her eyes, like rain fills the sky and she stumbled out the door.

Juan saw her silhouetted against the bright light, then she was gone. He leaned forward and pressed his head to the wooden bench in front of him hard enough to make it hurt. "Oh Lord," he groaned, but whether it was a prayer or a curse, he didn't know himself.

* * * * *

Rennie ran nearly all the way into town. The quaint village with its narrow, flower filled streets soothed her after a bit. She wandered about, trying to calm her nerves. The streets were quiet; the balmy spring air was soft on her cheeks.

After a while she started looking for something. She wasn't sure exactly what it was she wanted until she spotted the tiny store on the corner. It was a two-story shop, with hanging baskets of blue lobelia and pink petunias running riot around it. A bright green sweet-pea vine tangled up its waterspout, sprouting crimson blossoms above the wooden sign. The sign said "The Sphinx", and it was a bookshop.

The door chimes were miniature silver bells that tinkled when she pushed the door open. The shop was painted pale yellow. The walls were lined with books, of course, but also with cards, stationary, candles and glass trinkets. Silk flowers twined around a wrought iron staircase, which spiraled upstairs.

Rennie looked around, but nobody was in the shop. "Hello?" she called out uncertainly.

"I'm coming, dearie, I'm coming!" a masculine voice floated cheerfully downstairs.

Then down those stairs came first a long pair of scarlet clad legs, then a vivid green turtleneck, about which was draped a bright fuchsia scarf. The face peered down last, though the iron bars of the stairwell. It was a long, pale face with large, sherry-colored eyes and hair the color of gingersnaps cut short around a well-shaped head.

"Ohhh, have I got a new customer or what?" The voice was a light tenor, and it played up and down the scale from high to low, purring over each word as it left his mouth as if he couldn't bear to part with them. "My name is Sam, Sam I am." He said, coming all the way down the stairs and proffering a wiry hand to shake.

"Do you like Green Eggs and Ham?" laughed Rennie.

"I like *you* already. Now, don't tell me your name or your date of birth. I like to guess everything," Sam said, posing dramatically for a second in front of her then gliding over to his desk where he set up an electric kettle. He plugged it in and put two teacups on two plates, placing them on a lace-covered table in front of the bow window.

Rennie watched without saying anything. She turned instead to the wall of books and started to peruse it, running her finger lightly over the titles, reading them softly to herself.

"Okay, your name is Rennie and you're from Florida in the United States." Sam ignored Rennie's surprised gasp, cut two slices from a large chocolate cake, and placed them next to the teacups. "Mmm, this looks lovely. Miss Rose has really outdone herself this time. "I don't know your birthday, but I'll guess you're an Aries, with Scorpio rising. Am I right?"

Rennie caught Miss Rose's name and smiled. "You're right, but I don't know about Scorpio rising. I am an Aries though, how amazing! Now, let me guess. You're Samuel Sphinx, owner of the "Sphinx Book Shoppe" on Merry Street. And you buy all your tea things at Miss Rose's Tea Shoppe on High Street."

He smiled back at her, showing even, white teeth. "Perfect. I knew we'd get along. One lump or two?"

They sipped their tea, sitting at the cosy, table-for-four that was set up in the store's large bow window. A bench curved around the window on one side, and two wicker chairs with blue, velvet cushion were facing the table on the other side. Rennie sat on one chair; Samuel curled up on the other. He reminded Rennie so much of Mr. Marmalade, her much-missed cat, that she couldn't help smiling when she looked at him.

"It's a good thing you mentioned Miss Rose," said Rennie. "Otherwise I would have been completely flipped out. "

"We wouldn't want that, would we?" purred Sam. "More tea, darling?"

"Oh, yes, thank you."

"So. Let's talk serious here." Sam's accent was neither here nor there.

"Where are you from?" Rennie asked. "I never heard an accent like yours here."

Sam shrugged. "I'm Scotch-Irish, with a bit of English thrown in." He paused. "Just enough to make me civilized, you hear."

"What do you mean?" Rennie asked, stiffening a little.

"Oh, the English believe the Scotts and the Irish are savages. Didn't you know that?" He smiled brightly. "What's bothering you now? Why'd you come seeking out old Samuel?"

Rennie looked up, surprised. "How did you…?"

"Know something was bothering you? Easy, I saw your face as you walked in. '…So sorrowful the fragile mouth, so deeply gray the eyes. A stormy day, copper leaves in the wind, with pewter, glowering skies…' Did you like that? I made it up the minute I saw you." He beamed.

"Very pretty." Rennie said. "I wish I was as clever as you." She sighed. "I think that's what my problem is. My husband thinks I'm ignorant and I am." She bowed her head, hiding her blush behind her apricot hair.

"Today I asked him if the church was built when Jesus was alive. I feel so stupid. I wasn't really thinking when I spoke…"

"Anyone could make the same mistake!" cried Sam airily. "Churches all look old to me too." He peered at her closely.

"That wasn't the worst mistake I made."

"Oh? What could be worse? No, I'm just teasing. What happened?"

"It was a couple days after we got to England. We drove by Windsor and I saw the castle. I thought it was so beautiful. I said so, and then I said 'too bad they built it so close to the airport .' I realized my mistake right after the words left my mouth but it was too late. Our polo captain laughed himself sick and Juan just about snapped my head off."

"Well, it could have been worse. You could have added that land was cheaper near an airport." Sam chuckled.

"It's not funny," she said, her cheeks pink.

"You're right. Sorry. So, you want to learn about churches?" he asked. "I have just the right book for you. It's somewhere over here…"

He jumped up lightly and rummaged around the shelves a moment. "Ahh! Here we go. Don't be put off by the title, it looks mean but it isn't. It's an awful good read. You'll get through it in a week and come begging for more."

Rennie took it and giggled. "It's the Bible," she said.

"Yes, that's right. Never was there a better book written about Jesus. Now look here, it's a Bible, but it's for people like you."

"Ignorant?"

"No, silly. People who want to learn. A part tells you all about the book before you even read it. It's sort of a guide to the Bible, so any questions you have can be referred to here."

Rennie took the book and skimmed through it. "It looks like a children's book," she said. "It has photographs."

"Well, it is and it isn't. People seem to take more time explaining things to children so this book is a good place to start. It isn't a complete Bible, but it will be enough for now."

"I love the pictures. They look like something from National Geographic," said Rennie.

"Now, Mrs. Rose tells me your husband plays polo, am I right?"

"Yes." Rennie scraped up the last of the cake crumbs and carefully licked her fork.

"Can I give you some advice?" Sam had lost his bantering tone, his head cocked to the side.

Rennie put her fork down. "Of course."

"Well, polo isn't really a sport, you know."

"It isn't?" Rennie frowned.

"No. It's more a religion, a religion that goes back thousands of years. It is the oldest sport in the world. Its origins are lost in the mists of time, but people speculate that it came from hunting or from war. Early Persian texts speak of polo; Chinese paintings depict it. The Orient is its cradle, and like most things Oriental it is mysterious and many faceted. It used to be played by kings. In ancient times it was believed that the game was not over until someone died on the field."

"I didn't know that." Rennie said, amazed. "I thought polo came from England."

"The British army picked it up in India. They proceeded to civilize it and brought it back with them to England. It spread all over the Empire. The Argentineans are the undisputed masters of the game now, but without the kings of finance to provide for them the game would wither and die. Perhaps they realize this, perhaps they do not. At any rate, to be married to one of these "Princes of Polo" must be an exciting thing."

"Prince of Polo," murmured Rennie. "Yes, that would suit Juan, I think. Carlos, and Sebi too. Tom Wimsys would be the King of finance you spoke of. Without Tom there would be no Silver Bird team."

"I've given you food for thought, now for the advice. Never forget who the King is. Kings are notoriously fond of power games. At the same time, you must never forget who you really are. Moreover, you must always believe that all men are created equal, even polo players. You must keep your feet on the ground and don't try to impress people. Don't let anyone tell you you're not…" He paused. "Worthy. Yes, that's the word I was looking for. You have your own gifts, you don't have to be like everyone else to be happy. Okay? And if you're ever feeling sad you come see your friend Sam in the wonderful Sphinx Bookstore, you got that?"

Rennie bought the Bible, and Sam pressed a slim volume into her hand before she left. "You'll love it," he said. "Come back soon."

Rennie kissed him impulsively on the cheek and laughed when he pretended to swoon backwards. "Good-bye, and thank-you."

The book Sam had given her was called the "Maltese Cat ", written by Rudyard Kipling. She wondered why Sam had given her a book about a cat.

* * * * *

Rennie was so engrossed in the book she was reading she missed lunch and nearly missed the cocktail party. Juan finally dragged her downstairs, after having to tell her thirteen times to get changed.

During the party she floated around on Juan's arm, silent as a ghost, not saying a single word.

"Why don't you say something?" he hissed.

"Because I don't want to make a fool of myself," she whispered back. She hoped she was doing the right thing. She was determined to make Juan appreciate her.

"Well, you can talk about the weather, can't you?"

"You do the talking. I'll just hang onto your arm and smile, and everyone will think I'm a perfect lady. You'll see."

Juan became a bit exasperated but everyone did seem to think she was charming.

As they left Ronald Pouey patted Juan on the arm. "You have a lovely wife," he said heartily.

Rennie tried hard not to appear too smug.

* * * * *

She read late into the night and when Juan woke up at three a.m. he found her sleeping, the book pressed between her cheek and her pillow. Her hair billowed over her arms, and the soft glow of the reading lamp made her skin look like warm cream. He smiled tenderly and slid the book out from under her cheek and then he saw what she had been reading.

It was the Bible, a beautiful edition, with historical notations, photographs, and paintings from museums of the world illustrating it. He turned it over in his hands and opened it, flipping through the pages until he came to the "Gospel According to St. John". He read for a few moments and then softly closed the book. Rennie didn't stir.

He hadn't paid any attention to her when she'd come back from town. He'd been talking to Carlos and Sebi about their next polo game. When Rennie had disappeared into their room and not come down for lunch, he'd figured she was sulking. Rosa had sulked constantly, so he was used to it. When Rennie wouldn't change for the cocktail party, he'd been annoyed. He'd noticed her reading, but thought she was reading a fashion magazine.

What a fool he was. Slowly, he was starting to understand the quiet, gentle woman he'd married. Each day he found himself growing closer to her. It was both terrifying and wonderful. He resolved to apologise for being such a bastard in the church. It wasn't her fault she hadn't been brought up a good Catholic. He gently stroked Rennie's hair as she slept and his mouth curved into a smile.

The other book lying on the nightstand caught his attention and he picked it up. "The Maltese Cat," he read. He shrugged. Rennie must love cats.

Chapter Thirteen

The Beaufort Hounds were a strong team. Their captain was Sydney Trek, two goals, who'd made his fortune with a building company. He played with Carlos's ex-brother-in-law, Pedro Larson. Besides Pedro, who was rated nine goals, Sydney Trek played with another Argentine who was rated eight, and an Englishman rated three goals. The English player was a young man Sydney sent to Argentina every year to perfect his polo. The reason he was only three goals was largely due to Sydney's influence with the board of directors in the polo club.

Wearing their yellow and green polo jerseys, their ponies' legs wrapped in yellow and green saddle pads trimmed in yellow, the Beaufort Hounds cantered confidently onto the pitch.

In the line-up, Pedro Larson leaned over and hissed something to Carlos.

Carlos jostled his pony into position and hissed back, his expression evil.

Juan, right in back of them, frowned. It wasn't going to be a very fun game if these two started fighting.

Pedro looked furious and said something to Carlos, who laughed meanly and answered with a shrug.

Pedro looked nonplussed. "I'll kill the bastard!" he screamed.

Juan wondered what they had been quarrelling about, and hoped Pedro was kidding. However, he noticed that when the ball was thrown in Pedro slammed his horse into Carlos's, rocking his pony back on his heels. But Carlos had been ready and he managed to hit the ball up to Juan.

Juan took the ball up field and scored an easy goal. He had been expecting some opposition but no one challenged him. As he flicked the ball through the goal posts he looked around, feeling something was wrong.

Tom was playing number one, and he was riding off Sydney, who played back for the Beaufort Hounds. Sebi was with the English player, and Carlos was off his horse, as were the two other Beaufort players. There was Pedro—and for some reason he seemed intent on killing his own teammate. Luckily, Carlos was holding him by the shoulders. Juan guessed that Carlos had told Pedro what everyone had known for some time about his wife: that she was screwing his teammate.

He frowned. It wasn't very fair play. He'd known that maybe Carlos would say something if they were losing, or after the game just to be a jerk. But at the very *beginning* of the game?

It was the shortest game in the history of the club. Pedro managed to get in one good punch and he knocked out two of his own teammate's front teeth. Juan jumped off his horse and ran after him, intending to talk to him, but Pedro was livid. As Juan watched, Pedro stormed over to the stands, dragged his wife through the crowd and out to the parking lot. There he slapped her, stuffed her into his car, and drove off with a squeal of tires and a shower of gravel all over the protesting officials. Before he left he'd screamed at Carlos, "I'll get you for this, you bastard!"

Carlos turned to Juan. "How about a drink?" he asked. "I'm going to have a shot of whiskey."

"No thanks." Juan took his helmet off. "I guess I won't be needing this."

The crowd settled down to watch the second game while Tom and Sydney went into the polo club office to wrangle with the officials and to try to sort out the mess. Juan went back to the pony lines and wondered what the hell had gotten into Carlos.

When the dust settled, it was decided that the Beaufort team must forfeit their game to the Silver Birds. Pedro and

Carlos were both given warnings, and Pedro got suspended for one match. His teammate made excuses to fly back to Buenos Aires.

Juan was interested to see Pedro and his wife at the next polo game walking arm and arm, very lovey-dovey. She was wearing dark glasses, and he was nursing a split lip. Juan wondered if his wife had hit him in the mouth, and secretly hoped that she had.

* * * * *

A week later, the Silver Birds played the semi-finals of the Queen's Cup. The game was hard fought against the Mont-Rouge team from France. The French team played with Arnaud de Lancourt.

Juan was glad to see Arnaud. He liked the slim Frenchman, and he admired the sleek horse he rode.

"Are those horses from your farm?" he asked.

Arnaud nodded. "Yes, this one was actually Pierre's mare. I brought three of his over this season to sell. The rest are mine."

"How is your father?" asked Juan.

"Fine, thank you. How's your beautiful wife?"

"Fine thank you." He was surprised at the pang of jealousy he felt when Arnaud called Rennie beautiful, but then concluded he was uptight about the upcoming game. He nodded politely and they took their places in the line-up for the throw-in as the referee blew the whistle.

The Mont-Rouge team won five to two after a hard fought, low-scoring game. The horses were exhausted, and the players slumped in their saddles when the final bell rang.

Sebi had taken a bad fall and was nursing a bruised ribcage. Juan had gotten a crack on the right hand from an opponent's mallet. Even Carlos was limping when he climbed painfully down from his horse and headed off to the trophy presentation.

The Mont-Rouge team fared little better. Arnaud winced as he shook hands with Lady Tremain. He'd fallen and had put his hands out to break his fall. Now he was sure he'd sprained his wrist. His captain, Thierry Deschamps, had a bloody nose and it dripped down from his impressive moustache all over his red and white shirtfront. Madame Deschamps rushed over to her husband and stanched it with a towel, all the while vociferating at him in French. She took the silver trophy from Madame Tremain and tucked it into her voluminous handbag.

The two other French players had grass stains on their shirts and breeches from falls during the game. Sandrine Belheure, a woman pro, fluffed her short brown hair out and wiped a streak of dirt off her rosy cheeks. She was a rarity in the polo world, a professional woman player. But she was as tough as any other pro on the circuit, as Sebi had the misfortune to find out when they'd crashed together, resulting in a spectacular, somersaulting fall for both of them. Right now she glared at Sebi and told him that if her mare was lame because of the fall he'd be sorry the next time they played against each other.

Juan remembered the fall and shuddered. He had really thought Sebi was going to be killed. His horse missed landing on him by a mere quarter of an inch and Sebi was still shaking.

The only person unscathed was Tom. He was in a bad mood though, he hated to lose.

* * * * *

Rennie met Juan and Arnaud in the clubhouse bar. Arnaud kissed her soundly and told her that his father sent his greetings. Rennie turned pink with pleasure. They sat down, the men groaning slightly as they settled in their chairs. Arnaud massaged his wrist ruefully while Juan examined his right hand, flexing it and wondering if he shouldn't pack it in ice. Rennie took one look at the angry bruise and went to the bar. She came back with some ice-cubes wrapped in a tea towel.

"Here you go," she said. "I hope this helps."

"Thanks." Juan said gratefully. "I loved the horse you rode in the third chucker," he told Arnaud.

"The gray? Yes, she's very good."

Rennie nodded. "She made me think of the horse in the 'Maltese Cat'. I read that book the other day, it's really good."

Arnaud said, "I loved that book too."

"It's about a cat?" Juan asked.

"No, it's about a polo pony," giggled Rennie. "I thought it was a cat too. You have to read it. It's good, but I cried in the end."

"You're too soft-hearted," Juan said. He said it with a smile though. Rennie's empathy touched him.

"No, it does make you sad," said Arnaud, leaning over the table. He smiled at Rennie. "I cried too, honest. It was an excellent story."

Juan listened as Rennie and Arnaud talked about the book, but his mind wasn't on what they were saying. Rather he was watching Rennie's face as she spoke. He frowned. He was feeling something strange. It was an odd emotion, one he hadn't felt before. It had to do with the way she was looking at Arnaud. He didn't like it at all.

When Arnaud got up to go check his horses Juan actually felt relieved. It made him cross, and he snapped at Rennie. She just stared at him with bewilderment, making him feel even more like a cad.

Grumpily he leaned back in his chair, holding the icepack to his hand and watching the low rain clouds as they scraped their gray bellies on the treetops on the far side of the field. The colors of the clouds made him think of Rennie's eyes. As he watched, the clouds parted and the sun cast rays of light onto the ground.

"When I was little I used to think those rays were coming straight from God," said Rennie softly.

Juan was startled. "What did you say?"

She blushed. "Those rays of light you see through the clouds. I used to think it was God's grace. When I first heard those words, 'God's grace', I was sure it was referring to those shafts of light. They do look holy, don't they?"

Juan stared at her. The mixture of poetry and paganism was childish, but somehow touching. He looked back out the window. The rays of light were very lovely. He found himself smiling.

Chapter Fourteen

"Hey Rennie, you got some more letters." Tolly knocked on Rennie's bedroom door.

"Oh, thanks. Why don't you come in? Juan's at the stables and I'm just reading. Do you like to read?"

"Oh yes," Tolly nodded. She picked up a book and flipped through it. "This looks good," she said. "I like mysteries."

"I'll lend it to you when I'm done."

"What are you doing today?" Tolly asked, perching on the edge of her bed.

"Nothing."

"I bet Juan's excited about the finals."

Rennie groaned. "You can say that again. He can hardly sleep at night. He goes to the stables and hangs around the horses every spare minute, as if he's afraid they'll disappear or something if he's not staring straight at them."

"Your husband is so sexy," said Tolly. "If you don't mind me saying, I could eat him up for lunch."

Rennie grinned. "I eat him for breakfast lunch and dinner, and yes, he is sexy." She put her book down and stretched. "Just thinking about him makes me hot."

Tolly licked her lips. "Just thinking about you makes me hot."

"Are you gay?" Rennie asked.

"No. I'm bi. I swing both ways."

"Cool." Rennie said. "Do you have a steady boyfriend?"

"Actually, I'm married to a wonderful bloke. His name's Fred, and he and I love to go to the swinger bars in London. We belong to a club there called 'Switch Hitter.'"

"Tell me about it," Rennie said.

"On one condition," said Tolly.

"What's that?"

"I get to make you purr," said Tolly, a wicked grin on her face.

"Purr?"

"Yes, as in: pussy purrs when she's happy," said Tolly, slipping one hand between Rennie's legs.

"I don't think I can do this," said Rennie, drawing away with regret.

"Why?"

"I feel like I'm being unfaithful to my husband." Rennie blushed.

Tolly grinned. "Well, why don't we wait until he comes in?"

"I have a better idea." Rennie reached for the bedside phone and dialed Juan's cell phone. "Hi honey," she said. "Could you come to the room now? Yes? Great! But hurry, all right?"

She hung up and smiled at Tolly. "Someone's dreams are about to come true."

Tolly eyed her luscious body. "Yes—mine!"

Juan hurried to the house. He wondered what Rennie wanted. She'd sounded breathless. He opened the bedroom door, the room was empty.

"Where are you?" he called.

"Sit on the chair and close your eyes," came Rennie's voice from the bathroom. He complied, and then felt her presence as she came into the room. She stopped near him, and then he felt something going around his wrists, and realized he was being tied to the chair.

"Don't move," she whispered. She tied him to the arms of the chair, then she unzipped his pants and took his penis out. He was getting stiff by then, so it popped right out. She gave it a little kiss and laughed. "You can open your eyes now. But you can't move, all right? Do you promise?"

"Yes." Juan opened his eyes. In front of him, naked, was Rennie. She crossed to the bed, and to his shock, he saw another naked woman on it. Tolly! She smiled at Juan and stuck her tongue at him.

"Hi," she purred. She sat up, and Juan saw that it was true—Tolly was much curvier than Rennie. Her breasts were large with plum-colored nipples. Her veins showed in blue tracings beneath her translucent skin. Her waist was tiny, and her hips were nicely proportioned, with a lovely, rounded croup and full buttocks. Rennie knelt on the bed in front of her, and Tolly began stroking her breasts. Rennie reciprocated, taking Tolly's nipples in her fingers and squeezing them, and Juan could see them getting longer and harder.

Like his cock.

Juan was tied tightly, and couldn't reach down. Instead, he sat there, his penis standing straight up and so stiff it nearly hurt. It was strangely erotic being tied up. The feeling of being a voyeur, yet being helpless in front of Rennie was incredible. He was watching them, but they were controlling him. He couldn't move, but his cock strained into the air.

The two young women looked at him, identical, teasing smiles on their faces. Then Tolly reached between Rennie's legs, and Rennie uttered a little cry. She lay back, her knees raised and spread, so that Juan could see everything. He saw Tolly's fingers spread Rennie's pale outer lips and then stroke her darker inner lips until they were glistening with juice. Then Tolly inserted her finger, one, then two, and pumped in and out. Rennie twisted back and forth, her hands clutching Tolly's breasts as Tolly lay beside her, one shapely leg thrown over Rennie's thigh.

Tolly found Rennie's clit and massaged it, and suddenly Rennie arched her back and gave a sharp cry. Juan could actually see her cunt throbbing. The sight was more than he could stand. He felt himself just about to explode. Then Rennie took her hand and put it between Tolly's legs, and Juan saw her pale fingers disappear into Tolly's curly pubic hair.

It was enough.

With a ragged cry, he came, ejaculating helplessly, still tied to the chair. Embarrassment warred with pure lust. He'd never been so turned on. Just the sight of his come was making him hard again.

Rennie turned and saw his cock spurting into the air. Leaving Tolly, she left the bed and slid onto his lap. As soon as her hot cunt touched his penis, he was off again, stiffer than before, and coming just as soon as his erection was full. Rennie moved up and down, sheathing herself to the hilt on his shaft, while Tolly, her smile mischievous, offered him one of her luscious breasts, placing its nipple in his mouth, so that he could suck on it. She rubbed her cunt against his hands, still tied to the chair, and he twisted his wrist so that he could penetrate her with his fingers.

Her cunt was very wet. She didn't shave, and her pubic hair tickled his hand. His fingers slid into her hot, slick vagina, and Tolly moaned, pushing harder, until he felt a fast pulsing deep within her. He moved his fingers deeper, trying to figure out where that pulse was coming from. Was it an orgasm? He thought so, but he wasn't sure. Whatever it was, it was exciting.

Afterwards, they untied him, and led him to the bed. They lay down, and Rennie said, "Do whatever you wish."

Juan swallowed. He had come twice, but was already hard again. He lay on Rennie and penetrated her, thrusting against her while fingering Tolly's breasts and cunt. The feeling was incredible, and he felt himself starting to ejaculate again. He had hardly started when suddenly he felt something pressing against his anus. It was slick and slippery, and turning his head, he saw that Tolly had put a rubber over Rennie's vibrator and covered it with lubricant.

Rennie wrapped her legs around him , holding him tightly, and said with a grin, "So you'll know what it feels like."

Juan let himself be penetrated by Rennie's blue sparkly toy. His whole body was shaking when it was fully inserted. It felt odd and it even stung a little, but he lay atop Rennie, excited, but hardly daring to move. Then he did move, and it seemed to stroke him from the inside. A little cry escaped his lips and Rennie cupped his face in her hands.

"Are you okay?" she asked.

"Yes," he managed to gasp. He felt a fullness in his body that was totally unfamiliar. His cock twitched, buried in Rennie's hot pussy. The vibrator was strangely heavy. Then Tolly hit the button, and the vibrator went off.

So did Juan. He started spurting into Rennie, crying out with each thrust, while Tolly held him from behind, her body wrapped around his.

After that, it was an effort just to move. Juan managed to make it to the shower, and when he came back, he collapsed on the bed and fell asleep.

Chapter Fifteen

Rennie was humming as she went through her mail. After having sex with Juan and Tolly, she'd made Juan promise not to ever ask her to do it again. She'd adored it, she wasn't a hypocrite, but she didn't want her marriage to be like Tolly's. Tolly and she had talked about marriage at length. Tolly told her about the club where she and her husband went when they wanted to change partners. Rennie had been fascinated, but after thinking about it, decided it wasn't for her. Tolly said she loved her husband, but Rennie sometimes wondered. Especially the way Tolly went on about other men.

"Some people can deal with it, I suppose," Rennie had said to Juan. "But I just want to belong to you, and only you. I don't even want to make love to a woman again. It was something I'm glad I experienced, but it's over now. What do you think?"

Juan had smiled and kissed her deeply. "You fulfilled one of my dreams," he said. "I belong to you now, and only you."

So Rennie was in a good mood. Then she heard loud voices in the corridor. Intrigued, she opened the door and saw Lucia, hands on her hips, screaming at Carlos. He didn't look very concerned, even when Lucia stomped down the stairs, out of the house.

* * * * *

A little while later, Juan came back from the stables.

"What's up?" he asked.

"Lucia. I overheard her fighting. I asked her about it, and she said she's breaking up with Carlos."

Juan raised his eyebrows, now she had his attention. "Really? Did she say why?"

"She said she found out that he was cheating on her," said Rennie.

"So she found out about Sally." Juan yawned. "I wonder who told her?"

"What? You knew about that?" Rennie was shocked. "Why didn't you say anything? "

"To who?" Juan looked amused. "To Lucia? You think I should have told her? Why not just put an announcement in the Times?"

Rennie scowled. "You could have told me."

"I don't gossip, "said Juan.

Rennie flushed. "Sorry. "

"Is that all you have to tell me?"

"Yes," Rennie said, a bit put out.

"Fine, well if you'll excuse me I think I'll go down to lunch. In case you hadn't noticed, it's past noon. Why haven't you gotten dressed? Are you going to hang around forever in those old jogging pants?"

He left, with Rennie staring after him white-faced. She didn't have the nerve to tell him none of her clothes fit her anymore and she needed money to buy some.

Juan hadn't thought to ask her about the doctor's visit, although she was sure he hadn't forgotten. She'd had her first ultrasound. The fetus was now nearly four months old. When she stayed absolutely still she could sometimes feel a faint flutter in her womb, like the wings of a butterfly. The doctor had pointed out the baby's head. She saw its heart, beating away like mad. It had the requisite number of legs and arms, and had measured up just fine.

Then the doctor had told her it might be a boy. He could tell from the ultrasound. A boy. From one second to the next the fetus had gone from an intangible thought to a baby to a little boy. It was overwhelming. Then the doctor had patted her kindly on the shoulder and told her everything was perfect.

Everything was almost perfect. If only Juan would take the slightest interest in the baby. She wanted to tell him it was a boy, but she was afraid. It would make it too real for him. If only she could bring herself to talk about it, even if it was just to ask Juan for some money for new clothes. However, the very thought of asking Juan for money made her cringe. She had grown up knowing never to ask for anything from her mother. They simply had never had enough money. She'd done odd jobs to earn pocket money and the money she'd earned as a groom had gone towards the wedding. She had managed to put some away in a bank before she left, but she didn't have a credit card, and she didn't think to bring travelers checks.

When she came down to the dining room, she was wearing a wrap-around skirt and a loose tunic that hid her thickening waist. No one paid her a bit of attention, she thought bitterly. She could have come to dinner stark naked. All they talked about was the polo game.

The finals! They were tomorrow, she realized belatedly. No wonder Juan was on edge.

* * * * *

The day of the Gold Cup finals dawned bright and clear. Tom called the team together for a meeting right after breakfast.

Rennie walked to the village. She was feeling jittery because of the finals. The Gold Cup was the most coveted prize in Europe, and Tom had made it clear to the team that if they lost he'd be very upset.

Rennie kicked angrily at a leaf on the sidewalk. Why should Tom even care if he won or lost? Didn't he play for the fun of it? He'd made it to the finals, he should be thrilled. Instead, he was putting so much pressure on the team that Juan had gotten up in the middle of the night twice to be sick and he hadn't swallowed a thing for breakfast. Sebi was looking positively green and even Carlos had been snappish and tense.

Rennie sighed and turned the corner towards the bakery. Her heel caught in the curb grating and she pitched forward into the street. She threw out her hands and caught herself, but she landed with a hard jolt that skinned her knees. Her breath was knocked clear out of her and it was a minute before she could get up. Tears of pain sprang to her eyes but she brushed them quickly away. She looked up the road. Luckily, there had been no traffic, she thought. When she stood up again she was shaking.

"Goodness Rennie! Are you all right? My, you gave me a fright!" It was Miss Rose. She rushed out of her teashop and took Rennie by the shoulders. "Come on in and sit down dearie, you had a nasty tumble. Let me see your hands."

Rennie obediently held out her hands and let Miss Rose wipe away the gravel and apply disinfectant to her palms and to her knees.

"I'm sorry I scared you," Rennie said. "I think I broke my heel, that's all." She examined the faulty shoe and frowned. "It snapped right off. Good thing I have another pair." Suddenly she noticed her skirt. "Oh no, they're all wrong," Rennie wailed.

"What's the matter sweetheart?" Miss Rose waved to her waitress. "Stella, bring a tea for us." To Rennie she said, "Now, tell Miss Rose what the problem is."

Rennie tried to grin but the smile wobbled on her face. "It's going to sound silly."

"Nonsense. You tell me right now."

"I don't have a thing to wear to the finals. I was going to wear this skirt, but when I fell, I tore a hole in it and broke my shoes. The only other decent shoes I have are green, and I don't have anything to go with them. It's because of the baby. I'm getting fat, and nothing fits anymore." The last part of her sentence was lost in a wail and Rennie put her head on her arms and sobbed.

"There now, that's all right. Don't you have any maternity clothes? Probably not. Young girls your age don't think of things like that. Besides, nowadays you're all so thin. You're not fat at all you know. You're too skinny even. Now, now, don't carry on so. I'll tell you what. Why don't you drink your tea and I'll call my friend Deirdre at the little corner shop and have her pick out a few things for you to try on. All right?"

"I can't," Rennie cried anew. "I don't dare ask Juan for money for my clothes, what will he think?"

Miss Rose looked nonplussed. "He's your husband isn't her? The father of your child? Well?"

Rennie bit her lip. "Yes, but its not that easy. I never asked him for anything. I…I'm afraid to. I don't want him to regret…" She stopped, her face crimson. "I don't want him to regret marrying me," she finished finally.

"Why on earth should he do that?"

"Because, he was engaged to another girl and then he slept with me and I got pregnant." Rennie brushed the tears off her cheeks with the back of her hand. "And he never talks about the baby. We're just trying to get used to each other right now. It's all so overwhelming. I know he doesn't have much money. I don't want to start becoming a drain on his finances. I thought I could make do with what I had, letting out seams and leaving buttons unbuttoned. The problem is this damn final. Everyone will be all dressed up. I can't go in my unbuttoned jeans, or a torn skirt."

Miss Rose poured Rennie's tea for her and urged her to drink it. "Well," she said after a bit. "There is a second hand shop in town. Would you like to go there? They have lots of nice cast-offs. Maybe you can dig up something nice for the finals." Her voice was soothing.

She took a sip of tea and sighed. "If only you knew a young lady friend about your age just a tiny bit bigger than you with gorgeous clothes."

Suddenly she began to chuckle. "I have an idea," she said and started to laugh in earnest. "Come on now, drink your tea.

We're going to visit the person in this village with the most wonderful clothes."

* * * * *

Sam Sphinx looked up from the book he was reading. He peered through tiny gold-rimmed glasses that sat on the very end on his long nose. Today he was wearing a green velvet jacket with a turquoise silk lining. He had on a white linen shirt and his pants were black leather as soft and fine as kid gloves.

"What can I do for you ladies?" he asked in his deep, purring voice. "A book on the Scottish revolution? A red-hot romance that will steam your underwear off as you read it?" His smile was mildly ironic. "Don't tell me you finished that book of erotic poetry already, Miss Rose. I won't believe you."

Miss Rose snorted. "No books today Sam. We've got a marriage to save."

Sam raised his eyebrows. It was the first time Rennie saw him looking startled. "Well, judging from your track record I can see why Rennie wanted a second opinion, but what on earth can I do?"

"Dress the girl for the polo final!" Miss Rose waved in Sam's direction. "I've never seen you wearing the same thing twice, and some days I come in here three times. You must have trunks full of clothes upstairs, and poor Rennie tore a hole in her skirt a few minutes ago."

Sam opened his mouth and then shut it; he was at loss for words. Then he grinned and shrugged. "Well, I can't say you came to the wrong place." He got up off the chair and bowed to Rennie. "Will you follow me upstairs, my dear? We're about to turn Cinderella into the 'Belle of the Ball'. Or of the polo tournament at least."

Rennie was amazed at the quantity of clothes Sam had. There were silks, satins, velvets and laces, pants, shirts and scarves. There were shoes, boots and hats galore. Sam looked at Rennie critically, tipping his head from side to side and staring at her in a way that made her very nervous.

"What are you looking at?" she asked.

"Everything darling. Your hair, you skin, your eyes. I see you wrapped in gray chiffon, or in a salmon pink watered silk. All very flattering and completely unsuitable for a polo match." He sighed. "But for now, we need casual chic. Ah yes, here's what I was looking for."

He dipped into a drawer and unfolded a shirt with a band collar. It was made of raw silk, the color of butter. "Now don't tell me you don't look good in yellow," he said. "Because this yellow will suit your coloring perfectly."

He went to his closet and rifled through the rows and rows of pants hanging in perfectly pressed lines. "Hmmm, I think this will do…" He pulled out a pair of narrow, white linen pants.

Then he rummaged through his drawers and came up with a silk scarf. It was a floral print, in warm roses and cool greens. "Try this," he said.

Rennie went behind a folding Japanese screen and undressed, and Sam handed her the clothes over top. She dressed, marveling at the rich feel of the fabric against her skin. She was tall—Sam was only slightly taller. He was built like a dancer and his clothes fit her nearly perfectly, even with her thickening waist. She zipped up the pants and put the shirt on, smoothing it down over her hips.

"Let's see, don't keep me waiting!" Sam said.

Rennie walked back and forth in front of him as he examined the outfit. "It's very pretty," she ventured.

"Hmmm. It looks nice. But I want more than nice." He dove back into his closet and came up with a pale green sleeveless vest. It was made of silk and heavily embroidered with a multitude of birds and flowers. "Put this on over the shirt," he commanded. "And take off the scarf."

Rennie complied and he nodded in satisfaction. "That's better. The vest is just what it needed. Now, what size shoes do you wear?"

* * * * *

Juan was pacing back and forth in the room when she returned. He was a bundle of nerves and Rennie didn't dare speak a word to him. She was wearing the outfit Sam had lent her and she felt very glamorous, but Juan barely even glanced at her when she arrived. "Nice outfit," was his only comment.

"Thanks," Rennie said. He looked awful. His face was pale and he had circles under his eyes. She knew he hadn't slept at all last night. "Are you feeling better?" she asked.

"No, not really." He rubbed a hand over his face. "Do you mind riding with Carol? I'm going to the game with Carlos and Tom," he said, pulling on his white polo britches.

"Sure," said Rennie. She watched him leave the room, her heart heavy. He hadn't even given her a kiss before he left. Then she sighed. He must be a mass of nerves right now; she shouldn't be so egotistical. Still, a little kiss would have been nice. She picked up her purse and went to find Carol.

Rennie was thankful for her clothes when she arrived at the game and she even regretted not taking the hat Sam had offered. There were hundreds of people and everyone was beautifully turned out.

At the field Lucia disappeared, claiming she wanted to get a drink. Rennie sat between Alice and Carol. Rennie held her hands clasped over her stomach, leaning forward as if she was leaning into the game. She was hardly breathing. There was a vise of tension around her head and the muscles in her back and legs were frozen. Her mouth was drawn in a tight, thin line and whenever her husband hit the ball she flinched, almost as if she were the one he hit.

Juan scored nearly every goal. For some reason, Carlos was playing badly, missing plays, miss-hitting balls, and not getting along with his ponies. Sebi was a disaster; he'd already taken one tumble and had green grass stains all over his white breeches. Tom was shouting at everyone, further frazzling their nerves. It was unlike him, and the team was doing badly because of it. By the third chucker the Silver Birds were losing eight to six.

* * * * *

At halftime the spectators poured out onto the polo field to stomp divots. Alice darted through the crowd looking for the Queen or Prince Charles, whom she was determined to meet. She was disappointed though; the Prince was nowhere to be found. Not one member of the royal family could be seen, how boring. She turned and headed back, intending to get a piece of cake from the refreshment stand when she noticed Rennie standing by herself near the foot of the bleachers. Her face had a particular greenish look to it. Alice frowned.

"Are you all right?" she asked, tugging at Rennie's sleeve.

"I don't know," Rennie sounded faint. "I have the worst cramps. I think I'll go sit in the car." She turned and made her way towards the parking lot.

Alice went into the restaurant and grabbed some cake. As she went outside, she glanced towards the parking lot. There was Arnaud de Lancourt, the French polo player, and he seemed to be holding someone up. Someone who was sagging against his car. Alice gave a choked cry.

It was Rennie! What had happened? Did Arnaud hit her with his car? It certainly looked that way. Those Frenchmen were the worst drivers!

Chapter Sixteen

Arnaud caught Rennie just as she fell against his car. "Whoa! What's the matter?" he asked. "Lucky thing the car wasn't moving. Are you all right?"

Rennie shook her head. "I don't know," she was out of breath. "I don't feel well. Can you take me back to the house?" As a wave of pain shot through her back, she gasped and sweat popped out on her forehead.

Arnaud grabbed her arm. "No, I'm taking you to the clinic. Quick, get in my car. You look awful!"

"Thanks," Rennie grinned weakly. "You certainly have a way with...Oh!" She crumpled up in his arms. "I can't walk!" she wailed.

"What have you done to her?" It was Alice, who'd run over to Arnaud and was beating him with her fists.

"Nothing! Stop that you silly brat!"

"I'm not a brat!" Alice was furious.

"Get Juan!" cried Arnaud to Alice.

"I can't," she screamed. "He's playing now!"

"As soon as this chucker's finished go to the pony lines and tell Juan that Rennie's at the clinic in Midhurst, can you remember that?"

"But he's the only one scoring any goals for our team!" Alice complained. "If he leaves the team will lose for sure!"

"Alice!" Arnaud carried Rennie to his car and eased her into it. "Get going now!"

Alice poked her tongue at him and then ran off towards the stands. Arnaud hoped she'd get Juan. He wasn't sure what was the matter with Rennie but she looked dreadful. Her face was as white as paper and her skin cold to the touch and clammy.

At the clinic, the doctors took Rennie away and Arnaud sat down in the waiting room. He looked idly at an issue of *Country Life* and wondered what was keeping Juan. The minutes ticked by and became an hour. He cursed Alice under his breath and hoped that the silly girl would at least tell Juan *after* the game.

He didn't mind missing the game. He liked Rennie and it was the least he could do for Juan after what Juan had done for him when Pierre died. He remembered how sweet she'd been to his father who often asked about the willowy redhead. He hoped she would be all right. He knew she was pregnant, and figured it was just a little fainting spell. He didn't know it could be serious, so it was a shock when the nurse came out to get him, taking him for Rennie's husband.

"I'm so sorry," she said. "But she's lost the baby. There seem to be no complications and she'll be right as rain in a few days. She's been asking for you. Come in, you can see her now."

He walked into the room where Rennie lay. Her hair was spread over the pillow in an apricot cloud and her eyes had deep bruises under them. She tried to smile. "Hi."

"How do you feel?" he asked. He felt awkward standing by her bed so he drew up a chair and sat next to her. Quite naturally he reached over and took her hand.

"Lousy." She frowned. "It happened so fast. I didn't even realize what hit me. There were one or two horrible pains, and then the baby was gone." Tears had dried on her cheeks, leaving silvery trails. "But the doctors say I'll be fine. They think it's because I fell down this morning."

Her voice was slightly slurred and Arnaud realized she was drugged. Her eyelids kept closing, and she was fighting sleep. "Don't leave me," she murmured, and she closed her eyes.

He was startled. "Leave you? No, I'll stay."

Her voice was a whisper. "Juan? Are you there?"

"I'm here," said Arnaud. He knew she took him for Juan, but he didn't mind if it made her feel better.

"Thank you for staying with me. But, now that the baby's gone, don't leave me…please, don't leave me. I love you, even if you don't love me." Her eyelids fluttered briefly and she fell asleep as simply as a child.

His hand was still clasped in hers, she held it to her cheek as she slept. Arnaud gently eased his hand away and then smoothed a lock of hair. Her face lost its haunted look when she slept. He wondered why he hadn't noticed. Whenever he'd seen her before she'd always looked so worried. She shouldn't ever frown, he thought. She should always look peaceful like this.

* * * * *

He was sitting on the chair, leaning over her protectively when Juan came storming in. Without preamble he strode over and threw himself on Arnaud.

"You bastard!" he cried, and punched him. The blow glanced off Arnaud's cheekbone.

"Have you lost your mind?" Arnaud grabbed his arm and held him down. Juan was bigger than the Frenchman but Arnaud was wiry and he wasn't tired after a long, hard-fought polo game. "Just what do you think you're doing?" he hissed.

Juan glared at Arnaud. "Alice said you ran over Rennie with your car and the doctor told me she lost the baby." Suddenly his face crumpled. "Oh Dios mio, what have I done? I married Rennie because of the baby. I broke up with Rosa because of the baby. Now what do I do?"

Arnaud stared at him incredulously. "You don't marry someone for that reason alone," he said finally. "You must love her, look at her! Don't tell me you don't feel anything for her!"

"Of course I feel something for her." Juan sat down heavily. "Why did you have to run her over?"

"I didn't run her over!" Arnaud nearly shouted. "I found her collapsing in the parking lot on my car. She says she took a fall this morning, that's why she lost the baby!"

Juan looked at him bleakly. "Oh. I should have known. Alice is nothing but trouble. I'm sorry." He sat on the chair and put his face in his hands.

"No problem." Arnaud looked down at Juan, and noticed the grass stains on his shirt and the state of his britches. "Had a fall?" he asked.

"A big one." Juan put out his hand and flexed it, wincing.

"Fell on your hand?"

"No, I hurt it when I punched you."

"Serves you right," Arnaud spoke without rancor, rubbing his cheek. "So, who won?"

"They did. Sixteen to fifteen. We almost had them. We went in to extra time and had two extra chuckers. The goal posts were widened. Carlos missed a sixty-yard penalty shot." He shuddered. "And then the other team got the ball and scored. It bounced off Tom Wimsys's mallet. He's livid. Alice didn't tell me about Rennie until the trophy presentation was over and we all had time to get fired."

"You're off the team?"

"No, not really. We're still going to Deauville, but Tom Wimsys won't have the same team next year. Actually, Sebi and I might survive the deluge, but Carlos is out. That much is clear."

Arnaud winced. "Nice. It will be fun in Deauville with that sort of team spirit."

Juan laughed harshly. "Team spirit? Are you talking about polo? I never knew such a thing existed in that sport. Team spirit. That's a good one."

Both men were silent a while, watching Rennie sleep. Then Arnaud cleared his throat. "Um, I know this is none of my business, but, why does Rennie seem to think you'll leave her now that the baby's gone?"

"Probably because I asked her to marry me only when she told me she was pregnant. Before that I was engaged to someone else, and she knew it."

Arnaud looked at him severely. "She's been very unhappy lately."

Juan grimaced. "I suppose you think I've failed her in some way."

"I didn't say that."

"You thought it."

"Maybe. I'm sorry." Arnaud sat in the chair by the window. "So, what are you going to do now? Now that there's no baby dictating your actions?"

Juan flushed. "That's a bit below the belt, don't you think?"

"No. I don't. Rennie deserves someone who loves her, not someone whose sense of duty tells him when to get married and then makes him regret it. If you do regret it, let her go."

"What?"

"I said, let her go. It's not fair to torture her. She loves you. If you don't feel the same way, let her go." Arnaud took a deep breath. "And if you let her go, I'll be there for her. "

Juan stared at him. "You're in love with her?"

The Frenchman shrugged. "Does it matter to you?"

Juan felt a cold, white, rage boiling up in him. The feeling startled him. He took a moment to reply. "I think you'd better leave."

"Ah, so now your real feelings come to light." Arnaud was grinning widely.

Juan found he was halfway out of his chair and he sank back down. "All that was just a test?"

"Did it work? What are your feelings now?" Arnaud asked.

"You're right, I do love her. Now, what do I do?"

"You prove it," Arnaud said pointedly. "You make her smile again. And if you can't, you take my friendly advice and let her go."

Juan smiled crookedly, "Ah hell, what are friends for?"

* * * * *

Rennie didn't spend the night at the clinic. As soon as she woke up the doctor let Juan take her home.

They drove most of the way in silence. Juan had no idea what to say or where to start, and Rennie was too exhausted to talk. Most of the time she just stared out of the window. Juan glanced at her now and then and felt his chest tighten. Finally he cleared his throat and said, "We're going to my father's house tomorrow morning. We'll stay there for ten days. That way you can rest."

Rennie nodded. "That will be nice," she said softly. She stared out the window some more then said with sort of a sigh, "It hurts."

Juan winced. "I'm sorry," he said.

"It's not your fault." Rennie turned to face him. "It was because I fell. It's all my fault."

"Don't say that."

"It's true though. It is all my fault. It's my fault because I fell in love with you, and I couldn't say 'no' when I should have. If I had, none of this would have happened. You would be happily married to Rosa and I would be...I'd be back home I suppose. Doing nothing with my life." She turned to him, her face tragic. "I can't help it though. I do love you. And I'm glad we're married."

She wasn't crying, Juan noticed with something like admiration. There was a rare determination that seemed to illuminate her. He started to glimpse the steel she was made of.

"I don't love Rosa," Juan said. He lowered his chin and stared at the road. "I never did. And you were the one who made me realize that."

"Do you love me?" she asked quietly.

"I think so. I don't know, I don't know what I feel tonight. I think I'm too tired, too numb, and too shocked," he said. There was a long pause. "The nurse said the baby was a boy."

Rennie sighed. "It wasn't really a baby though, was it? It won't even get a name or a funeral. There's nothing left of it. The doctors just took it away and I never even got to see it."

Juan was stunned to feel tears on his cheeks. He hadn't cried in so long. Quickly he brushed them away. Rennie was looking out her window. He hoped she hadn't noticed. "I won't forget him," he said gently, when he found his voice again.

Rennie reached over and touched his hand. "Thank you," she said. "For keeping your side of the bargain." Then she was silent for the rest of the trip and Juan could only wonder what she'd meant by that.

* * * * *

Juan helped her out of the car and half carried her up the stairs to their bedroom. The big house was silent. The rest of the team was not there, they had stayed in Midhurst for the traditional polo ball, to be held that very evening.

Juan had just asked Arnaud to give his regrets to Tom Wimsys. Arnaud had agreed. He was going to the ball with an English heiress.

Arnaud was having a bit of trouble with his date. He had been persuaded by his patron to take Elizabeth to the ball. Elizabeth had begged and pleaded until her father had given in. Elizabeth's father was Arnaud's patron's boss. It hadn't been difficult to persuade Arnaud to bring Elizabeth, but there were a few problems. For one thing, she was only fifteen. In addition, her father told Arnaud that if he brought her back drunk he'd make sure he never played polo again.

Right now Elizabeth was whining.

"I want some champagne. It's not fair to bring me to a ball and expect me to drink soda."

"Have some orange juice," suggested Arnaud.

"I want champagne."

"Your father doesn't want you to drink."

"Screw him."

Arnaud eyed the petulant blonde hanging onto his arm. His patience was wearing dangerously thin. "If you are going to complain all evening I will simply load you back into my car and drive you home, is that clear? Now, let's go dance. This is a ball, isn't it? And you do want everyone to see your new dress, don't you?"

Elizabeth looked down at her light blue silk dress. It had a ridiculously low-cut bodice that nearly showed the tips of her pink nipples. Arnaud was grateful for the fact that she was such a little bore, if she'd been nice he'd have a hard time controlling himself around her. She might only be fifteen, but she was ravishing, and she knew it.

She arched her back and wiggled her hips. "I love to dance," she said.

Arnaud suppressed a shudder. Moreover, her voice was like someone raking their fingernails across a blackboard. He should have no trouble keeping his hands off her.

Elizabeth had no such qualms. She draped herself around Arnaud's neck. "I think French accents are so sexy," she said. "Can you talk some more French to me? It really turns me on."

Arnaud sighed heavily and then said, "*Espèce de petite pute, tu es sans doute le plus vulgaire des filles que j'ai eu le malheur de sortir avec. Ta robe est indécente, et ta voix est épouvantable.*"

"Ooh, that's *so* sexy," said Elizabeth. "I wish I knew what you were saying, but I get all wet just listening to you."

* * * * *

Alice was sitting in the corner of the room. She'd overheard Arnaud speaking to Elizabeth and it had cheered her up immensely. She thought that anyone who could call that plump blonde a little whore and say she was vulgar wasn't all bad. Her French was sketchy, but obviously better than Elizabeth's.

She began to regret telling Juan that Arnaud ran Rennie over with the car. Juan had reacted badly. First, his face had gone all white, as if the blood had drained out of it. Then it had gone sort of greenish and tears had actually appeared in his eyes. He'd cursed in Spanish, which Alice understood perfectly, and then he'd run off toward the parking lot, leaving his polo bag behind, along with his sticks and his trophy. Alice had packed everything up for him and had gotten Sebi to help her. Sebi had been so frantic with worry, he'd insisted on calling the clinic.

That was how Alice had found out about Rennie losing the baby. It made her sad. Carol, her stepmother, had just shrugged when she'd heard about it, saying "that sort of thing happens all the time. Rennie will be fine and have other children." Alice had been shocked, but even her father had taken the whole thing lightly, which was one of the reasons she was sitting by herself in the corner.

She'd gotten in an awful row with him on the field, because all he could do was complain about losing his stupid game, while Rennie had just lost a baby. When she'd had the effrontery to tell her father that, he'd put on his "patient, talking to a little child" voice and told her not to be dramatic. She'd fussed even more; he'd lost his temper, and he'd slapped her. Taken aback and wanting to make amends, he'd called the house and found out that Juan and Rennie were back, but that they were leaving in the morning for someplace called Snowdonia.

Alice thought it was a beautiful name and wished she could go there too.

Chapter Seventeen

Rennie packed the last of her clothes into her new suitcase. "I'm set," she said.

Juan poked his head into the room. He took his toothbrush out of his mouth and frowned at her. "What are you doing standing up? I thought I told you I'd do that!" He looked worried.

"I'm fine." Rennie closed the suitcase. "The doctor told me not to take baths for three weeks, and we have to be careful to use rubbers until I can take the Pill or we decide to have another baby. But otherwise everything is fine."

Juan put his toothbrush down and came into the room. He was wearing his bathrobe, and nothing else. It swung open when he walked, showing his flat chest and muscular torso. Rennie felt a rush of pure desire and her nipples tingled. When he took her in his arms, she laid her head against his chest and despite herself, tears slid down her cheeks.

"*Mi bonita,*" he whispered tenderly. "*Te amo mucho. Por favor, no llorés mas.*"

"I'm not crying because I'm sad," said Rennie. She nuzzled Juan's collarbone. "Well, part of me is sad. But mostly, I'm so happy I...I could cry," she finished, feeling ridiculous. "Honestly, don't mind me."

His arms tightened around her shoulders. "That's okay. I don't mind. You can cry if you want to." His voice was half laughing, half serious.

Rennie snuggled deeper into his arms. That was it. Half laughter, half tears. They had both been shocked by her miscarriage, but it had shown them what they really felt about each other.

"I can read your mind," said Juan. He drew her to the bed and made her sit down. "Rest, please."

"What was I thinking?" Rennie asked, looking up at him. God, he was so handsome. And he loved her. Her heart swelled with joy.

"Your eyes are glowing. You must be thinking of..." Juan paused and his eyes twinkled. "Of Mr. Marmalade, your cat."

"How did you guess?" Rennie leaned back against the pillows. She was tired. Yesterday she'd slept all day. Juan had surprised her. He'd gone shopping and had bought her a new suitcase and a new coat. The suitcase was beautiful tan leather, and the coat was made of soft, supple, pale gray wool lined with dark gray silk.

This morning they were leaving for Wales, and she'd wanted to leave before the others came back from Cowdray. She didn't want to see the Wimsyses, Carlos or Sebi before Deauville. She knew it was because she was too shy, and that she was being almost rude, leaving so soon, but Juan had agreed, and now they were in rush.

There was a knock on the door, and Tolly peeped in. "Everything all right?" she asked. "Baggage all set? I'll send James up then." She looked at Rennie, an anxious expression on her face. "How are you feeling, luv?"

"I'm fine, Tolly, thank you."

"Shall I bring up some more scones or tea?" She looked at their tray. "You've finished everything. Would you like some orange juice?"

"I'd love a bottle of mineral water." Rennie looked at her bedside table. "I still have a few antibiotics to take."

"Right, I'll be back in a tick." Tolly hurried off.

Juan sat next to her and took her hand. "We'll have more," he said. His face was shadowed, so Rennie couldn't see his expression, but she knew how sad he was. She hugged him.

"We'll have lots more. And this time, we'll decide when. It won't be a surprise."

Juan shrugged. "Babies are always a surprise, but they're always precious." He gave a crooked grin. "We Argentines are all mad about children. For us, they are very important, and they are always welcome. I'll be the happiest man on earth when you have my baby. This I promise you." He paused, looked at their entwined fingers.

"I was foolish," he said softly. "I tried to convince myself that I was doing a noble thing by marrying you, and I never realized that I was being egotistical. In fact, I was in love with you, and never wanted to admit it. I wanted to have you near me on my terms. I'm sorry. I made you very unhappy."

"No, Juan…"

He put his finger on her lips. "But I'll make up for it, I promise."

She took his hand and kissed it. "You already have. You did do something noble when you married me. You could have gone back to Argentina and forgotten all about me."

"Never." Juan was adamant. He grinned. "When I go back to Argentina, you're coming with me. I can't wait to show you my estancia, and the house I have near the mountains. It is totally surrounded by wilderness."

"Sounds scary," said Rennie.

"No, it's fantastic. You'll love it." He looked up as another knock sounded. "Come it."

It was Tolly and James. Tolly had Rennie's water, and James got the suitcases and took them downstairs.

Rennie took her pills and then Juan, still treating her as if she were made of porcelain, helped her to her feet and slipped her coat over her shoulders. She couldn't help staring at her image in the full-length mirror. The coat was so beautiful. It hung straight down to her calves, and was light yet warm.

Juan watched her as she admired the coat. He admired Rennie, though. The pale gray wool set off her delicate coloring. She looked at him and his breath caught in his throat. He'd bought the coat because the color had reminded him of Rennie's eyes. They were clear as stars now, and staring at him with her heart shining through. Some day, he thought, we'll have a little girl with eyes like that. He imagined himself holding a little girl's hand, and hearing a soft voice saying, 'Papa, I love you.'

He coughed to hide his emotion, and bent to pick up his own coat and the car keys. "Shall we go?" he asked.

Rennie gave one last look around the room. "I'll always remember this place," she said. She turned to Juan. "It was a beautiful honeymoon, thank you."

Juan raised his eyebrows in surprise. "What? You think it's over? I have news for you, mujer, the honeymoon has just started."

Rennie's warm giggle tickled his ears. "Well, don't forget the rubbers then," she said with a mischievous grin.

Juan's penis stiffened and he had to reach down and adjust things before he could leave the room. He grinned. Life was sweet, and getting sweeter.

* * * * *

Rupert was waiting for them at the cottage. He'd prepared their room, and Rennie was touched to see he'd filled all the vases in the house with flowers for her.

After they got settled, they went to the living room where Rupert had prepared tea for them. Juan picked up the book Rennie had brought downstairs. "The Maltese Cat. Did you finish this yet?" he asked her.

"Yes. Go ahead and read it, you'll love it," said Rennie. She turned to Rupert. "It is so peaceful here. I feel completely at home. Thank you for having us."

"Here, let me get you some more tea," he said, his face turning a bit red.

Rennie laughed. "If I drink any more tea I'll turn into a tea leaf. I'm fine."

"So, your mother is coming tomorrow." Rupert stared at the fire. "I haven't seen her in so long," he said.

"I think it's so cool that you knew her," said Rennie. "What was she like?"

Rupert smiled. "Shy, like you. Tall and slender, and she had class. She was class personified. Some people thought she was a snob, but she simply had beautiful manners. I was on the English jumping team, and we weren't looking forward to competing against her, I'll tell you that. She and the Sergeant were an incredible pair."

Rennie blinked. If she didn't know better, she would have thought Rupert had a crush on her mother. The idea made her lips curl in a smile.

Juan caught her look and asked, "What's so funny?"

"Oh, nothing," Rennie said. "Do you want me to come to the airport tomorrow?"

"No, you stay here and…"

"Rest. I know." Rennie rolled her eyes. "I'm rested enough. I feel fine. I feel better than fine. I want to go riding tomorrow and…"

"No!" both men cried at the same time. Juan looked stern.

"No riding until next month." His mouth was set in a firm line, and Rennie knew better than to argue. She decided to change the subject.

"Don't forget the shopping list when you leave tomorrow," she said sweetly.

Juan looked up from the book. "Shopping list," he repeated, a blank look on his face.

Rennie batted her eyelashes. "Shopping list," she repeated, and ran the tip of her tongue around her lips. "Rubbers," she mouthed silently. She loved it when Juan's ears turned bright red like that.

Chapter Eighteen

Marilyn was exhausted after her trip over the Atlantic. The plane had been late because of a strike, her bags had been the last ones out, and her favorite pair of sunglasses had been stolen when she'd put them down on the counter for a just a second.

Even so, she looked stunning, decided Juan, who'd come to pick her up at Heathrow. She wore a light beige linen skirt with an ice-blue jacket slung over her arm. Her shirt was white cotton, rolled up at the sleeves because of the heat, and a plain straw hat was pinned firmly to her blonde chignon.

She didn't recognize him at first. She stared right at him, then seemed to realize with a start who he was. "How's Rennie?" she asked right off, then, "Oh Juan, I'm sorry. How nice of you to come get me. It's so good to see you." She gave him a quick, hard hug and to Juan's consternation, burst into tears.

"Rennie's fine," he said, holding her close and patting her back. "She's waiting for you at the farm. Don't cry," he said awkwardly. "Rennie's just fine, honest."

Marilyn backed away, wiping her face. "I'm worn out, that's all."

"Here let me take your bags. We have a bit of a drive in front of us, we're going to my father's farm. I took Rennie last night. We'll spend the week there before going to Deauville."

Marilyn nodded. "So, how was your season?"

"Good." Juan shrugged. "We came in second overall in the gold cup, third in the Queen's cup. Mr. Wimsys should be content."

"But he isn't?"

"Well, no. That sort of man never is. Look how many times he's changed wives," joked Juan.

"But you've got to play with him." Marilyn got into the car and sat back with a sigh. "I hope you don't mind if I fall asleep."

"Only if you snore," said Juan.

Marilyn looked sideways at her son-in-law. His face was a study in concentration as he eased the car onto the motorway. The window was open to let in some air, and the wind blew his hair back, revealing a high, pale forehead. His eyes were hazel. Marilyn had forgotten what he looked like. She had a few pictures from the wedding but Juan had been very tense that day and it had shown in the set of his face. Now he was more relaxed and she saw the determined bone structure. He had a square chin and a wide, mobile, mouth. His face reflected his moods perfectly. It was a sensuous face, but his eyes had a keen gaze that Marilyn found reassuring.

Gathering her courage she asked, "How are you and Rennie doing?"

"Fine." Juan shot her a penetrating glance. "But that's not quite what you meant, was it?"

She blushed. "I didn't mean to pry," she said.

"I know." Juan shifted gears and swung around a slower car. "I know what you meant. You wondered if now that there's no baby I'm going to change my mind about being married." He smiled crookedly. "You aren't the first person to wonder about that."

"Oh?"

"I won't lie to you, I married Rennie because I wanted to assume my responsibility. Many marriages have been based on less and they've worked out fine." Marilyn bristled, but he shook his head. "Let me finish. I was engaged to a girl, had been since I was fourteen. It sounds romantic and foolish perhaps, but that's how it was. Then I met your daughter and I fell in love, but I didn't realize it at first. It took a while for it to sink in. I'm remarkably thick sometimes. But I do love her and we intend to stay together. Your daughter is a good person and I've begun to understand just how rare and precious a truly good person is."

Marilyn smiled. "She *is* good, isn't she? And I'm glad you love her, because I know how much she cares for you. Her letters were full of nothing but news about you; your polo games, your thoughts and doings."

Juan shook his head. "She needs to have more interest in herself."

"She has no self-esteem," said Marilyn. "I'm afraid that's my fault. I never had enough time for her—I had to work. I didn't have a family to fall back on and her father died before she was born. She felt his absence very strongly." She yawned and blinked. "I'm sorry, but I can't keep my eyes open another second."

"Go to sleep. I'll wake you when we get to the village, and if you need anything I'll stop at the store." Juan sighed. "I hope my father's cleaned up your room for you. The farmhouse is large but most of the rooms have been closed off for ages. I built a fire in your room before I left this morning so it won't be damp, but the bed needed airing out and there was nothing in the bathroom; no soap, no towels, no toilet paper. Even so…" He broke off and looked at Marilyn. She was sound asleep.

"Okay, so I'm a very boring guy," he murmured.

* * * * *

When he got to the village he woke her up. She gazed around sleepily, yawning and blinking her eyes. "Where are we? It's very pretty here."

"We're in Wales, in the village nearest to the farm. If you want anything, now's the time to ask, because we're rather isolated."

"No, I don't need anything. Unless you want something."

Juan felt his ears get hot. "Well, I do need something in the drug-store, but I'll just be a second."

"I'll come with you, then I can look around."

191

Juan went to the counter, then, making sure Marilyn was out of earshot, lowered his voice and asked for some rubbers.

"Rubbers sir?" echoed the salesgirl in a chirpy voice. "What size do you need?"

Marilyn had jerked her head up when the salesgirl had called out the word '*rubbers*'. Now she stared at the salesgirl, a fascinated expression on her face. Juan's face was burning.

"Size?" he asked, his voice cracking a bit. "Uh, what sizes do you have?"

"Well, small, medium and large. It depends, you see. Would you like to see one?" The salesgirl was all business.

"See one? I suppose so."

"What size do you want to see sir?" She was smiling brightly.

Juan tried not to look at Marilyn. His face must be like a tomato. Juan shuffled his feet and frowned. "Um, may I see a medium?" he muttered.

The salesgirl nodded and said to Juan, "follow me." She walked up the aisle and stopped right next to Marilyn who was busy picking out hair color-cream. "Here you are. What color do you want?"

Juan wanted the floor to swallow him up. "Co—color? Any color."

The salesgirl took a little packet down off a shelf and unwrapped it. Juan risked a glance at Marilyn. She seemed totally intrigued, her eyes fixed on the packet.

The salesgirl shook it out and held up a blue, plastic pair of baby's rubber training pants for him to see.

"This is the medium, it's for a one-year-old to an eighteen-month-old baby. The large size is for two or three-year-olds. The smalls are for newborns."

Juan stared, absolutely flabbergasted.

Marilyn choked and sputtered. "I'm sorry," she gasped. "I'll wait in the car!" She fled laughing hysterically.

Juan thought he'd never been so embarrassed. "I didn't exactly mean that," he said. "What you call rubbers we call training pants. What I need is more along the lines of birth control for men, if you see what I mean."

Now it was the salesgirl's turn to blush. "Oh, that!" she giggled. "We call them condoms, or French letters if you want the slang. Next time you'll know."

"Thanks." Juan sighed. Part of him was relieved Rennie wasn't pregnant any more. But part of him was still mourning for the son he'd never know. He realized, logically, that he and Rennie had lots of time to have children, but there was still a pang of deep sadness there.

In the car, Marilyn was still shaking with giggles. "I'm really sorry,"she said when Juan came back. "When she asked you what size you wanted…" She broke off with a shriek of laughter.

Juan looked at her through lowered lashes. "I didn't know what to say. I wasn't about to ask for a large, that would have been a bit presumptuous." His knew his cheeks were still red.

"And small would have been embarrassing," Marilyn wiped her eyes. "Did you finally get what you wanted?" He liked the way her fair skin showed her emotions. So like Rennie, he thought.

"Yes, thank you." Juan grinned at her.

"Well!" said Marilyn, wiping her eyes and getting her breath back. "It certainly is beautiful here." She rolled down her window to get some air. "Where exactly are we?"

"Snowdonia."

"What a lovely name."

"The farm is just beyond those hills. On a clear day like today we can see the sea."

"I hope your father doesn't mind me coming like this," said Marilyn worriedly.

"He doesn't. As a matter of fact he's looking forward to meeting you again."

"Again?" Marilyn looked blank. "I know him?"

"You met him once years ago. But you probably don't remember him."

"What's his name?"

"Rupert. Rupert Allistair."

Marilyn shook her head. "I'm sorry, I don't remember. I don't have a very good memory. I'm sure when I see him it will all come back to me..." Her voice trailed off and she stared out over the rolling hills. "How pretty."

Juan shrugged. "You get used to it."

* * * * *

Dinner was a casual affair. They simply tossed lamb chops on the kitchen fireplace grill.

The electricity had gone off and the only light in the room came from an oil lamp hanging over the scarred wooden table. Judging from the ring of black on the ceiling, it was used often. The fire had burned down and the window was open wide, letting in the cool night breeze.

Rennie curled up on an armchair. She stared sleepily at the glowing embers. Her gray eyes and pale hair picking up glints of gold from the flickering light around her.

Marilyn was glad to see that she was feeling better. She had sobbed bitterly in her mother's arms but afterwards they talked about it and Rennie admitted it was a huge weight off her shoulders. She wasn't quite ready to assume the responsibility of raising a child just yet, not when she had just left off being a child herself. She was going to travel all over the world with Juan and they were going to get to know each other before turning their attention to a baby.

Juan was reading a slim book. He would glance now and then at Rennie, and they'd smile at each other, as if sharing some secret joke. The title was 'Maltese Cat'. Juan was like a cat himself. He sat bonelessly on the chair, his head tilted a bit to the side and the shadows made his almond eyes even more slanted. He turned the pages with strong, capable hands that were only a bit scarred from polo.

Rupert was pouring over his accounts. He chewed on the eraser of his pencil and frowned. The firelight made him look devilish. His green eyes glittered and his hair, tied back in a long ponytail caught the firelight and turned from silver to gold.

Marilyn watched him out of the corner of her eye. She was still trying to remember where she'd seen him. His greeting had been polite, if a little distant. She'd noticed his gray ponytail and his green eyes, but he didn't remind her of anyone from the past.

"How was your trip?" he asked.

Marilyn shrugged. "All right. Like most trips. Long and tiring."

Rupert smiled. "Well, it's good to have you here. I adore my daughter-in-law, I'll have you know."

It was a moment before Marilyn realized he was talking about Rennie. "Oh!" she said. "I'm glad. Sorry, I'm a bit out of it."

"If you're tired you can go to bed," he said suddenly, and Marilyn blushed, because she'd been staring at him.

"That's all right, I'm fine."

"I apologize about the electricity. It goes on and off like that. I have to redo the whole electric system here. I think my grandfather had it done before the war. The first war, that is. When the circuits melt I have to replace the lead wires. Right now, we're a bit short on wire. I'll get some tomorrow when I go to town. Luckily, it's summertime. The heat goes off with the electricity. It's a bother in the winter." Rupert chuckled.

"It's not funny Papa," Juan said sharply. "You could have fixed up the farm anytime you wanted."

Rupert looked surprised. "But I like it this way."

"So do I," Marilyn hastened to say before Juan could reply. She'd seen the quick flash of anger in Rupert's eyes. "I think it's very romantic," she finished lamely.

"Thank you Marilyn, but Juan's right. I should get it done. Usually I don't mind. We're just a bunch of bachelors on the farm, and in the winter, the hunters are a tough bunch. They love to, what do you Americans say? Rough it, right?"

"I like it too," said Rennie from the depths of her chair. "It *is* romantic. Look at the light, it's just a soft glow. Moreover, the stars are much brighter without electric lights all around. I feel like I can reach up and touch them."

Juan stared at all of them, incredulous. "You're just backwards, that's all. The twenty-first century is here and you're still living in the stone age."

"I prefer to think of it as the Renaissance," said Rupert, closing his account book with a snap and putting it on a tall stack of magazines behind him. "We have a little electricity, our heat is erratic, but we're making progress."

"Progress?" Juan snorted, but his mouth twisted into a smile. "I suppose you could call it that. The last time I was here the toilets were outside in a little wooden house."

"See?" Rupert leaned back in his chair and lit a cigarette. The smoke curled up over his head in a lazy, blue spiral. "You have to understand, son, that all the money I make goes back into the farm. Not into minor comforts like heat and electric light. I buy breeding stock, good tractors, a new truck. Last year I invested in a new aviary to raise pheasants. I haven't the extra money to fix up the house. I admit that I'm not in any tearing hurry. I don't have a woman living with me to complain about not having hot water."

"Wait a minute," Marilyn said. "You don't have hot water?"

"Well, there might be some left. The heater is erratic, but it does work occasionally. Usually just enough for one shower though."

Marilyn stood up. "Well, if you'll excuse me, I'm putting first dibs on the shower."

Rennie laughed. "He's just kidding Mom, he has lots of hot water. He didn't say that the water comes from a hot spring. It's *always* hot. This house was built on the site of some ancient Roman baths."

"I take back the Renaissance," Rupert said, winking at Rennie. "We live in Roman style."

* * * * *

Rupert and Marilyn took the jeep the next morning to tour the farm.

"Don't you ride anymore?" asked Rupert.

Marilyn shook her head. "No, I don't."

"Bad back?"

She shot him a curious look. "Yes. It happened when Rennie was born—something to do with a breech birth. How did you know?"

"Oh, I think I heard about it years ago, I can't remember. Or maybe Juan told me."

"Juan told me that you knew me. I'm sorry, but I don't remember when we met."

"I was in Italy when you won the silver medal. I was with the riding team from England. I saw you there and thought you were the most wonderful rider I'd ever seen. And your horse, he was incredible."

"I think I remember now. You've changed, your hair was darker and much shorter."

Rupert chuckled, and then grew serious. "It was more than twenty years ago. Life seems to go by so quickly, doesn't it? My wife was expecting our third child when I was in Rome. She was here on the farm. We didn't move to Argentina until a year later. Juan was the only one of our children born there."

"You have four children?"

"Three. Our eldest son died."

"I'm very sorry. It must be terrible to lose a child." She thought a moment about her daughter's loss, but then sighed. Rennie would have others. Rupert had lost a beloved son.

Rupert just nodded.

Marilyn was silent, thinking back. The memory of Rome was both painful and bittersweet. The death of her mother, the Sergeant, her silver medal, the flight home. Everything was blended together and colored with sorrow. The medal was hiding in a drawer at home. She'd never gotten any joy from it. Her face grew still.

Rupert stopped the jeep on the crest of a hill. "This is the highest point on the farm. From here you can see down in the hollow where the house and barns are, and over there is the sea."

Marilyn shaded her eyes and looked. "I didn't know it was that color here. I expected something more, more..."

"Sedate?" suggested Rupert.

"It looks like the Caribbean."

"In the summertime, yes. But in the winter it's slate blue, or pewter gray. It changes you see. It's the Gulf Stream, all the way from Patagonia. It brings us a temperate climate, although we're pretty far north."

Marilyn got out of the jeep to stretch her legs. The long grass waved around her, deep, green and inviting. Wildflowers danced in the breeze, and the heady buzzing of bees was everywhere. "Do you have bee hives?" she asked. *Everything was so lovely here*, she thought. *This is what I've always dreamed of.*

"No, but my neighbor does. He sells honey and beeswax products. My candles all come from his shop."

"That explains the scent of honey last night. I thought it was from the flowers outside."

"The rosebush climbs right into the window, practically. I'm not much of a gardener. I prune only when I feel I'm being invaded." Rupert laughed.

Marilyn bent down to pick a cornflower. "I think it's perfect. I wish…" she broke off suddenly and blushed. She was being silly.

"You wish what?" Rupert asked.

"Nothing."

"Yes, go on, tell me, what do you wish?"

"I wish I could stay forever."Marilyn shrugged self-consciously. "I sound like a child, don't I? I see something pretty and I want it. I've always been selfish like that."

"You can't own the view, or the ocean or the wildflowers," said Rupert. "You love beauty, that's all. It isn't selfish."

"Perhaps. But it's always been my downfall." She grinned wryly.

"Rennie's father was beautiful, eh?" Rupert said gently.

Marilyn stared at Rupert. Rupert's expression was compassionate, and Marilyn found herself wishing she could tell him everything. "Did you know him?" she asked.

"Enough."

"I was so young, and he was so handsome. It was easy for him to have me. I didn't pay the slightest attention to any of my friends, or family."

"What happened?"

"He died. It was too sudden, we didn't have the chance to find out we were totally wrong for each other," she said. "I've been going on and on about myself. I'm sorry." Suddenly self conscious, Marilyn wandered across the meadow, picking flowers to add to her bouquet. She was faintly embarrassed having confided in Rupert. At the same time, she felt as if she'd always known him. It was uncanny how she was drawn to him.

"I didn't mean to be nosy," apologized Rupert.

"That's all right." Marilyn smiled. "I don't really mind. Here, in England, all that seems so far away."

"We're in Wales," said Rupert. "Better not let the natives here hear you say you're in England. They're a touchy lot."

"Are you Welsh?"

"Yes, I grew up here. It was good to come back."

"When did you come back?"

"Right after my wife died."

"Do you miss Argentina?" Marilyn broached this subject delicately, knowing it might bring painful memories of his wife and son.

"No, I miss my sons, although they're good letter writers. I miss the estancia, and my friends but I don't miss Argentina. It was always too big for me. I always felt a bit out of place and part of me has always been right here in Wales. Do you miss your home?"

"I miss William's Hall, the house I grew up in. I miss my father and mother, though they're both gone now. I miss the Sergeant and sometimes I miss my husband, but I don't miss Florida at all. I live there but I think I hate it." She laughed ruefully.

Rupert nodded. "Are you going to Deauville with Rennie and Juan?"

"No. I don't have the finances to spend any more time in Europe. My boss gave me a week off, no more."

"Your boss? What do you do?"

"I do manicures," said Marilyn, trying not to notice his horrified expression. "It's really quite interesting."

There was a long silence, then Rupert said, "I read about the Sergeant and your husband when the accident happened."

Marilyn plucked at a daisy, shredding the petals. "That was years ago."

"I have a good memory."

"You must." She sighed.

"You were brilliant." Rupert surprised her with the passion in his voice.

"Perhaps." Marilyn's grin was wry.

"No, you were truly brilliant."

"I don't think about that part of my life anymore. What's the use? The page is turned, I try and look forward." She wished he'd speak of something else. The past was depressing.

"And what's in front of you?" Rupert asked. He took her arm gently and turned her towards him. "Look at us. Two fools, living in the past and not admitting it to anyone." He leaned towards her and kissed her on the lips. "I've wanted to do that since I first saw you. You had on tan riding pants and a white cotton sweater. Your hair was pulled back in a long, blonde ponytail and you were riding the Sergeant."

Marilyn pulled away sharply. "I'm not a fool and I don't live in the past. What's gone is gone." She decided on a white lie. "I have a boyfriend in Florida and I'm quite happy."

"A boyfriend? What does he do?"

Marilyn reddened. The lie was getting more complicated. Now she had to invent a job for her fictitious boyfriend. "He has a charter fishing boat."

"Are you going to get married?"

"No."

"Why not?"

"Because," Marilyn floundered for words, "because I don't love him, I suppose. We never discussed marriage." For a second she got angry with her make-believe boyfriend. How could he never have asked her to marry him? Maybe she could invent another lover. That would teach him.

"How long have you known him?"

Oh no, more questions! "What is this? The Inquisition? I've known him for about a year, why?"

"And before that? Did you have a boyfriend before that?"

Stung, she replied, "Yes! I'm not a nun! What about you?"

"Nobody. No one since my wife died." Rupert sat down in the grass, pulling Marilyn down beside him. "I have never been able to simply date someone because I was lonely or because they were there. I have to be in love. I was madly in love with my wife, too much so, I think. I was even jealous of my own children. I wanted her undivided attention. She could never give it to me though. To tell you the truth, I think I smothered her. I asked for too much. I was wildly jealous and I made her life unbearable. When she died, I was able to step back and see what I'd done. I promised myself I wouldn't love anyone like that again."

"You can't keep that sort of a promise," Marilyn said gently.

"I can. I'm a determined sort of character. And what I want, I usually get."

"I'm not. I'm one of those people who float through life doing what other people want them to do. I don't have any personality whatsoever. Maybe if I had things would have been different."

Rupert looked at her through narrowed eyes. She was leaning back on her elbows, her eyes closed, face to the sun. Her hair fell in a golden cascade to the ground behind her. Her shirt was unbuttoned just enough to show a bit of lacy bra. He closed his own eyes then and lay back in the grass with a small groan. Personality or not, she was damn sexy. Moreover, she had no interest in him at all.

He was surprised then, when she leaned over him and kissed him firmly on the mouth. His mouth opened to hers and he pulled her over on top of him. They rolled in the tall grass, startling butterflies and dragonflies in their sudden haste. He thought he wouldn't be able to get his pants off fast enough. He did though, and she pulled her skirt up, dragging her underwear off with a little laugh that made him even harder. His penis throbbed with an aching need.

Her legs were long and tanned, and she spread her knees wide, arching her back and holding her arms out to him. He had time to catch sight of her golden pubic hair, pink labia and then her hands caught his shirt and she pulled him to her.

They came together half-dressed, with Marilyn's bouquet of wildflowers crushed between them as he thrust into her. His cock slid into her cunt as if it were made for it. She bucked against him, and he groaned, all hope of control fleeing as her hips rose and fell. His cock jerked and he came, driving into her, cries torn out of his throat.

The Queen Anne's lace tickled Rupert's nose and he sneezed at the worst possible moment, making Marilyn erupt in gales of laughter. She lay beneath him, shaking with the force of her orgasm coupled with hilarity.

"I never did anything like that before," she said dreamily, sitting up and tucking her breast back into her bra.

Rupert plucked a daisy out of her hair and kissed her. "That's good. I'd hate to think you did this sort of thing every weekend."

"Mmmm, I think I'd like to."

"Is that a proposal?"

Marilyn nodded. "For once in my life I'm going to do something *I* want to do. There's just one thing *you* have to do."

"What's that?"

"Get the heat fixed before winter. I've never spent winter in a cold climate and I don't want to freeze to death."

"Are you serious?" Rupert sat up suddenly, his eyes wide. "Are you quite, quite serious?" he repeated incredulously.

Marilyn imitated his accent. "Quite." She finished dressing and sat beside him. "I don't want to spend the rest of my life alone and I don't want to let anything else go by me. I've missed enough. If you'll have me, I'll stay. And when we get tired of each other I'll go. It will be as simple as that."

Rupert shook his head. "Nothing's as simple as that. I'll tell you what. We'll live together for a year and if it works out we'll get married."

"Old fashioned, aren't you?"

"Quite." He couldn't stop grinning.

* * * * *

When Rennie and Juan left for Deauville, Marilyn flew back to Florida with Rupert. He wanted to see the "Land of the Retired American ", and she wanted to sell the apartment and quit her job.

"Nice place," said Rupert, when he walked into the apartment. He sat in the same wicker chair Juan had sat in and looked at the photo albums. "In a way it's a pity to sell this place. It's part of an old house, isn't it? You probably can't get these old wooden floorboards in many American houses, especially here in Florida."

"What are you thinking of?"

"Keeping it and renting it out. We can come here for some sunshine in the wintertime. It would be nice. You'll see, after four months of frost and drizzle, you'll want nothing more than to lie in the hot sun, if only for an hour."

Marilyn tilted her head to one side. "Yes, I think that would be possible. And it will make me feel horribly rich. I can say to people, 'I'm off to spend a few days in my apartment in Palm Beach'. They'll think I'm a terrible snob."

"What about your job?"

"What about it? I quit, remember? I don't even have to clear out my desk. I don't have one."

"You won't miss it?"

"You're kidding, right?"

"Move over, I'm going to help you pack. If you persist in putting fragile things on the bottom of the trunk you're not going to have anything left when you get back home."

"Home." Marilyn smiled. "It's funny but I do think of Wales as home now. And after only three weeks there. Here, you finish this closet while I call a real estate agency. I'm going to rent the apartment out furnished, that way I don't even have to bother about the furniture."

"Americans are so practical it scares me sometimes."

"What about Mr. Marmalade?" Marilyn looked at the cat, sitting in a patch of sunlight.

"He'll love the farm, you'll see. He'll be running it in no time, bossing the sheep dogs around and catching mice. Jude will appreciate some help, I'm sure."

"Mice?" Marilyn cried. "You didn't tell me you had mice!"

"You're not scared of a wee mouse, are you?" Rupert asked, looking worried.

Marilyn tried not to laugh, but it bubbled out anyway. "Your expression was priceless!" she said. "No, not to worry. Wee mousies won't scare me. Big rats, maybe, but Mr. Marmalade will protect me."

"I will too," said Rupert, giving her a quick hug. "From mice and rats and bats and..."

Marilyn put her hand over his mouth. "If you want me to come to Wales, you won't say another word." She lowered her voice. "I'm afraid you're going to say spiders, and I have a phobia about those creatures." She shuddered.

Rupert nodded. "There are no spiders in Wales. As a matter of fact, it's the only country in the world without them. And if you do by any small chance catch sight of one, all you have to do is scream, and I'll come and rescue you."

"Perfect." Marilyn patted Mr. Marmalade. "You will love your new home," she told him.

Rupert finished cleaning out the closet and started sifting through the photo albums in the dresser drawer. "We'll put these in a box and ship them. Is this William's Hall?" He pointed to a picture of a graceful mansion surrounded by a low stone wall.

Marilyn peered over his shoulder. "Yes, that's where I grew up."

"Don't you want to go back before we leave? Are you close to your family?"

"No. I'm afraid I haven't been back since I was twenty. I fought with my stepmother and my sisters prefer to ignore me. I was cut out of the family. I would love to go back, of course. But I won't."

"Why not?" Rupert asked. "I would. Hell, that was all so long ago. Why don't you just walk in?"

"Because there's nothing there for me anymore. I've learned to get along without them. You've heard that expression 'you can chose your friends but not your family'. Well, it's true. However, you can choose not to be a part of your family. Sometimes families can poison your existence. In some cases, it's better to cut all ties. I think Rennie is better off not knowing her step-grandmother or her aunts. My sisters are all weak-minded and mean. They can only see as far ahead as the next social dance or ball. Their lives are made up of dinner parties with people they hardly know and various husbands, lovers, and divorces."

"How can you know about them if you haven't been in touch? Maybe they've changed?"

"I said I cut myself off from my family but I still have friends in Virginia. We write. I get news."

"Your spies."

"I suppose." She sounded tired. "I know it sounds petty. Yet, I've always been too proud to beg. I won't go back uninvited. They've always known where to find me. I sent everyone invitations to Rennie's wedding. I didn't get a single answer. It has to go both ways."

"I'm sorry."

"Oh, don't be. Here, grab a towel. Let's go to the beach. It's hot, I feel like a swim."

At the beach, they swam out past the breakers, floating in the deeper water.

"I can't get over how few people are here," said Rupert.

"It's August," said Marilyn.

"Well, that suits me anyhow. There's something I've always been meaning to do. But first, I need to be able to stand up." Rupert swam to Marilyn and untied her bikini top. Then he slipped his hand into her bikini bottom. She grinned and opened her legs. He slipped a finger into her, feeling gently for her clit, and then, loosening his shorts, he took his penis out.

In the water, weightless, Marilyn lay on her back and let Rupert position himself between her legs. He lowered himself so that his face was in the water, and he clamped his mouth over her cunt, licking until he had to come up for air. He slid a finger into her vagina, and she writhed against him. He loved to see his finger disappearing into her flesh. Excitement made his cock stiff, and he gave a look around, making sure no one was about. It was, after all, a public beach. But that just added piquancy to the act. Feeling like a naughty schoolboy, he entered her, then they floated a while, letting the swells move them up and down.

Rupert pushed Marilyn's bathing suit top aside. Her breasts were white against her tan body, and he cupped them in his hands. He put his feet to the sandy seabed, and then using it for purchase, thrust hard against her body. His cock loved her cunt, it swelled and hardened even more, making him groan with pleasure. She was getting slipperier; he could feel her start to tremble. Now she was rocking against him, and one hand dove down to fondle her own clit. The sight drove him crazy. He watched as she floated, her nipples now erect, her hand rubbing her own clit, until she came, arching her back and wrapping her legs tightly around his waist. When he felt she'd finished, he let himself go. Digging his toes into the soft sand, he held her to him and spurted into her, ejaculating with a hoarse cry.

They let the waves carry them back to shore, and lay for a moment in the surf, getting their breath back.

"We won't be doing that much in Wales," said Rupert.

"Of course we will," she said. "We'll be making love every day, if I have my way."

"I mean, not in the ocean," he said with a leer at her breasts. "Once a day sounds fine to me. And twice, sometimes if you want. And you better fix your swimsuit, or you'll get arrested."

Marilyn retied her top and sat up, a faint blush on her cheeks. "Well, as long as we agree." She smiled at him and gave him a hard kiss.

"I love you," said Rupert, taking her into his arms. "I've been waiting to say that. You've come along at the right time."

"Hmmm," said Marilyn, reaching into his shorts and stroking him until he was hard again. "I think I've come at the right time too."

Chapter Nineteen

Rennie and Juan were on the beach as well, that third day of August. They were on the other side of the Atlantic, walking arm in arm, kicking idly at the seaweed and flotsam the tide had left on the shingle.

"God it's cold here." Rennie looked at the green water crashing in a white froth on the dark gray sand and shivered.

Juan pulled his jacket closer around his neck. "The wind is out of the north. It'll get warm later on in the month, I promise."

"Well, I still won't swim in that water. It looks like sludge. When's our first game?"

"In three days."

Juan picked up a piece of driftwood and tossed it into the seething ocean.

"What shall we do tonight?" Rennie asked.

"We'll go to Arnaud de Lancourt's house in the country. He invited us for dinner."

"Good idea." Rennie grabbed Juan around the waist and pulled him to her. "Give me a kiss, you handsome devil you." Her hair whipped around their faces, hiding them.

He reached his hands into her shirtfront and cupped her breasts. "Hey! Your hands a freezing!" Rennie shrieked and pushed him away, then dashed off. "Try and catch me!"

He did, laughing into the wind. Seagulls screamed and wheeled around them, their wings held stiffly outstretched, a thousand white birds against a dark gray sky.

There was a fishing boat, dragged up on the beach. Rennie sat in the lee of the wind and took off her shoes, digging her feet into the cool sand. Juan sat beside her and slipped his hands into her shirt again. Her nipples hardened immediately against his palms and he rubbed them.

Rennie gave a little giggle of delight. A rush of heat between her legs made her moan and she raised herself on her knees and unbuttoned her jeans. Panting, she slid them off. Juan moved in front of her and put his jacket on the ground beneath her. He pushed her onto her back, and then he put his mouth onto her clit and sucked, all the while stroking her breasts beneath her shirt.

Her juices were making her cunt slick. Juan sighed happily and buried his face between her legs. Her pubic hair was starting to grow in again, and it was slightly scratchy. The feel and taste of her silky flesh was divine. Juan moved his face from side to side, licking and sucking until Rennie was calling his name over and over, her hips humping against the sand. "Oh Juan!" she gasped. "Harder, please, Juan, please."

His cock was throbbing and so hard that he had trouble getting his pants unbuttoned. He pulled a rubber out of his pocket, dropped it in the sand, and cursed with impatience. Rennie giggled, and he grinned, abashed.

He opened the foil package and smoothed the rubber over his penis. "Okay, now just calm down," he told his cock sternly. He didn't think it was going to listen to him. He was hard as granite and twitching with eagerness.

Kneeling in front of her, he took her legs and put them on his shoulders. Her legs were spread and his cock was pointing straight at her. He took a deep breath, then he slowly thrust into her wide-open cunt. She leaned back on her elbows, her hair in the sand, and she raised her hips, sheathing herself on his cock. She was so tight and slippery, and so sexy with her legs up and wide, her head tipped back, Juan had to struggle for control. When he pulled out, the cold air came into contact with his cock so that when he thrust into her cunt, it seemed even hotter. The air was cool, but Rennie was hot.

She closed her eyes, and her fingers dug into the sand. "I'm coming," she gasped, and she bucked against him, grabbing him with her hands and pulling him into her.

"Now?" Juan asked, leaning over her, his body sheltering hers. He felt her legs start to tremble and he thrust his cock into her, sheathing to the hilt. He looked down. The sight of his cock buried in her beautiful pussy was intoxicating. He would never get enough of her.

"Now!" she cried. Her legs slid off his shoulders and she lay flat on the ground, lifting her hips into the air. Her whole body shook, and he felt tremors massaging his cock within her cunt.

He slammed into her, his body screaming for release. In a second, his cock was exploding into her, his seed shooting out of his body so hard he thought he'd faint. He hoped the rubber wouldn't burst. Again and again he convulsed against her, his hips arching into hers, his cock driving into her cunt.

When he finally stopped, he felt as if his whole body was wrung out. He brushed his hands over Rennie's breasts, and kissed her tenderly on the mouth.

"I love you," he whispered.

"I love you too," she said. "But I'm starting to get cold. Would you let me get dressed now?"

"Only if you let me undress you when we get back to the hotel."

She chucked softly. "Oh yeah? And just what do you have in mind?"

Juan raised his head and gave her a sexy wink. "A shower. And a blue sparkly vibrator."

Rennie blushed, and Juan laughed, kissing her on the nose.

* * * * *

That night at the de Lancourt's house, Rennie saw a real French chateau, a moat, a thoroughbred racing stable, and two of the sweetest dogs she'd ever met. Their names were Plume and Ficelle, and they were Brittany Spaniels. They had large, brown Spaniel eyes and long silky coats. One had black and white spots and one was red and white. They were elderly dogs that slept on embroidered cushions near a large fireplace.

She loved the de Lancourt's house. It was a small brick cottage with a thatched roof. The whole cottage was filled with silver trophies, hunting trophies, and pictures of Arnaud and Pierre growing up.

The pictures showed their whole life and Rennie looked on as they grew up before her eyes from one frame to the next. She stopped at the chimney where the last photo of Pierre stood. It had been taken in Palm Beach. He was sitting on a polo pony, and his head was turned a bit away from the camera. He had been laughing at something someone had said.

"He was so handsome," sighed Rennie.

Baron Delancourt smiled. "He was, wasn't he?"

Rennie blushed. "Arnaud is handsome too," she said quickly. Then she bent down to pet the dogs.

Arnaud and Juan spoke together about horses, and polo. Rennie admired the beautiful house and tried to concentrate on everything she saw so that she would always remember it. If she had a house someday, this was how she wanted it to look. Warm, cozy, inviting.

She looked over at Juan and smiled. In the candlelight, his hair gleamed and his eyes had romantic shadows around them. He caught her look and winked. Then he lowered his chin and mouthed, "later."

She blushed. They were getting on so well it was practically sinful. She'd never felt so secure. Juan made her feel as if she were finally alive. News from her mother was in the same vein. Rupert and she were already talking marriage. Marilyn wrote to her daughter that she'd never been so happy in her entire life.

Juan took a sip of excellent Bordeaux wine and glanced at Rennie again. His life had taken another turn, and he found himself looking forward to the future. The future was going to be in Wales, working with his father on the farm, playing polo during the polo season, and Rennie. His wife. The sweetest woman he'd ever met. To think he'd almost ruined it. He raised his glass to her, then to Arnaud who was watching them with a wide grin on his handsome face.

"A toast," said Arnaud, standing up. "To Juan and Rennie, may their lives be long, sweet and fruitful. And to the French Gold Cup. May my team beat the Silver Birds and win."

He drank his wine and winked. "Next year you can play on my team, and then you can win."

Rennie smiled again, her face lighting up. The Deauville polo season was shaping up to be a fun one. If only the sun came out it would be perfect.

The End

Enjoy this excerpt from
My Fair Pixie
© Copyright Samantha Winston, 2005

My Fair Pixie

What does a five hundred year old, incredibly cultured male vampire want? Sebastian Montgomery Chateaufix stared at the mirror and wondered. His reflection eluded him as usual but that didn't matter. What mattered was the fact that in five hundred years he hadn't found what really eluded him—a soul mate. For some reason, he seemed to be attracted to bimbos.

He stared a little more at the mirror, and realized he was dangerously close to whining. *Why is it,* he mused, *that most of our kind spend our time on earth whining?* Last night had been the last straw. At what should have been the party of the season with laughter making the sparkling chandeliers shiver, his guests had wandered about moaning and complaining about everything. Everyone whined, and the werewolves were the worst. Hear one whining werewolf and you want to lock them all in the kennels. Which reminded him—he'd better go set Luster loose before the damn creature gnawed through the bars. He pulled the curtain open a bit and glanced out the window. The sun had set. He could go out now. He flung his cloak over his shoulders and glided out the door.

Luster sat in the kennels glaring at him. Now in human form, he looked puny but furious. "I hope you're satisfied. I missed the full moon last night and now I'll have to wait another month before I can go visit my wife."

Sebastian shrugged. "You should have thought of that before ruining my party. I had intended the roast goose for everyone. Eating all the food and whining I might have put up with, but then you started humping the guests' legs as they sat at the table, and that amused no one, I can assure you."

Luster sighed. "You're right, Seb. I'm sorry. But you should know by now that black tie dinner parties are no place for werewolves when it's the full moon. Besides, it's not my fault Penelope Gangrein was in heat. We lost our heads."

"Well, no hard feelings." Sebastian held the door open. "Your clothes are in the guest bedroom. You can use the shower and clean up before going home."

"Thanks Seb." Luster headed towards the manor and then looked back over his shoulder. "What are you up to tonight?"

"Nothing in particular. I don't have any plans."

"Look, I want to make it up to you. In my jacket I have a ticket to a new show—a dating game show. It's a sort of entertainment for humans, and you look like you need a change of scenery."

Sebastian raised his eyebrows. "Thank you, Luster. I accept with pleasure." A dating show, whatever that was, sounded like just the thing to cheer him up. He changed into a bat and flew to his room to get into some dressier clothes, grab his car keys and find Luster's ticket. Then he strolled down the carpeted staircase to the first floor and told his butler not to expect him for dinner. In the garage, he jumped in his Porsche and headed toward the city. The night was young. Before he hit the show, he'd grab a quick bite to eat.

There were a couple places he knew of where he could sink his fangs into someone's neck without being seen. Joggers sometimes ran alone, at night, through the park. He left his car in the brightly lit parking lot and trotted over to the jogging track. A small section of it passed through a densely wooded area. He flew to a low branch and waited.

You'd think they'd learn, he mused as he dropped out of a tree in front of a hapless jogger. He grabbed him, and with his supernatural strength, held him still while he filled his belly. Not too full, didn't want to kill him. The jogger's blood tasted a tad bit odd.

He finished drinking and asked him sternly, "Did you take any drugs tonight?"

The man looked at him vaguely and mumbled, "I…took a Viagra pill and washed it down with a glass of red wine. That's all."

Sebastian used a simple spell to make the jogger forget what had happened. The bite marks were hardly visible. He kept his fangs needle sharp. Professional pride hadn't been dampened despite his depression. Then he checked the address on the ticket and got back in his car. Viagra? He had no idea what Viagra did to vampires. Well, at least he hadn't been on LSD or anything. Usually he preferred joggers because they tried to stay healthy and their blood showed it.

His vision blurred slightly as he pulled up to the studio in front of the valet parking. Frowning, he stood still a moment, leaning against a lamppost. That damn jogger had been stuffed full of alcohol—he'd lied! *One glass of red wine my foot!* Sebastian shook his head. It was amazing he'd been able to stay on his feet and jog.

About the author:

Samantha Winston is the pen name for Jennifer Macaire, an American freelance writer/illustrator. She was born in Kingston, NY and lived in Samoa, California and the Virgin Islands before moving to France. She attended Parsons school of design for fine art, and Palm Beach Junior College for art and English literature. She worked for five years as a model for Elite. Married to a professional polo player, she has three children. After settling in France, she started writing full time and published short stories in such magazines as Polo Magazine, PKA's Advocate, The Bear Deluxe, Nuketown, The Eclipse, Anotherealm, Linnaean Street, Inkspin, Literary Potpourri, Mind Caviar and the Vestal Review. One of her short stories was nominated for the Pushcart Prize. In June 2002 she won the 3am/Harper Collins flash fiction contest for her story 'There are Geckos'.

Samantha_Winston@hotmail.com

Samantha welcomes mail from readers. You can write to her c/o Ellora's Cave Publishing at 1056 Home Ave. Akron, Oh. 44310-3502.

Why an electronic book?

We live in the Information Age—an exciting time in the history of human civilization in which technology rules supreme and continues to progress in leaps and bounds every minute of every hour of every day. For a multitude of reasons, more and more avid literary fans are opting to purchase e-books instead of paperbacks. The question to those not yet initiated to the world of electronic reading is simply: *why?*

1. *Price.* An electronic title at Ellora's Cave Publishing and Cerridwen Press runs anywhere from 40-75% less than the cover price of the <u>exact same title</u> in paperback format. Why? Cold mathematics. It is less expensive to publish an e-book than it is to publish a paperback, so the savings are passed along to the consumer.

2. *Space.* Running out of room to house your paperback books? That is one worry you will never have with electronic novels. For a low one-time cost, you can purchase a handheld computer designed specifically for e-reading purposes. Many e-readers are larger than the average handheld, giving you plenty of screen room. Better yet, hundreds of titles can be stored within your new library—a single microchip. (Please note that Ellora's Cave and Cerridwen Press does not endorse any specific brands. You can check our website at www.ellorascave.com or

www.cerridwenpress.com for customer recommendations we make available to new consumers.)

3. *Mobility*. Because your new library now consists of only a microchip, your entire cache of books can be taken with you wherever you go.

4. *Personal preferences are accounted for*. Are the words you are currently reading too small? Too large? Too...**ANNOYING**? Paperback books cannot be modified according to personal preferences, but e-books can.

5. *Instant gratification*. Is it the middle of the night and all the bookstores are closed? Are you tired of waiting days—sometimes weeks—for online and offline bookstores to ship the novels you bought? Ellora's Cave Publishing sells instantaneous downloads 24 hours a day, 7 days a week, 365 days a year. Our e-book delivery system is 100% automated, meaning your order is filled as soon as you pay for it.

Those are a few of the top reasons why electronic novels are displacing paperbacks for many an avid reader. As always, Ellora's Cave and Cerridwen Press welcomes your questions and comments. We invite you to email us at service@ellorascave.com, service@cerridwenpress.com or write to us directly at: 1056 Home Ave. Akron OH 44310-3502.

THE
☥ ELLORA'S CAVE ☥
LIBRARY

Stay up to date with Ellora's Cave Titles in
Print with our Quarterly Catalog.

TO RECIEVE A CATALOG,
SEND AN EMAIL WITH YOUR NAME
AND MAILING ADDRESS TO:

CATALOG@ELLORASCAVE.COM
OR SEND A LETTER OR POSTCARD
WITH YOUR MAILING ADDRESS TO:

CATALOG REQUEST
c/o ELLORA'S CAVE PUBLISHING, INC.
1056 HOME AVENUE
AKRON, OHIO 44310-3502